What readers are sayin...

'Grabs hold and doesn't let go.' – *Michael Dax, Berkshire, England*

'Emotional and touching ... told from the heart, with great love and compassion for animals.'
– *Sheila Belshaw, author of* Fly with a Miracle

'[Lewis] understands dogs, that's obvious, but he also has the ability to make them come alive on the page.'
– *Jared Conway, Malaga, Spain*

'I couldn't stop reading this! ... Brilliant!'
– *A.L. Skip Mahaffey, author of* Adventures With My Father

'An amazing insight into the thoughts, humour and emotions of our four-legged friends.' – *Helen Jackson, Auckland, New Zealand*

'Wonderfully different.' – *Susan Bennett, Victoria, Australia*

'One of those reads that lingers in the back of the mind. I can see this on film.' – *Melanie Comley, Normandy, France*

'Emotionally highly charged and full of the right ingredients – what more could readers want?'
– *Tony Bayliss, Wolverhampton, England*

'[An] amazingly tender and touching story ... [Lewis has] a gift to be able to express so well what an animal might be thinking.'
– *J.V. Douglas, Longview, Texas, USA*

'The cover is brilliant and the contents do not let the cover down.'
– *Lisa W.B., author of* A Fine Line: A Balance to Survive

'I haven't read a dog book since I read Jack London's classic work ... I shall refer to your book as *White Fang 2*.' – *Barry Wenlock, Nepal*

'This book is one to be treasured ... a delightful story of a dog whose spirit will not be stifled.' – *Sally-Ann Mair, Peebles, Scotland*

‘A wonderful tale of hope and love.’
– Dawn Evans, Upington, Northern Cape, South Africa

‘What dog lover could resist this? ... [A] story with an integrity that does full justice to a much-loved animal’s fighting spirit and joy for life.’ – *Cas Peace, author of* For the Love of Daisy

‘Beautifully written.’ – *Lynne Morley, Llanfechain, Wales*

‘Incredible writing ... by someone who really loves and knows his dogs ... a beautiful, poignant read.’ – *Katy Roberts, Brighton, England*

‘Quite enchanting.’ – *Sarah Guy, Reading, Berkshire*

‘You will fall for Nelson’s charms ... I was gripped from the first chapter ... a rollercoaster ride of emotion.’
– Paula Duff, Sheinton, Shropshire

‘The images [Lewis] portrays are just astounding ... flows and reads like a movie. I was captivated.’ – *Marianna V., Philadelphia, USA*

‘Appealing and easy to get lost in.’
– Jane Finch, author of Squirrel Island

‘An amazing story of two brave dogs ... very funny as well as emotionally satisfying.’ – *Gerry McCullough, Belfast, N. Ireland*

‘James Herbert did this before, with *Fluke*, but not as well.’
– Andrew Wright, Sussex, England

‘An endearing, heart-warming story.’
– Sandra Garcia, Johannesburg, South Africa

‘Some of the most gripping, emotional work I’ve read ... expertly woven.’ – *Thomas J. Winton, Hobe Sound, Florida, USA*

‘Very accessible, touching and immediate.’
– Elizabeth Jasper, Andalucia, Spain

‘Utterly fantastic ... *Marley and Me* all over again (but in a good way, not a copycat way).’ – *Andrew Morgan, Ashford, England*

‘A pure Disney movie in words.’ – *Frank McGrath, Dublin, Ireland*

IF ONLY I COULD TALK

A CANINE ADVENTURE

IF ONLY I COULD TALK

A CANINE ADVENTURE

TONY LEWIS

Matador
5 Weir Road
Kibworth Beauchamp
Leicester LE8 0LQ, UK
Tel: (+44) 116 279 2299
Fax: (+44) 116 279 2277
Email: books@troubador.co.uk
Web: www.troubador.co.uk/matador

ISBN 978 1848763 791

British Library Cataloguing in Publication Data.
A catalogue record for this book is available from the British Library.

Typeset in Georgia by Troubador Publishing Ltd, Leicester, UK
Printed and bound in Great Britain by the MPG Books Group

Matador is an imprint of Troubador Publishing Ltd

Written in very fond memory of …

… two family members dearly missed. Selfless, mild-mannered and considerate, they possessed an inimitable *joie de vivre* that was a privilege to share. They both adored life, revelling in its most simple of pleasures. To them, these were life's great luxuries. One of their more eccentric habits was to seize any opportunity to run naked along the shallow waters of an evening shoreline, a setting sun caressing their backs – carefree of all life's stress and worry …

… perfectly normal behaviour for a couple of dogs.

For Carter and Jinny

Three and a half years ago, rural England, the middle of June

The house is ablaze. Inside, an eight-year-old Labrador-Whippet cross is trapped. Outside, Rascal, a small terrier, can do nothing to help his best friend.

Nelson can't breathe any more. His throat and lungs are choked. The heat is overpowering. These are surely his final breaths. With every breath, he wheezes and coughs. He retches uncontrollably.

~ *Why can't I breathe? What's happening? Why are my eyes hurting so much?*

Nelson can't see anything at all now. His eyes are shut tight. He can't keep them open any more. He is weak and dizzy, unsteady on his paws.

He stumbles into the wall again. He staggers around the room and collides with the table. The smoky air is solid and heavy. Everything is blurred. He is confused and *very* scared. He cries out in anguish.

~ *Why is it so hot?*

He has tried calling for help but nobody hears. Can't get out. Trapped. There is no one to rescue him – except Rascal. But Rascal can't possibly help.

It's getting hotter and hotter. Smokier and smokier. Each time Nelson inhales, he sucks in a painful breath. He knows he has to breathe to stay alive, but the air he takes in is thick and poisonous. What choice does he have?

He collapses on the floor.

Nelson can hear Rascal outside. He tries to open his eyes to find him. Sees him through the smoke and the glass. He is in the garden. Frantically spinning around in tight circles, barking in fear and panic. Their eyes meet, and Nelson pleads for Rascal to save him. Rascal yelps in anguish, turns and disappears to look for help from someone – again.

He returns alone. Again. The dismay in his eyes tells Nelson he still hasn't found anyone. Fears he never will. Rascal calls out to Nelson not to give up.

With all the strength left in him, Nelson struggles desperately and manages to stand up. He staggers clumsily past the window and to the back door again. He pushes and paws hopelessly at the wood but still it doesn't budge, resisting his feeble efforts. He has already tried jumping up to the handle but he is too exhausted now. Even if he could reach it, what then?

He shuffles back to the window and scratches at the glass ineffectively with his paw. His efforts are useless. Pointless.

Death is tapping on his shoulders, pushing him into the floor. Can't fight it any longer. The heat is unbearable. Flames fill the kitchen. His chest is agony. So tight. He staggers around the room in circles, helplessly, completely disorientated. There is no relief. His legs are weak, shaking. His body trembles.

He wants desperately to talk to Rascal but he has too little energy left. He tries to call out but his voice is a senseless whisper, a meaningless rasp. His head hangs low. He doesn't have the will left to lift it.

Nelson wants to tell Rascal everything. Things he should have told him before. Things that Rascal will never know – so much more than Nelson ever had the chance or the strength of mind to tell him. To tell *them*. But it's already too late.

He reaches the window again and collapses against it. The two dogs look at each other through the thick glass. Something unmistakably final passes between them. Nelson's farewell message is transmitted. Rascal yelps with sadness and despair but Nelson doesn't have the energy to communicate. He has given up.

Rascal approaches the glass and touches it with his moist snout.

He recoils – the glass is too hot for his sensitive nose. Only a few centimetres separate them. His frightened eyes fix Nelson a pleading regard. Rascal's nose is as close to the glass as he can bear it, and he lifts a delicate paw. He places it against the windowpane, trembling nervously – his leathery paw ignores the temperature. His head is cocked to one side and his ears are tucked back.

With what little willpower he has left, Nelson lifts his own paw and places it against the glass. Against Rascal's small paw. They stare into each other's eyes, neither of them blinking.

But Nelson is too weak to hold his leaden paw up. It slides slowly down the glass to the floor. He lies down and places his snout between his front legs and whimpers. He knows Rascal can hear him. But will he understand? He pants violently. He knows he shouldn't, but he can't help it. He is sure he will pass out soon. He does hope so. *Please let me die*, he tells himself.

Nelson manages to force his eyes open and looks at Rascal one more time. Rascal jumps up against the glass and scratches frantically with both paws, yelping loudly. Trying to dig through the barrier between them. A barrier so invisible yet one which signifies life or death. Life on Rascal's side, and death on Nelson's.

Rascal senses Nelson's utter resignation and lowers his paws. He lies down slowly and faces him. Like Nelson, Rascal pushes his snout down between his paws. He looks straight at Nelson. Into him. Rascal's nose is wet and shiny. Nelson's is dry and scorched. What a time for Nelson to feel jealousy.

Rascal's exhaled breath gathers in a cloud on the windowpane and fogs Nelson's view. The more Rascal breathes the hazier he becomes to Nelson, as if drifting away, leaving him behind. Like all the others did ...

Nelson doesn't want to die a pathetic death in front of Rascal. He can't let Rascal see him like this. With all his determination and self-pride, he regains his paws. He turns away from Rascal and stumbles slowly to his basket. He climbs in, collapses heavily and curls into a tight ball. He tucks his snout deeply under his thigh. His eyes fall closed and he doesn't look back. He can hear Rascal begging him to keep battling. He can hear the desperate calls and his claws scraping the window. But Nelson can't bring himself to look at Rascal again. Not now. It hurts too much to lose him. To lose them all.

A final whimper escapes from Nelson's basket.

~ *Where are my guardians when I need them most?*

Part 1

The Nelson Touch

~ 1 ~

Richard and Françoise arrived home from the hospital to discover Rascal at the front of their house barking hysterically. Black smoke was billowing from the side.

'Oh, *mon Dieu! Rich*ard!'

'Quick!' he shouted. 'Call the fire brigade! Nelson. He's inside.'

Françoise didn't react. Her eyes were wide.

Richard dug into his trouser pocket, fumbling in panic. He pulled out his mobile as he rushed along the path to the back of the house. Still groggy and disorientated from the tests at the hospital, his hands trembled so much that before he managed to press any keys, he dropped the phone onto the concrete path. It landed heavily and the back cover fell loose. The battery dropped out and slipped down into the outside drain.

'Bloody hell! Pull yourself together, man,' he shouted. 'Quick, Fran, give me your phone.'

'I haven't got it with me – I left it in the house.'

'Damn! Get next-door, quick! I'll try and get the dog out.'

Françoise ran next-door. There was nobody home so she hammered on the door of the next house along the road. They were home, thank God.

Richard was at the kitchen window. He cupped his hands over his face to see inside. Thick dark smoke filled the room and blackened the windows. He saw heavy flames over the cooker, licking high against the walls. The kitchen units were ablaze. In a split second, Richard knew exactly what had caused the fire.

Smoke poured out through the top panes of the kitchen windows in heavy funnels – the two windows they opened on warm days – and it swirled out through the cooker extractor vent. He ran to the back door. There, smoke was filtering through the keyhole. He squinted through the patio doors. There were no flames, but the heavy fog of smoke impeded his view and he could see nothing of Nelson. Rascal was next to him jumping up at the window and trying to scratch his way through. He used both paws against the glass, scratching manically.

'Come on, Rascal. Good dog. Out of the way.'

Richard grabbed the door handle and turned the key. He pushed the door inwards. The tremendous heat and the escaping smoke hit them both in the face. Man and dog jumped back.

Françoise arrived at the back door to find Richard coughing in the dissipating smoke. Desperate anguish was etched across her face. Rascal suddenly jumped out from behind Richard and ran in through the door.

'Rascal, no!' shouted Richard and set off after him.

Only seconds later, Richard emerged from the house, coughing and spluttering and rubbing his eyes. His face was already black.

'I can't see a damned thing in there, Fran, it's just too smoky. I can't get anywhere near the kitchen, the heat is overpowering.'

'Nelson?'

'I can't see him!'

'What about Rascal?'

'I don't know.'

Rascal immediately jumped out from the house, snorting heavily. He shook his little head as he sneezed repeatedly. Françoise ran to the outside tap and turned it on, cupping some water in her hands for the dog to drink. Rascal lapped gratefully at the water. As soon as her palm was empty, he spun round and ran straight back into the house.

'*Rich*ard! We have to get them out of there. Quickly!'

'I can't get inside! It's *too* hot.'

'We can't leave Nelson. He will die.'

Richard said quietly, 'I think we might already be too late.'

'*Non!* I will not hear such words, *Rich*ard! He is not dead. I will go in and get him myself!'

Richard pulled his wife back and said, 'No! You can't go inside. The kitchen is on fire, for God's sake! I can't see a damned thing for the smoke. We have no choice. We'll have to wait for the fire brigade. You can't breathe in there.'

Françoise sank against Richard, ineffectual and useless.

Rascal appeared in the doorway. He ran straight to the outside tap, which Françoise had neglected to turn off. He tilted his head to one side and drank eagerly from the cascading water. Then he ran past them again and back into the smoke.

'No, Rascal, no!' begged Richard.

Richard ran quickly to the tap and dampened his handkerchief. Covering his nose and mouth, he ducked in after the dog.

Rascal was first to come out, retching again. A moment or two passed before Richard exited ... alone. Suddenly, Rascal's ears twitched and he set off at speed along the path to the front of the house. Richard said quietly to his wife he thought he'd seen Nelson, but couldn't reach him. He thought he was in his basket, hidden under his blankets, but that could have been just the way they had settled.

Rascal appeared again. He was followed by a group of firemen running up the path. They shouted rapid questions at the couple and immediately headed in through the back door – Rascal was close on their heels, but Richard grabbed him and held him tightly. Another fireman ran up the path, past the couple. Rascal yapped at him to hurry up and get his friend out.

'Please bring our dog out,' asked Françoise meekly, echoing Rascal's thoughts.

'I think he's in the dining room. In his basket ...' added Richard, still catching his breath.

Before he entered, the fireman removed the breathing apparatus from his face, looked at them doubtfully, but said: 'We'll get him out for you, don't worry.'

Then he disappeared into the fire.

Richard and Françoise stayed close to the kitchen door and waited. And waited. Richard was crouching down and he held Rascal safely by the collar, stroking him absent-mindedly. All three watched helplessly while the firemen fought the fire. Already, unbidden thoughts were swimming around in Richard's head. Why did he rush off to the hospital? The cooker ... How could we be so stupid? ... If only I'd had those bloody migraines sorted out sooner ... Please, Nelson, come out alive ... please.

He could feel one of his headaches coming on. He winced and tried to ignore the pain in the back of his neck and in his temples. No, not now – not now! he grimaced.

Within only a short period – but an eternity to Richard and Françoise – the fire was successfully extinguished and the firemen emerged through the smoke. One of them carried the limp form of a dog across his chest. Nelson sagged lifelessly in the man's arms. The fireman walked beyond the couple and placed the dog gently on the grass. He removed his helmet and breathing apparatus and turned to them.

'I'm sorry,' he said. 'Really sorry. I don't think your dog's made it.'

He arranged Nelson's body on the lawn. The lawn where Nelson had spent many an afternoon sprawled out in the sun, a half-eaten chew by his side. The fireman stood up and looked at Richard and Françoise again. He bit his lower lip and repeated, 'Very sorry. I really am.' Then he left to help his colleagues finish off and pack away their equipment.

Richard walked nervously over to their dog and crouched down beside him. Nelson lay on his right side, his legs splayed. He stroked the motionless body affectionately from head to tail, caressing the fur. He noticed that Nelson had not been burnt in the fire, but each time he stroked the dog, his hand was blackened. But he didn't care about that. He had – *they* had – lost a dear friend. The guilt was already beginning to surface above all the other emotions.

Richard tickled Nelson behind his ear, and rubbed the ticklish rib on his left side. Nelson's back leg didn't twitch at all. No response. Richard crouched lower and uttered soft words into the dog's ear, and gently opened one of Nelson's eyes in a forlorn search for any indication of life. There was none. He placed a palm on Nelson's ribcage but he felt no soft thump under his fingers. He leant closer still and put his cheek against his dog's face and whispered, 'Oh, Nelson, I'm sorry. I'm so very sorry.'

Françoise placed a hand on her husband's shoulder. Tears running down her face, she spoke softly.

'It's not your fault, *chéri*. It's mine. *Chéri*, the firemen need us for a minute.'

Richard stood up slowly and they approached the fireman, who was standing patiently in the background. He was very sorry to have to interrupt, but he needed to ask them a few questions about the circumstances of the fire before they packed up and left. It wouldn't take long, he assured them.

~ ~ ~ ~ ~

Rascal lay on the far side of the lawn. He knew he was expected to keep a respectful distance while Richard was with Nelson. But now that his friend had been left all alone, he padded cautiously – one slow paw at a time – over to the body. He sniffed at Nelson and circled him slowly. He checked round the dog, twitching his nose over Nelson's whole body. There was something about Nelson that Rascal had never smelt before – a foreboding odour. It was very unpleasant and Rascal didn't like it at all. His snout curled up at the sides when he inhaled. He knew what it must signify and he hung his head low, as if to stop the smell from entering his nostrils.

Rascal put his left leg on Nelson's body and pawed his friend's flank delicately. Normally this would have received a response from Nelson, a playful snap that said, *Hey, paws off, kiddo!* But there was nothing.

He circled a few more times and then approached Nelson's face. He put his head alongside Nelson's snout and sniffed. Then he lowered his face and rested his chin on Nelson's neck. He whimpered a last goodbye to his best friend. Rascal rose again and walked back round to Nelson's side. Pushing apart his friend's legs, he made himself a niche large enough to lie in. He curled up alongside the still warm body and buried his face into Nelson's armpit, one ear flopping onto Nelson's motionless ribcage.

Françoise happened to look over her shoulder and she saw Rascal snuggled up against Nelson. Her knees buckled and she began to quietly weep.

Rascal stole a glance at Françoise. Through that simple eye contact, an intensity shot between them as if they spoke the same tongue. Rascal turned his face away from her and pushed a heavy head back into Nelson's body. He sighed the heaviest of sighs and closed his eyes.

~ ~ ~ ~ ~

The firemen were beginning to leave. The one who had brought Nelson out of the house approached Richard and Françoise to offer his condolences again.

'I had one a bit like yours. I lost mine too. She was run over. I know it's of no help, but—'

Everyone turned when they heard Rascal. He was standing with both his front paws up on Nelson's chest and was barking incessantly with such venom. He had a wild look in his eyes, the fur on his back was bristled stiff and his tail was erect. He threw his head backwards and, with each ferocious bark, his jaws snapped open and closed.

Richard shouted at Rascal. The pain in his head was excruciating. He ran to pull Rascal off Nelson's body, his head pounding as he bent down. But before he reached him, the little dog jumped clear and began running in erratic circles round Nelson.

'Rascal! Stop that. Leave him alone, for God's sake,' cried Richard. 'Stop it!'

Rascal snapped dismissively at Richard and continued barking. He was just centimetres from Nelson and he barked directly into the dog's face.

'He has gone mad, *Rich*ard,' said Françoise. 'Is ... is ... this how dogs show their grief?'

Richard didn't answer. He was still trying to grab hold of Rascal. Still trying to ignore the pain and the spinning sensation he was feeling. Go away, he told his migraine again. I haven't time for you now – not now!

'I have no idea,' offered the fireman. 'I've never seen behaviour like that before.'

Rascal turned his attention to Françoise and began jumping up at her, barking and snapping at her ankles. Richard commanded him to stop and to sit down but Rascal ignored him. His eyes had a distant but insistent glaze in them and he held a paw high, jabbing it heavily against Françoise's shin.

'Quick!' yelled the fireman. 'Get your vet on the phone now!' He was crouching down with his head on Nelson's body, an ear on his chest. 'Your dog's still breathing.'

~ 2 ~

The fireman stroked and caressed Nelson. He lay still, not responding to the touch. But he was alive! The fireman crouched closer to Nelson's ear.

'Well, blow me, dog! I never would have thought it possible. You must be one hell of a fighter. Hang in there, bud.'

Rascal stood behind the fireman, still barking, his tail swinging frantically side to side. The fireman turned to him and beckoned him over.

'Come here, little man, come on.'

Rascal approached and pushed his snout against Nelson's face, nudging him insistently, with his tail wagging out of control.

'I think you might have just saved this dog's life,' the fireman said, and ruffled Rascal's head, a huge smile beaming across his blackened face. 'If he pulls through this, he'll owe you one. Now, you stay here and watch over your pal.'

It was one of the few instructions that Rascal didn't ignore.

~ ~ ~ ~ ~

Nelson spent three days in the oxygen unit at the vet's practice. He was alive and breathing. But that was all. Those days and nights were long ones for Richard and Françoise; particularly for Richard. Although he hadn't experienced any more migraines since the fire – and it had been several months since his previous fainting episode in the garden – he had not mentioned this most recent headache to his wife. Didn't want to worry her; it was probably a one-off. She had enough on her mind. But what Richard found sickeningly ironic was that he had rushed off to the hospital for some 'ridiculous' test that had proved utterly ineffective. Strapped to a sophisticated bed unit, he had been lifted and rotated upside down, and left there in a bizarre attempt to induce one of his headaches and dizzy spells. In the space of a few short hours, Richard's life had, quite literally, been turned upside down – twice!

The vet would not commit either way as to whether Nelson would pull through. His heart was working but it was terribly weak, and the vet admitted it was truly amazing the dog was even still alive. For him to have survived was definitely a positive sign. The vet was giving Nelson water by syringe, but he was not eating at all. He said he would be able to tell them in probably a day or two if Nelson stood a fighting chance. Meanwhile, all they could do was wait ... and hope.

They had not been allowed to even touch or hold Nelson yet, as he was contained within his pure environment. They visited the surgery twice daily and they took Rascal with them most times. They hoped a canine presence – that of Nelson's best friend – would help pull him through. It was heartbreaking to see their dog inside a box-like Perspex unit connected to all manner of tubes and electrical wires. They wanted desperately to rip all the cables out, to throw the top off the oxygen unit and reach inside to hold Nelson close. To stroke and caress him back to life. But they had to be content with touching the unit and whispering through it. Richard saw that Françoise was even stroking its transparent sides.

'He knows we're here,' he said to his wife. 'I'm sure of it.'

Rascal sat impatiently at their side, tail wagging. He looked up to where Nelson lay; over to Richard; to Françoise, and back again. His hairy face jerked up and down, craning for any indication of what was happening, his eyes both inquisitive and beseeching. Françoise reached down and tickled behind his ears and said: 'He will be okay, Rascal. He will make it. He has to.'

~ ~ ~ ~ ~

On the morning of the fourth day, Richard and Françoise arrived at the practice only minutes after it opened and they rushed straight in to see Nelson. The oxygen unit was empty; Nelson had gone. They both panicked and Françoise immediately began to cry. Richard felt a headache forming. Back to haunt him. He ordered it to go away.

The vet appeared through the open doorway. He quickly approached the couple and apologised to them for finding the unit empty. He had not expected them to arrive quite so early to visit Nelson. But their panic and tears were not necessary, he assured them. There was good news: Nelson was off the critical list.

Richard's head pain left him almost as quickly as it had arrived. He massaged the back of his neck and felt what he called his 'golf ball' lump softening. Françoise never noticed; she was already following the vet. Richard breathed two huge sighs of relief. One for himself, and one for Nelson.

The vet escorted the couple into another room, where Nelson lay on his side on a bed with his legs outstretched. His head was propped up on a little pillow. His eyes were closed, his body flaccid, and he did not move a muscle. But, there, unmistakably, on his chest was a steady rise and fall. The wonderful sight lifted the couple's hearts. Nelson hadn't given up.

But with Nelson's miraculous improvement, the couple finally appreciated just how much the recent events had affected them both – more than they'd had the chance to realise earlier. They were both exhausted. And there was so much to do. Not only had they almost lost Nelson, but they had come frighteningly close to losing their home, for heaven's sake. It would have to be emptied, scrubbed and cleaned, bottom to top. Smoke had escaped through the internal kitchen door and had spread through to the hallway, the lounge, and even upstairs to the bedrooms and bathroom. The kitchen units and their contents were burnt beyond use and the cooker was a snarled mess. Everything in the house was covered in a sooty film – even their clothes in the wardrobes, and paperwork in the drawers.

They had to spend several days with their friends, Tom and Gill, who lived nearby, because the insurance company instructed them that they must not touch or move anything in the house until the company's assessors had been. But all that had been merely peripheral to them when they thought of their beloved Nelson, lying in a plastic box.

~ ~ ~ ~ ~

On the morning of the sixth day, the vet telephoned and told them the worst news. The vet spoke and Françoise listened, her face contorting with every word she heard. It was what they had feared the most. They had dared to hope but the phone call shattered those hopes.

The vet could do no more for the dog, he apologised sincerely. Nelson had not improved, and he thought it was time now for them to let him go peacefully and accept that their dog would not be coming home. Françoise took only a moment to compose herself.

'But he *will* be coming home, *monsieur*,' she said with a resoluteness in her voice, not realising she had slipped into her native French politesse. 'We want to bring him home with us. His place is here. With us.'

Although the finality of the news hit the couple hard, they had been bracing themselves for it every day – every time that damned phone rang. Would it be the vet, or would it be the hospital with another appointment for Richard?

During the sleepless hours of the previous nights, Richard and Françoise had come to their decision. It was a painful one, but they had to think of Nelson. It would be unfair and cruel to prolong his suffering indefinitely. They had agreed that if the vet advised them it was only right to let him go, then that is what they would do. But they had already flatly rejected the idea of a cremation – Nelson would be coming home.

Guilt began to consume them both from the inside out. It seeped from every pore, every minute of the day. Neither of them could switch it off. Sleep was the only escape, but sleep came hard. Richard knew if he hadn't had to rush off to the damned hospital at such short notice, none of this would have happened. It was his fault. But he couldn't shoulder the blame alone. He couldn't handle it. And he simply could not bring himself to blame his wife, so he shifted some of his guilt onto the NHS.

Françoise knew what her husband must be feeling. She knew he would never voice it, but she knew. Oh yes, she knew. For her, the guilt was equally intense, if not more so. If only she hadn't been so stupid as to forget to turn off the cooker. *Idiot!* How could she ever forgive herself? How could Nelson?

'This is not your fault, *chéri*,' she had said. 'For goodness sake, you had to go to the *docteur* for those tests. What is *my* excuse?'

Richard and Françoise arrived at the practice just before noon. They did not take Rascal with them. They stood with Nelson and stroked him tenderly, each placing a hand on him and gently caressing his head, tickling behind his ear, massaging his flank.

'Do you remember ...' said Richard, '... the day when we first found him? The look of surprise on your face when he ...'

Françoise smiled thinly and interrupted her husband.

'Yes, of course. But you should have seen your face, *mon chéri*, when he showed you he didn't want to wear that lead. Now *that* was a picture.'

Richard moved his hand onto Nelson's chest to feel it gently rise; then fall; then rise again. Françoise put her palm on top of Richard's. Together they felt their dog breathe.

'It ... it doesn't seem right, *Rich*ard. To put him to slee— to ... He is still breathing. He is still alive. Maybe there *is* a chance ... a little hope. I just feel ... How can we give up on him when he hasn't given up on us?'

The vet entered the room. He asked if they had made their decision. Yes, they had. Yet, by the end of the conversation, they had changed their minds completely.

Although the vet was still adamant that it was the right decision to release Nelson from his suffering, he had also spoken of a possible hope. He knew of several dog owners who had used homoeopathic treatments and medicines, and even acupuncture, to help their pets. He admitted it was not something he practised himself, so he could not advocate such treatments, but if they were truly determined, then he would be willing to discharge Nelson into their care. He said he had spoken with a fireman who claimed he knew of Nelson's ordeal. He had called in once or twice to see the dog, and he told the vet that he himself was a firm believer in homeopathic treatments. He had left his name and address, and a list of websites and phone numbers for companies specialising in these types of medicines for animals.

The couple's minds were in turmoil.

'There's always hope,' the vet said, 'as long as he is still breathing. But there might come a day when you must face it, I'm afraid. If he hasn't improved soon – and I mean very soon – then please do bring him back in. It would be cruel, otherwise. Especially if he still won't take on any food. But, yes – there is *always* hope.'

~ ~ ~ ~ ~

They returned home and did their best to settle Nelson back in amid the chaos.

Although the cooker was unusable, the fridge and sink were undamaged and had been attended to by the cleaning contractor. Richard and Françoise bought minimal kitchen crockery and utensils, and had stocked the fridge with a few essentials; they would be living off ready-meals and takeaways for a while. The dining furniture had been taken away for cleaning, so they used a small camping table and chairs borrowed from Tom and Gill. They borrowed bedding from the neighbours, and bought Nelson a new basket and blankets. The list went on. The house smelt terribly of smoke and, no matter how much they cleaned and sprayed the rooms, it would be months and more before the smell would disappear completely.

Nelson had to be lifted in and out of his bed; he was unable to move at all by himself. Richard placed him in his basket in the sunshine because the weather was so good. And even though it was summertime, he put on the central heating in the evenings to keep Nelson warm.

He was taking in so little water it worried the couple, and still he would accept no food. Although his resultant movements were only minimal, they still had to clean him up afterwards. Richard bought a second basket and some extra blankets to ensure Nelson always had a clean bed.

The couple had desperately wanted to have Rascal around – they believed his presence might help Nelson recover, but the vet had advised strongly against it for the time being. He had said that Nelson needed to take things *very* slowly indeed and Rascal's boundless energy and enthusiasm might not be the ideal cure they had envisaged. He warned that Nelson was still much too fragile to cope with so much excitement so soon. Richard and Françoise certainly didn't agree with the decision, but Nelson would have to do this on his own without any help at all from his friend. Rascal too would have disagreed.

After two days, and for the first time in over a week, Nelson opened his eyes. Françoise was with him and she watched them slowly open.

'*Chéri! Rich*ard! Quick, come here! He has opened his eyes. Oh, *merci, Dieu.*'

They sat down in the sun lounge for the rest of the afternoon and attended to Nelson. Nelson's eyes opened and closed lethargically. He looked at Richard and Françoise, not showing any signs of recognition.

'*Rich*ard? Do you ... do you think he knows who we are? What if—?'

'Yes, Fran! He does. Of course he recognises us. Don't you, lad? Eh, Nelson?'

Richard thought he saw a tiny flicker in one of Nelson's eyes. But maybe not.

After a few days more, Richard was woken just after dawn by strange sounds from Nelson's basket at the foot of their bed. He was vomiting violently, his chest heaving in spasms. The vomit was black.

Watching Nelson, it made Richard realise their decision to bring him home may not have been the right one. It was extremely upsetting to witness their dog vomiting from one end, and unable to control the other. It wasn't dignified. If Nelson's life was to end, Richard wanted him to be able to leave this world nobly – not like that.

Françoise reassured him.

'No, *Rich*ard. This is a good sign. It means the detoxification medicines are doing their work. They are clearing his lungs for him. He is going to be all right; I can feel it. I *can*!'

'I hope you're right, darling. I hope you're right.'

Richard went to the kitchen and prepared some crushed-up Weetabix and milk for Nelson. He put it into one of the food syringes and took it, along with a syringe of water, back to the bedroom. The dog accepted the water gratefully, but when Richard emptied the food syringe into Nelson's mouth, it dribbled back out and into his basket.

'Patience, *chéri*,' said Françoise. 'Have patience. He will not let us down. He is a tough dog.'

Richard sighed and rubbed his temple. He then massaged the back of his neck.

'*Chéri*, are you having one of your headaches again?'

'No, dear,' lied Richard. 'Just tired, that's all.'

She knew he was keeping things from her, but she said nothing.

They got up and dressed, and Richard placed Nelson in the sun lounge in a clean basket, where he could look out through the window if he wanted, on to a gently warming sun.

They tried to busy themselves with other things but it was too difficult to concentrate. Nelson spent much of the morning vomiting and retching, and then he started to have violent sneezing fits. In the rays of the sun that pierced the glass, the couple could see mists of black mucus being ejected from Nelson's nose. There were black stains on the wallpaper and window glass.

'Are you sure we're doing the right thing, Fran?'

'I am positive, *Rich*ard. He is getting better. He is, *chéri*, he is. He will be back out into the fields with Rascal before you know it.'

~ 3 ~

The days came and the nights went. The uncertainty stayed.

And then a breakthrough.

Richard tried to give Nelson some water from the palm of his hand rather than from the large syringe. He lifted Nelson's head and held his palm under the dog's mouth. With only a little encouragement, Nelson obliged and lapped the water slowly.

'Good boy. Good boy. That's more like it.'

Richard gave him more water until the dog stopped lapping. Then he tried feeding him. This time the food stayed in the dog's mouth. Richard lowered his head and saw Nelson's throat muscles working.

'Good boy, good lad,' he whispered in a voice shaky with emotion. 'Was that good? Do you want some more, Nelson?'

The dog's ears flicked and the tip of his tail twitched. Richard was sure he'd seen it. He had. The tail moved.

'Fran! Come and see this, quick.'

From the corner of his eye, Nelson spotted Françoise dash into the room. His tail wagged again. Françoise turned on her heels, ran to the lounge and cried her heart out. A few moments later, she returned, knelt down and gave Nelson a long, gentle hug. Richard refuelled the syringe and winked at him.

'Good lad, Nelson. I bet you could murder some KFC chicken strips now, eh, lad? Well, once you're up and running, we'll treat each other, shall we? Here, have a bit more.'

Late in the afternoon, Françoise sat with Nelson for an hour or more. She wanted to see if any of his strength had returned yet. She placed her hands under his body and delicately tried lifting him up in his basket, onto his feet. But his legs were still too weak to support even his diminished weight and whenever she relaxed her hold, he slumped back down. So, she tried again. Then again. And again.

Early in the evening, midway through dinner, they heard a little yelp from within the sun lounge. They panicked, jumped up and rushed to investigate. They found Nelson lying facing the back door, his tail swishing from side to side impatiently. He looked up over his shoulder at them and yelped again, this time a little louder.

'Do you think our dog is asking to go outside, Fran?' asked Richard with a joyous smile on his face. 'Good lad, Nelson. Well done! Do you want to go out?'

Nelson yapped again and his tail sprang to life.

Françoise whispered to her husband, 'Well, go on then, *chéri*, help the poor dog up. He is desperate, *le petit*.'

Richard assisted Nelson to his feet and the two of them shuffled out into the garden. He hovered over the dog while it took care of its duties and then they shuffled back into the house.

There were three bowls by Nelson's basket – one was for food, one for milk and one for water. The food bowl was still new and empty; it had not been used yet. Richard kept his hands under Nelson's chest and guided the dog slowly to the water bowl for a drink. He was surprised when Nelson pulled and steered him sideways a little to the bowl full of milk. He began lapping eagerly at it.

'Fran? Why don't we put some food in his bow—?'

'I am already on the way, *chéri*.'

Françoise returned quickly, filled the bowl and took over from Richard. She supported Nelson while he finished his milk. When his thirst was quenched, Nelson eagerly guided her left a little and started gingerly exploring the food bowl with his nose. He took his first mouthful. And then another. He didn't leave a morsel to waste; the bowl was licked and polished, clean as new again. Then he emptied the water bowl. When he had finished, Nelson wandered slowly, with Françoise's support, to his basket. He carefully lifted his left paw and placed it in the bed. His right paw followed and he climbed in. Françoise felt her hands being twisted in a slow circle as Nelson sought comfort. He flopped down and sighed heavily. He sneezed twice, throwing black snot onto her shirt, sighed once again, and looked at them as if to say: *That's much better! Right, I'll get some sleep now, I'm exhausted.*

It might have been coincidence. It might have been Richard's wishful thinking. It could simply have been the positivity of Nelson's improvement, or it could even have been the sight of Françoise crying with joy. But whatever it was, Richard was convinced he felt a sudden easing in his head and neck. Perhaps he would not need to go back to the hospital for further tests after all.

~ ~ ~ ~ ~

A few days later, Richard returned from town with, as promised, a family bucket from KFC. He excitedly cut up the chicken into morsels and sat down on the floor next to Nelson in his basket. Nelson caught the aroma of the chicken and lifted his head, his nostrils glistening damp and anticipative.

'Look at his nose twitching away, Fran. He can't wait.'

He fed each piece to the dog, one by one, from the palm of his hand. Nelson eagerly swallowed it all. Richard reached into his own food package and passed a single French fry to Nelson. He knew Nelson didn't like the soggy KFC fries at all; he usually turned his nose up at them.

'How about one of these, lad? Fancy a chip?'

Nelson sniffed it, curled his lip and turned away.

'That's my boy. Don't let your standards slip.'

The syringes were put away – never to be used again.

Nelson still was unable to walk unaided, but he whimpered when he wanted to go outside. His voice was coming back slowly, and the feeble yelp had progressed to a beseeching yap – Richard said he thought it sounded remarkably similar to Rascal's bark – and he had regained almost full control of his bodily functions. There was noticeably more strength in his legs, and the couple could see and feel Nelson tentatively placing each paw on the ground to test his own confidence.

Days turned to weeks.

Richard was still waiting for further developments from the failed inducement tests he had undergone on the day of the fire, so they were still worrisome times. The latest specialist had proposed Richard might benefit from an even more in-depth MRI scan, to see if it would show up anything that the first one five months ago had missed. He also thought it would be a prudent idea to conduct a full cerebral angiogram. It had, after all, been almost a year since Richard's first headache and they were still no nearer to a diagnosis.

This particular specialist, a new member on the hospital team, was as keen as Françoise to find an answer and a cure. It was, once again, a tiresome matter of waiting for an appointment. Richard had already persevered with months of doctors, appointments, tests, tests and more tests, so what difference would another few weeks make? And if he were just a little honest with himself, he wasn't particularly relishing the prospect of going through another MRI scan, or having tubes threaded up through his body and being filled up with dye. And if he were truly honest, it petrified him.

For once, the appointment came quickly – a matter of days. Richard was still unconvinced it was all necessary.

'But, Fran,' he insisted. 'I haven't had a headache or a dizzy spell for weeks now.' He knew it was only a small untruth, but he corrected himself anyway. 'Not since Nelson started eating again. Do we really nee—?'

Françoise's look was all it took to answer the question.

So, a few days later, they went to the hospital again. Françoise waited patiently – trying hard not to worry too much – until, finally, Richard emerged ... in a wheelchair. Françoise's eyes were wide and wild. She covered her mouth with her hands and took a deep breath, which she held as Richard was pushed towards her. Her palms were sweating.

'Fran!' bellowed Richard down the long, echoing corridor. 'Fran, don't panic, dear. Everything's okay. Everything's okay. It's all fine.'

When he eventually reached her, and she saw the beaming smile and excitement in his eyes, she finally exhaled. The nurse left them and Richard began.

'Calm down, old girl – no need to worry your lovely self. All's well that ends well. Finally, we get an answer. Good old NHS, eh? It might take them a while, but they get there in the end. It seems, my dear, that I have a little lump at the base of my skull. No, no, don't panic, darling. It's not a tumour! No, it seems that my resident golf ball is actually an aneurysm. Do you know that word in English, dear? Yes, of course you do. Well, anyway, I have a small aneurysm that had ruptured. But it's not a tumour, thank God, so don't fret.

'I'm rather glad I had that angiogram done now, Fran. It was fascinating to see – all that coloured ink flowing around my body. Apparently, it's just a small aneurysm with the tiniest of ruptures, which I presume is why that first scan missed it. I'm actually a very lucky fellow indeed. If it had been a bigger one, and that had haemorrhaged, we might not be having this little chat. So, things have worked out quite well, haven't they? Anyway, I could even see the little bleeder on the photos. Amazing! More a little pea than a golf ball, really. It *is* still leaking a little bit, they said, but it has almost healed. All on its own. The doctors said it has been trying to heal itself for the past ... God knows how long. Well, ever since my first spell, I suppose.

'They've assured me there's no serious risk any more, but they want to keep me in for a few days for recuperation and observation. They've told me I'll have to stay in bed – horizontal – *for a whole week*, so that the rupture can heal itself properly. It won't have the chance, otherwise, if I'm moving around all the time, you see. Flat on my back for a week, twenty-four hours a day, doing nothing at all. Doctor's orders! What do you think about all that then, dear? You're not saying much.'

Françoise was so relieved that, for a long moment, she found it hard to say anything at all. It was too much to take in.

'Whatever it takes, *chéri*. What *ever* it takes. I'm so relieved we finally know what it is. *Merci, Dieu*. You might even enjoy it, you old devil: all those young nurses looking after you.'

Richard failed to suppress a smile. 'But what about you and Nelson?'

'We'll be fine. We'll keep each other company. Don't worry, you'll be able to see him when you come home. I'll tell him the wonderful news for you.'

Although he was putting on an amazingly brave face for his wife, Richard's guilt rose and manifested itself again. He accepted that he would have to leave Françoise to nurse Nelson alone. He was abandoning them both. Abandoning Nelson again! Why hadn't he gone to the doctor's much sooner, the old fool?

After five long but successful days in hospital, the doctors were happy to release Richard. The rupture had fully healed, the swelling had dissipated and the checks they had made indicated that all was well. No complications. It was fantastic news. Richard could go home again to his wife. He could see Nelson again. They could get on with their lives.

At home, husband and wife chose to gloss over the events. Françoise's only demand was to make Richard promise that if he ever again felt the slightest headache coming on – no matter how small – he would tell her. He assured her he had learnt his lesson the hard way. By the end of that week, Richard was doing well, and Nelson even better: he could walk a few metres almost unaided. One mid-afternoon, Richard was washing up, whistling merrily, when he heard Nelson yap.

'Just a minute, lad. I'll be there in a tick,' he shouted. 'Do you want to go out? Just let me fin—'

Another yap.

'All right, lad, I'm coming. Just let me—'

Several yaps. And some more.

Richard let the plate fall back into the soapy water and hurried into the sun lounge.

The patio door was already open. Outside on the lawn lay Nelson, flat on his back, all four legs in the air. Dancing round him in circles was Rascal. It was Rascal making all the noise, overwhelmed at seeing his friend again.

Françoise had often joked about Richard's inability or unwillingness to show his emotions. 'Typical man, typical *English*man', she had said many a time, but if she had seen him standing in the patio doorway, she would have changed her mind. Tears rolled down his cheeks.

Rascal jumped up and down like a dancing horse. Forwards, backwards and then forwards again, all the while barking. He ran at Nelson as if to jump on him but, stopping short, he grabbed hold of Nelson's back leg and began chewing and pulling at it. Nelson lay still and let Rascal chew for a moment; then he yapped once at his friend. He gave Rascal a look that said, *Enjoy it while you can, you little shrimp. I'll be back on my paws soon, and then there'll be trouble!*

But Rascal wasn't going to wait anything like as long as that. He nibbled Nelson's leg persistently. Then he swapped over and chewed the other one. He pushed his snout into Nelson's neck and nudged him. Nelson let out another little yap.

'Rascal,' said Gill. 'Leave him alone. He doesn't want to play. Here, boy!'

Richard hadn't noticed Gill and Tom standing by the gate to the back garden. He rubbed his eyes and cheeks self-consciously and wiped the tears onto his shirt.

'Sorry, Gill. Tom. I didn't see you both there.'

'No need to apologise, Richard,' Gill replied. 'I'm welling up, myself. How's he doing then? And how are *you*? Françoise told me the good news.'

'Better by the minute, I would say. Both of us!'

'Hi, Richard,' said Tom. 'Welcome home! You must be relieved it's finally all over. Or are you missing the attentions of all those nurses?' Tom smiled at Richard and then looked over to Rascal, who was still pestering Nelson. 'Rascal! Here!'

'No – it's okay,' replied Richard. 'Leave them. He only wants to play.'

Nelson realised there was no respite from Rascal's enthusiastic onslaught. Preventative action needed to be taken. He wriggled himself over and rolled onto his belly. He pushed his legs hard into the grass, trying to force himself upwards. Rascal backed away, still yapping excitedly.

Françoise appeared in the doorway.

'What is all this noise about? What is going—? How did—? Did he get there all by himself? Look, *Rich*ard, he is trying to stand up.'

Nelson knew he could do it, but this time he had an audience, and a point to prove. He was determined. Slowly, and with great effort, he pushed himself up, paw by paw, into a standing position. Then he stretched. His tongue hung loosely from his mouth and he was panting rapidly. Not wanting to overdo his exertions too much in one session, he immediately sat down heavily on the grass, his rear quarters lopsided and loose. He faced the humans, tongue hanging out of his jaw.

Rascal voiced his approval and went to sit alongside his friend, bolt upright as if on parade.

'Oh, oh. Look at them both,' said Françoise behind cupped hands. 'Look at them. They are like two bookends. Wait – while I get the camera. I want a photograph of this.'

'Never mind the camera, darling. Do we have any champagne?'

'I ... I don't know. If we do, it will be in the fridge in the garage, *chéri*. Do you think it is a good idea? You are still on those tablets, remember.'

'Fran, my dear! If I can't have a glass of the old bubbly to celebrate this little black miracle in front of me, I might as well be in a wooden box.'

~ ~ ~ ~ ~

The months passed, and before they realised it, a full year had come and gone since the fire. Summer had returned almost as quickly as Nelson had.

Nelson was noticeably slower and definitely more relaxed now. Rascal slowed down accordingly. He must have sensed that his time with his pal would not be quite as it was before. He was dealing with an older dog; the events had surely accelerated his friend towards retirement in a slightly higher gear than normal. Nelson was no longer able to keep up with Rascal for quite as long when they raced along the shoreline or chased rabbits through the woods.

Nelson, for his part, could not have been happier. The flick of an ear and the blink of an eye said as much. He must have appreciated Rascal *finally* treating him with a little more respect. The message in Nelson's eyes was, '*and about time too!*'. The sparkle was truly back, his nose carried a glistening sheen, and his tail made up for lost time. And, of course, he had a new regular treat to look forward to. Once a week, Richard would dash off to town, returning with the forbidden fruits of KFC – he soon discovered Nelson had developed an insatiable appetite for the side order of baked beans. Richard still felt responsible for events and it was the least he could do to assuage some of the guilt by providing for their faithful dog in any way he could.

He and Françoise loved to watch Rascal and Nelson run together in the fields, and they often called in at Tom and Gill's to collect Rascal so the two dogs could frolic. And sometimes at the weekends, a certain fireman called at the house and took Nelson out for a long walk – Nelson had a new friend.

Richard's own recuperation was as absolute as Nelson's. He took further strength from the knowledge that their dog was fitter and healthier than they could have ever dreamed possible, and it humbled them both to hear the vet's comments that he had never seen a dog pull through such an experience nor make such an astounding recovery.

'But,' he said, and it was a big 'but'; he admitted it was impossible to say what effect the whole ordeal had on Nelson's mind and how his brain had coped after being starved of oxygen. 'Put it this way,' the vet had said, 'don't enter him for the London Marathon this year. But do give him plenty of exercise. Keep him active, like before. Let *him* be the one to decide how far he wants to go with this. He's in charge now. But most of all – enjoy him! He's an amazing animal, and he deserves all the love you can give him.'

What was very clear to them all was that Nelson was back doing what he loved best – living life to the full, and enjoying whatever it chose to throw at him. Even if that did mean an unruly Patterdale-cross called Rascal.

One year became the next, and two years became three.

Summer said its annual farewells and handed over to autumn. The coolness of winter soon returned. But inside, Richard and Françoise were warmed through by Nelson's presence. They treated every new day with Nelson as another special one; one to savour the company of their unique four-legged friend. They would never fully know what true effects the events had on Nelson; they could only ever guess. There was only one member of the household who really knew that. Françoise often found herself telling Richard that she wished, oh, how she wished, that Nelson could somehow let them know how he truly felt. When she sat with him, caressing him delicately behind his ears where he loved it, she looked deep into his eyes, those big twinkling eyes full of life, emotion and meaning. And she would ask him in a quiet, yet insistent voice: 'What are you thinking, Nelson, *mon petit*? If only you could talk.'

Part 2

Four Paws and a Tale

~ 4 ~

The present day, a fine December morning

Nelson lies snug and comfortable in his basket, with his chin propped up on the side. He gazes vacantly out through the patio window as a gentle December dawn taps on the glass. He finds himself contemplating his life with a warm feeling inside. He couldn't be happier, and his tail twitches with contentment.

It's been three and a half years since the fire, he tells himself. Three and a half wonderful years that he wouldn't have lived if it hadn't been for Rascal.

He has been awake for some time, pondering, daydreaming, and reviewing his mixed fortune down the line. He has no cause for complaint. He has had an unforgettable life. Christmas is not far off again; but Nelson won't be here to celebrate this one. He has made a choice. His head is in a bit of a whirl, and when he tries to organise his thoughts, his mind fills to overflowing with a confused blur of memories. But he has plenty of time, as it will be a good while before his guardians surface for the day.

Three and a half years. A long time ago – twenty-five years on his canine calendar! – but still he has bad dreams about the fire from time to time. He whimpers and yelps in his sleep and wakes up trembling, panting, his paws clammy. Occasionally he even wakes Richard and Françoise with his cries. He twitches and kicks with his back legs during his dreams, perhaps fighting with the fire demons in his sleep. When he wakes, his covers are tangled and twisted, kicked out of bed onto the floor. Often, he finds himself out of his basket and at the other side of the room by the window, whining quietly for help from an invisible presence outside. And although it is his own reflection in the glass, Nelson imagines Rascal outside, pawing urgently at the window. Nelson longs for the day his terrible dreams finally stop. He wants to remember the wonderful times, not the fire.

After he turned away from Rascal at the window and collapsed in his basket, he had but few recollections of the days that immediately followed the fire. Yet, one particular scene does keep coming back to Nelson. He can picture Rascal jumping up and down on him and shouting loudly in his ears. Nelson remembers being on his side, legs splayed and trying so hard to lift a leg to push Rascal away, but he had no strength. He couldn't even open his eyes to plead with Rascal to leave him alone. All he wanted to do was to lie still and die.

What he recalled next was being in a strange new place and squeezing his eyes tightly closed against a painfully intense light. He wanted desperately to lift his paws to cover his eyelids because the light penetrated them mercilessly. But his legs were too heavy, and he didn't even have the energy to turn his head and body away. Yet, he sensed a cleanliness and a purity around him in that place. Something calming. But through his eyelids, the stabbing light pierced that calm. He wondered if that was what dying was all about.

He could hear noises and voices, but they were not all faint and wispy, or drifting, as they are in his dreams now. They were all mixed up, loud and echoing. They hurt his head. But he knew them. One in particular was a dog's voice. A female dog's voice. It was so familiar and he heard it calling to him. Nelson tried to open his eyes to see where the voices came from but he couldn't; they were weighed down and glued tightly closed.

But he *was* alive. He knew he was!

As time passed, Nelson regained most of his strength and finally started to feel his true self again. His legs performed when his brain asked them to, and his road to recovery meant he could at last cock a leg without assistance from his guardians. This was a very important statement of independence for Nelson, and it meant his poor guardians didn't get a soaking from his clumsy three-legged spraying, which must have pleased them too.

The months passed slowly by. Those months became trouble-free years, life returned almost to normal for him and things were like they used to be – except that Rascal didn't insist on Nelson squirming around on dead seagulls as much any more, for which he told Rascal he was grateful. He was back to being his old self, although with a little more emphasis on the old. But what exactly is that 'old self'?

Nelson is almost but not quite up to knee-height on an average human; soot black and, some would say, a handsomely unique cross between a Labrador and a Whippet – a purebred pedigree cross-breed of mixed parentage and origin. He has some of the girth of the Labrador but the legs of the Whippet. That isn't to say he resembles a Labrador on stilts, but it does mean he is very fast. His four-paw drive is supremely efficient, as any retreating rabbit will verify. Well, it *was*. Nowadays, he is somewhat slower. He can still give Rascal a run for his money along the seafront, but only over shorter distances – anything more than an hour and this old pooch is prematurely pooped. And as for the rabbits, well, Nelson had to take early retirement from that pastime as they are simply too nimble and nifty for him these days.

Nelson noticed, too, that Rascal gives him a little head start on their races nowadays by pretending to sniff a tree, or by joining the dots along a female's trail for a while. He always catches him up soon after and snaps impatiently at Nelson's heels, tongue hanging out, with a cheeky grin on his face. After running a few teasing circles round Nelson and shouting his usual jovial obscenities – which shall not be repeated – Rascal overtakes. He speeds off with a lightning acceleration that always amazes Nelson, Rascal's nostrils dribbling, and saliva splashing poor old Nelson in the face.

For Nelson is old now, and he would be the first to admit it. He is almost twelve after all. Not a bad age, he tells himself. He knows his time has not been wasted, and he is a fairly wise old hound now. He didn't get this far by being just any dopey old Basset. Well, not all the time, anyway.

His current moniker is indeed Nelson, but he did have other names while living with his previous guardians, both here in England and, *naturellement*, back when he was a pup in the heart of the French Alps, where his then guardians, the Morettis, called him Ombré. So what cruel and complicated turn of events forced what was once a tiny, mischievous ball of pup-fluff into the harsh reality of northern France? And how, some eight years ago, did Ombré ever come to put his Gallic paws on English soil in the first place?

Alone and scared, Ombré had been forced to live a lonely stray's existence, roaming the streets of a city not far from the Normandy coast. He spent his days getting into all sorts of trouble, going hungry and wishing he had never been born. He hated crying himself to sleep every night, and waking up shivering in the cold, the wind and the rain. If it hadn't been for old Bazou, he would have given up completely. He continued his despondent wanderings, forsaken by the world. Even *maman* had stopped watching over him.

Resorting to stealing and scavenging from waste bins, Ombré found himself in a large truck park. Plodding dejectedly from truck to truck, driver to driver, he was looking for no more than a friendly greeting or an affectionate tickle of his ears. He found neither. He spotted an old truck at the far side of the park with one of its rear doors open so, with nothing better to do, he went to investigate. He stood behind it, raised his snout and lifted a paw to concentrate. From inside, a magnetic cocktail of delightful aromas tickled his nostrils and pulled Ombré irresistibly towards it. When he threw his paws up against the back, stretching high to see what was inside, his excitement and desperation suddenly took control of his rationale. He catapulted himself up into the welcoming darkness where he could hide from life's pitiless reign.

Ombré fell into a deep and much needed slumber. He slept so soundly that he never even heard the back door of the truck being swung closed. The gentle rumble of the engine and the rocking of the truck as it travelled many a motorway kilometre served as a perfect remedy to his cold, sleepless nights. When the truck was driven onto the tunnel train, Ombré was blissfully lost in a wonderfully vivid dream about his mountain strolls with Belle. When he finally woke, long hours after departing the truck park, he realised he was trapped, en route to separation from his native France – destination England. In fact, he was already on English territory with no way of turning back.

~ 5 ~

The driver of the delightfully smelly old truck had no idea he had a four-legged stowaway in the back – not until Ombré finally succeeded in making his presence known somewhere in England. Ombré had been only slightly concerned while being thrown about in the back of the truck, and he was in no great rush to abandon the creature comforts of his colossal bed. But he was hungry again and extremely thirsty.

He had shouted repeatedly at the top of his voice and scratched on the walls of the truck, but there was never any response. All the fluffy old tartan blankets surrounding him acted as soundproofing and his calls remained unheard. In the back of the vehicle were hundreds and hundreds of them, all thrown on top of one another in huge piles – en route to a charity warehouse.

In the rear corner of the truck, plugged into an electrical outlet, Ombré had discovered the driver's very well stocked cool box. Ombré circled it, pawing at it and sniffing the sides. Even with the lid firmly on, he could smell there was food inside. Food that he must eat. Fortunately for him, Ombré had mastered a rather clever trick he first learnt as a youngster when he still resided in the Alps with the Moretti family. He could prise the lid off a cool box in under twenty seconds. He had watched the Morettis do it so many times during their family picnics together and he had studied their movements conscientiously. He soon discovered he could do the same with his snout and paws. Putting the lid back on was altogether more difficult, so he never bothered with that. He was ever-pleased with this skill, but his guardians didn't always seem too enamoured of his dexterity.

That day in the blanket truck was during a particularly hard time of his life and, although theft was not something he was prone to, food and water were his priority. He hadn't eaten for days and the previous drink he'd had was some oily water from a puddle in the truck park. Fortunately for Ombré, the cool box was similar to the one the Morettis had. His ravenous hunger took over and he pushed his snout and a paw into the lip between the lid and base. When he lifted the lid off, his culinary desires came instantly true; it was brimming with cheese, dried sausage and cured ham. He hadn't seen so much meat since the day he was banned from the local butcher in his Alpine village.

Before long, he had finished off the meat, and had greedily chomped away on the final morsel of cheese. He left nothing to waste, except for one vacuum-pack of *jambon de pays* that he was unable to open. He mopped up every little bit of spillage; the wooden floor of the truck was bone dry. He had even licked all the various wrappings clean of their taste. He was a very full dog and more than ready for another good nap. His thirst still bothered him, but the strong pull of sleep took his mind off it temporarily. Ombré climbed onto the mountain of tartan – the biggest bed he had ever seen.

His bedding had a wonderful aroma to it too. The blankets had come from various holiday parks in southern France, and the smells lingered on – to Ombré's distinct pleasure. They smelt of people, barbecues, sun cream, beer and wine, and there were grains of fine sand embedded in them. There were hundreds more smells besides, so he had a good sniff around before settling down to sleep again. The pleasant mix of male and female odour had his senses alert, and that unmistakable whiff of human sleep was a delight in his nostrils. It took him some time to absorb it all. It took him even longer to rearrange the blankets for the ultimate comfort before he was finally forced to give in and collapse onto his full stomach. He turned only one cursory circle and flopped down with a gaping yawn, a sigh of fulfilment, and a deeply resonant burp. Normally, he would complete two full circles before properly settling down – sufficient for him to attain his usual back-to-the-womb comfort, but he skipped the routine that day.

~ Finally! he said to himself. A good meal and a comfortable sleep, somewhere it doesn't rain.

Things were looking promising for Ombré, and he drifted off to sleep, already wondering what adventure would befall him next.

He was brutally woken by an explosive shouting.

His big flappy ears are, much like his snout, highly sensitive receptors, so he was shocked by the piercing volume to which they were being subjected. He was instantly alert, his feral instincts taking over. From his sleeping place high up on the blankets, he blinked to focus, and looked down to the back of the truck. He saw the bulging red features of the driver, waving his arms above his head. He had a face the complexion of corned beef and he screamed profanities at Ombré with a look of sheer rage – a look that was backed up by his actions when he reached up into the back of the truck and grabbed a large broom.

Ombré had already had a few disagreements with brooms, mops and various gardening implements in the past, so he was very keen to diffuse the situation with minimum fuss and pain on his part. He climbed nervously down from his bed and walked slowly to the back of the truck, one eye on the driver, his other on the gyrating broom. He flicked his tail to half-mast and wagged it a little for the driver to see. Ombré was at a complete loss as to what the driver's display of bursting blood vessels was for; Ombré thought he had done him a good turn or two. He had cleaned up all the spilt contents of his cool box, he had polished the truck floor clean, and he was keeping the driver's bed warm for him. There was even some food left for him.

The driver still hadn't climbed into the back of the truck, so Ombré's elevated position enabled them to look at each other as equals – or so he hoped. He turned and stood slightly sideways on to the driver and looked at him with his head angled rather than facing him eyeball to eyeball. This should show him I mean no harm at all, decided Ombré. He lowered his head ever so slightly, bared his neck to the man and wagged his tail. Not a tail held high and erect, but no, more a *Hi, pleased to meet you* wag.

Ombré's tactics didn't appear to be working. Understanding dog-speak clearly wasn't the truck driver's forte and he continued to rant wildly in an alien tongue Ombré did not comprehend. However, a raised broom is the same in any language. Ombré dropped his head even lower so his chin was almost scraping the floor; he retracted his tail and tucked it tightly between his thighs to show the man that Ombré accepted he was in charge.

Maybe it was the language barrier but, without further warning, the jabbing broom hit Ombré hard and square on his shoulder.

~ *Aïe!* Oww! he cried out in pain.

Ombré was thrown backwards against the blankets. Because the man was bigger and stronger, Ombré's natural instinct was to show his submission even further. If his lowered head and retracted tail hadn't worked as hoped, then there was clearly a superiority struggle in the making unless he quickly diffused it. And Ombré knew who would lose. The driver had not accepted his earlier submissive displays and still believed him to be a threat, so Ombré knew he would have to demonstrate total submission and respect. He had no choice. So, he lay down slowly on his side, lifted one of his back legs high in the air and he urinated.

Not much came out – nothing more than a squirt and a dribble. It was all he could muster, and he was very disappointed. Ombré reasoned that the driver must have mistaken this as a feeble gesture and an insincere display of respect on his part, because he became even more enraged. He climbed up into the truck, still screaming and shouting, and he advanced rapidly, thrusting the broom at Ombré with a vicious stabbing motion. Ombré was cornered with nowhere else to go. He darted backwards and uphill onto the top of the blankets where he presumed the madman couldn't reach him or swing at him.

He was wrong, and the driver started pulling himself clumsily up the blankets. From his summit, Ombré called down to the man to tell him he didn't mean any disrespect, and there was no need for them to fight. The driver ignored him, and swung the broom, catching Ombré a skimming blow on his right ear. He dodged sideways just before the next swipe arrived. He quickly jumped down off the blankets and skidded across the wooden floor, ignoring the splinters that he felt entering the leathery pads of his paws. He hurdled the scattered blankets and ran for the back of the truck, throwing himself out of that door like a Greyhound from its starting cage. As he flew mid-air, he looked over his shoulder and he felt the broom thudding heavily under his rear quarters, which propelled him forwards. Luckily, he landed on all fours on the ground behind the truck. He darted left and right, back and forth, trying to decide which way to run.

When he was a safe distance clear he stopped running and turned to look back at the truck to witness the man still waving the broom and hurling incessant verbal abuse. He turned quickly away, showed the man his *derrière* with as much contempt as he could communicate and ran off quickly into the bushes. He lay down on the grass, took a paw in his mouth and licked his wounds clean. He jogged deeper into the trees away from harm. But where was he jogging to? More immediately, what was he going to do when he got 'there'?

It was not that Ombré wasn't relieved to be far away from his previous so-called guardian. When he had finally managed to escape from Alphonse's farm in Normandy, his sole intention had been to hit the road as quickly as possible and run, run, run, far, far away. But perhaps not quite as far as England! How did he manage to get himself into such a predicament? And how would he get himself out of it? The answer would come in the most unexpected of forms.

~ 6 ~

Ombré had been an illegal immigrant in England for around two weeks following his broom-propelled ejection from the blanket truck. He was on his own yet again. Back to lonely days and long, cold nights in the rain, always hungry, thirsty, and in search of nothing more than an affectionate stroke or cuddle. Someone who gave a damn about him. It seemed to him that nobody did any more. He had almost given up, had no further interest in life, no motivation to do anything. He spent dreary days wandering around without real purpose, desperately looking for somewhere to hide, or a large rock under which to disappear.

Eventually, he stumbled upon a peaceful place that was ideal for the purpose because it was so deserted. Ombré flopped down under a large tree and huffed discontentedly, letting his soulless eyes close. He pressed his chin down onto his outstretched paws, blinked his eyes open again and stared over his snout into the distance. Far away. Far away from there. Back to the Alps and to Belle.

He had effectively been on his own for almost four months. He was tired of chasing his past, and despaired of looking forlornly for his future. He needed some companionship. His tail was a pathetically disjointed extension of his sadness, and it hung loosely behind him. It was as if it didn't belong to him any more.

He started to cry himself to sleep. When he could cry no more, he was relieved to feel his eyes finally grow heavy as he slipped into a fitful slumber. He prayed they wouldn't open again.

But unfortunately they did, when a group of little birds landed on the branches directly above him and started chirping and chatting among themselves as if they had something to celebrate in this awful world. Ombré was in no mood at all for such melodic merriment, so he tried to block out the noise. No matter how much he folded and covered his ears with his paws, however hard he tried to ignore their singsong, the tuneful interlude actually served to lift his spirits a little. Until, that is, he felt something sticky slap onto the top of his head. He sprang to his feet and jumped up at the tree, shouting at the birds to show a little respect for his predicament, but they laughed at him and flew away. Ombré did his best to scrape the offering from his head but he couldn't quite reach it, so he had to let it go crusty. Inexplicably, this amused him and had the effect of cheering him up further. It showed that someone was aware of his existence, even if it was proven by launching droppings on his head.

He jumped up into the air and called after the birds, this time to thank them for snapping him out of his trance, but they were long gone. He shouted anyway – it helped to pass the time. He ran round the tree in circles, shouting at no one or nothing in particular. Then he ran up and down the grass, shouting at the sky, at every tree and at every bird he saw. He ran and ran until he was exhausted. His voice was hoarse with all the shouting. He spotted two people walking along a path, so he ran past them and yapped a *Bonjour!* as he sped by.

He sprinted from one corner of the park to the next and back again, with a spring in his legs that he hadn't used for too long. When he returned to his tree to check if his new bird friends had come back, he spotted the two people again, so he bade them *Au revoir* and *Bonne journée*, but they gave him a strange look and scurried off.

~ Life's not so bad after all, he told himself as he collapsed in a contented heap under the shade of his tree.

Ombré was innocently unaware of the fact, but the place he had chosen as his retreat was a sprawling cemetery. To him, it was simply a large park. He cherished the rolling expanse of manicured grass, dotted with big old trees and what he thought were just big stones. There was plenty of space for him to find peace and solitude. It was very clean and tidy, he noticed, and ever so quiet. He decided he might as well rest up there for a few days to see if he could hatch a plan. He would have to lay down some house rules with those birds first, though.

His retreat was somewhere outside of a small village and Ombré was overjoyed to discover that there was easy access to drinking water, and he could find plentiful food from a local eatery. And he was always assured a good night's sleep because his park was curiously deserted after dusk. During the day, he watched people come and go in small numbers. It was never very crowded except when a large group of people turned up. But, Ombré observed, they never stayed long. At night, the park was his. Even the birds were absent.

He bumped into Timothy and his father purely by chance early one evening. It was a rather unorthodox beginning to their relationship, but the boy and his father would soon form part of Ombré's tight clan, a united little pack.

Ombré was napping in the shade of a large, round-topped stone, when a small boy spoke to him and disturbed his contented state. He yawned widely, smacked his jaws noisily and gave himself a good waking-up shake and a full stretch. What did the little boy want?

The boy repeated his words but Ombré was unable to deduce whether it was a question, a request or an instruction. The words were spoken slowly, as though deliberately drawn out and stretched, but they were devoid of emotion. There wasn't the slightest change in tone to help Ombré. And as it was all in English, he had little hope of working out what Timothy wanted. He communicated his confusion with a short yap and a tilt of his head.

~ *Je te comprends pas!* I don't understand you!

Timothy's mannerisms and stilted way of speaking were entirely due to his condition; he lived with a form of autism. His father, David, was struggling bravely to cope with an autistic son, but after the recent loss of his wife, he found things almost unbearable. Impossible sometimes. Together, he and Rosie had nurtured Timothy as a team and had brought the boy up with all the love and special attention they could give him. But now that he was forced to do it alone, David was struggling to cope with the harsh reality of his wife's fatal mugging and with Timothy's eternal condition. Their future was as uncertain as that of Ombré.

Timothy spoke to Ombré again, his monotonic diction confusing and annoying the dog.

Ombré yapped at him impatiently.

~ Look! I have no idea at all what you are talking about, little boy. *Je suis français* and you are not making any sense to me.

He had just been woken from a beautiful dream, and the boy's interruption annoyed him so much that he voiced his discontent. If Ombré's *maman* had ever seen him behave in such a despicable way, she would have cuffed him hard on the snout and denied him his milk rations. But Ombré had, just that day, convinced himself he really could survive without humans. They had done him no favours recently, so he had resolved to stay independent of them for a while. They didn't care about him, so he didn't care about them. Simple!

He trotted away from Timothy, a defiant bounce in his step, tail held high. He headed over to a big shady tree on the far side of the cemetery, where he answered a few calls of nature. He glanced dismissively over his shoulder but he saw the boy was just centimetres behind him, hovering over him with an impassive look on his face. Ombré felt that the boy was now disciplining him, but it was still impossible for him to be sure. He shouted his annoyance again.

~ Look, boy! Leave me alone will you, he snapped at the boy's heels, and took his leave again, this time running fast so that Timothy couldn't keep up.

The strange little boy left him alone after that and Ombré didn't see him for a couple of days. Not a particularly inspirational first encounter, not one overflowing with future promise. But that was Ombré's fault; the boy had caught him at a confusing moment, torn between dependence and independence, and he was unfairly tetchy. Blatantly rude, in fact.

Ombré returned to his private ponderings.

In the light evening breeze, a few damp leaves were falling off the trees and floating lazily to the ground. The air was fresh and moist; a light rain had fallen earlier. Ombré started to amuse himself by jumping up in the air and trying to catch the leaves before they landed. He trapped a good few in his snapping jaws but most fluttered around too much. Some landed on his nose and some fell onto his head and stuck. It felt good to play games, a release from his troubles, as during the previous months he had forgotten how to enjoy himself. And he much preferred the leaves to the bird droppings.

People generally came and went quietly in ones or twos. Some gave him a little laugh or smile and then carried on their own walk. A few gave him the clucking-tongue greeting that many humans use. Traditionally, Ombré would have approached them, introduced himself and his tail properly and had a preliminary sniff. But for that short time in his new environment, he actually felt very happy to be on his own, free of all obligation. For the first time in too long, he carried his head above his heart. He was still very wary of meeting another Alphonse, though.

He had discovered some well-stocked waste bins behind the village pub, only a short sprint away, and there was certainly more than enough water in his park – a gross understatement in itself. Twice each day, a very strange thing happened, one that took Ombré a long moment to accept. The first time he witnessed the phenomenon, it caught him completely off guard and scared him senseless. He was minding his own business, dozing off quite successfully, when suddenly he felt a wet sensation dribbling forcibly down between his legs. Never since being a puppy with a bladder that had a mind of its own had this happened to him. Within seconds, he was soaking wet down there. This worried him greatly because he'd just had a wee – well, eleven of them, to be precise.

He twisted his head round and down to investigate. When his nose was closer to what he presumed was his faulty valve, he sniffed hard. It had none of his usual odour, so he shunted his carriage slightly sideways to investigate more and received a face full of powerful jet spray. He jumped up in shock and stared in disbelief at a jettisoning fountain of water coming up from the grass. He jumped clear, stood back and shouted angrily at the fountain, with his front paws spread and his damp backside high in the air.

Once he had calmed down a little, he looked around him for some clues. Slowly, it became apparent what was going on and he cursed his innocence. Scattered over a large area, covering much of his park, lots more little fountains of water were spurting from the grass at regular distances. How ignorant could I have been? he thought. It's obvious what is happening, you fool! Never had he experienced such a thing back in France, so it must have been a weather pattern particular only to England. It was raining upwards, of course.

~ What a magical place this is, he sighed. I love it here.

At first, the novice in him tried to drink the water as soon as it spurted powerfully from the grass, but he received a good old soaking with that technique. He quickly learnt that if he positioned himself correctly, the water spray would arc through the air and all he had to do was gobble at the fine mist when it came down again. And he got a free shower for the price. Ombré had great fun running from one spray to another, pouncing on them, stamping them down with his paws, nosediving into the fountains and drinking the cool water. It was so refreshing. Passers-by watched him and laughed but he was having too much fun to pay them any lengthy attention. He called to a few and showed off his paw-stamping moves.

One particular afternoon a few days later, he hadn't noticed his frolics were being closely watched until he heard a familiar little voice. He recognised it instantly. The same dull words.

'Have you come to see your dead mother too, Mister Dog?'

~ 7 ~

It was the same toneless question the boy had asked the previous time they met. Ombré looked up at Timothy quizzically. Timothy repeated his words.

'Have you come to see your dead mother too, Mister Dog?'

What was the boy saying to Ombré in that alien language of his? There was still nothing to give the baffled dog a clue.

Ombré was in a much better frame of mind this time, so he was much more courteous to the boy. He sat down in front of Timothy with an inviting yap. He pricked up his ears and tilted them forwards to attempt to understand the foreign tongue. He didn't grasp a single thing. Timothy carried on talking regardless. And when Timothy spoke, he had a habit of not stopping. Ombré would soon begin to wonder if the boy ever needed to pause for breath.

'Is your mother dead too? My mother is. She died when somebody killed her when she was taking some money from a hole in a wall. At first I did not understand why there was a hole in a wall with money in it and I did not understand how mother knew there was some money in the hole but father explained it to me. My mother was my best friend but because mother is not with us any more my best friend now is my father.'

Ombré looked up at Timothy, wide-eyed. Timothy paused only briefly and then continued chatting.

'You look very cute when you look up at me with your head leaning to one side like that, Mister Dog. Do you have a best friend, Mister Dog? I can be your best friend if you want me to. I do not have many best friends but that is because people think I am a bit weird. Father says I am not weird but I am just different. People call me names all the time but it does not upset me but I know it upsets father when I tell him what happens to me on the way home from special school. The teachers at special school say that my condition is called autism but father likes to say I am artistic and not autistic. I know he only says that because he finds it difficult to cope with me.'

Timothy stopped talking and suddenly pointed to the other side of the cemetery. Ombré looked up at his waving finger excitedly and wagged his tail. He never understood why humans wiggled an extended index finger like that, but it often led to something interesting – or food! – hence the enthusiastic tail.

'Look, Mister Dog. Father is over there putting some flowers on the grave. No you silly dog not on the end of my finger. He is over there look.'

Ombré jumped up at Timothy's finger. Did the boy want him to sniff it? To nibble it? What?

'No you silly dog you are not supposed to look at my finger. The flowers we bring for mother are always very pretty and they smell beautiful just like mother was. But soon they will be dead like mother is now so we will come back and we will bring some more for her.'

Timothy knelt down and looked at Ombré expectantly. Ombré's ears twitched in anticipation of something but he was unsure what. A tiny whimper escaped.

~ *Quoi?* Why are you looking at me like that?

It was starting to go dusk. Ombré was extremely hungry, and it was almost time for his usual running of the gauntlet behind the village pub. He looked at the boy with apologetic eyes and made as though to leave, wagging his tail to the right, just once or twice, to let the boy know he was in a good mood and had very much enjoyed meeting him. He would have loved to stay but there could well be some leftover spare ribs or a half-finished roast chicken waiting for him in the bins. He stood up and turned away from Timothy.

Timothy spoke as Ombré was in mid-turn.

'Do not go yet, Mister Dog. Please stay here with me until father returns. He is a little sad now but I would like you to meet him. You will like father. I do.'

Ombré continued to walk away, but stopped when he heard the same words following him.

'Do not go yet, Mister Dog. Please stay here with me until father returns. He is a little sad now but I would like you to meet him. You will like father. I do.'

Ombré reversed a little and turned to face the boy. He sat down again and, with a big sigh, whined politely that he was very sorry for being rude but he really did have to dash, otherwise those mangy cats would steal his food again.

'I do not know about you, Mister Dog, but I am very hungry and ready for my dinner. I am having fish fingers and mashed potatoes and mushy peas for dinner. Big plastic green mushy peas. That is my best favourite meal ever.'

Timothy knelt down on the grass in front of Ombré and placed a cupped hand tenderly on either side of Ombré's face. Timothy was always comfortable and at ease with animals, but he feared being touched by humans, and refused to touch a fellow human being back. He found it difficult to trust them, and it scared him if anybody came too close – even his mother and father. His father had always found this one of the more difficult symptoms of his son's condition – especially under recent circumstances. David desperately wanted to be able to hold Timothy close. He needed to share the pain of their loss, to heal the cavernous wound that Rosie's departure had cleaved in his heart. But Timothy was unable to let him. David had always been a career-orientated man, but his sole ambition now was to one day be able to share a big father-son hug.

Ombré didn't flinch or pull back when Timothy touched him. He let the little boy clasp his head between small hands. Timothy held Ombré's head delicately, all the time looking into his eyes. Ombré returned his stare. He felt Timothy's fingers stroking him behind his jawbones, in the fleshy bit under his ears, and he closed his eyes in utter pleasure. He blinked and blinked as Timothy fixed him a gaze. It felt so good to be touched, to again feel a human's tender caress. *Mon Dieu!* How he had missed that. Ombré thought he might drop off at any moment but he was determined to stay awake to enjoy the attention for as long as he could. His hunger was forgotten; the cats could dine well tonight. He could feel his eyes twitching and his snout nodding and drooping, but luckily Timothy held Ombré's head upright with his palms.

Timothy leaned his face closer. Then he moved his head from side to side and back, his nose lightly touching Ombré's damp snout as he did so. A shiver rippled through Ombré's body, from the tip of his snout, downwards and backwards, and he felt it spasm through him and eject from his twitching tail. Timothy looked him square in his blinking eyes.

'This is what Eskimos do to say hello, Mister Dog. Would you like a hug now? Father says that hugs always help people with their sadness so shall we try one because you look a little bit sad to me? Father tries to hug me sometimes but it scares me and makes me go all shaky and nervous. I do not really know what sadness feels like but I know I am not happy that mother is dead. I think I must miss her a lot. Father says I do.'

Ombré was still recovering from the shock of the snout-thing when the boy moved in even closer and put his face against his. He squeezed Ombré in his tiny arms.

'Now that we have introduced ourselves properly, Mister Dog, and we are best friends I need to tell you a few important things. I remember from the other time I saw you that you have some very bad manners. I asked father if it is okay to do a wee on the gravestones and the trees in the cemetery and he said no it is very impolite and that I should show more respect. I think father thought I meant was it okay if I do the wee and not you so I had to explain it to him because he is a little bit slow sometimes. You did a lot of wee on trees and some on the gravestones but you must not do that even if you are a dog. Father told me that dogs do not know about cemeteries and gravestones and that you probably thought they were just big stones so I will forgive you but only if you promise not to do it again especially on the grave of mother. And father says that when two people make an agreement they usually shake hands. But because you are a dog I will shake your paw and you can shake my hand. Father and I make hundreds of agreements but we never shake hands because it means I have to touch him. I have noticed something about you, Mister Dog. You have very big ears. And you have a funny little white patch on your chest. Should we make an agreement then, Mister Dog? Shake my hand if you want to.'

Timothy held out his right hand in front of Ombré. He opened his palm and wiggled his fingers. Ombré was becoming increasingly worried about this boy's intentions. First, the pointing-finger thing and then the erogenous stroking. Then came the snout-snuffling and full body squeeze. What are these hands going to do to me next? he thought.

~ What are you *doing*? Ombré asked with a twitch of his ears.

He tensed his front legs and folded his ears back.

~ Don't you come any closer with those hands. I'm not ready for you yet.

Ombré backed up a little, shuffling awkwardly. Timothy leant forwards with his hand and wiggled his outstretched fingers again.

Ombré felt one of his paws lifting up. Hey, wait, he told himself. I didn't do that! It lifted higher and pushed itself forwards into the boy's hand. Timothy grasped it firmly and shook it up and down, up and down. Ombré made only a disconcerted and weak attempt to pull it backwards and free of the grip but Timothy easily held on to him and shook his leg over and over again. Ombré wasn't at all conscious of the fact that Timothy was still speaking to him; he was too preoccupied watching his paw bounce up and down, fearful that his shoulder could be dislocated at any moment.

'Good then, Mister Dog. We have an agreement now. We have made an agreement of gentlemen. Now that we are best friends we can see each other when father and I come to visit mother. We come every few days. Do you have a name, Mister Dog? You are not wearing a collar but you must have a name. Unless you are a wild dog but I do not think you are. Is your name Patch like your little white patch? I hope not because Patch is a boring name. You must have a name. I do. There are lots of different names that people call me but my real proper name is Timothy. Or Tim if you are really lazy with your words like father is. Mother always used to call me Timothy but father always calls me Tim. Sometimes he calls me son but he never calls me moon.

'I asked father if I had to stop liking mother now because she is dead or if I am allowed to carry on liking her. He said if I really wanted to I could try to like her even more than when she was at home with us. I liked it a lot when she was at home with us. She made me fish fingers and mashed potatoes and mushy peas for dinner. And she made me raspberry jam and ready salted crisp sandwiches for lunch at special school. But I did not like her just for that of course. And father said if I ever wanted to think about mother then all I had to do was close my eyes and look for her. But all I saw were little silver speckles and black spots so father told me not to close my eyes so tightly. And then I saw her. And she was very beautiful. But when I opened them again she went away. But she always comes back when I close them. Watch.'

Ombré broke free from his trance, looked up and watched the boy opening and closing his eyes slowly but rhythmically while he spoke. Ombré felt himself almost hypnotised by the boy's actions. Timothy repeated this several times and then looked down at Ombré.

'You can have your paw back now if you want, Mister Dog, because I think we understand each other. Do you see those little birds in the tree over there? When we come here I always bring them some birdseed and feed them. They are my best friends too and I like to give them little gifts. I can give you a little present next time we see each other if you like but I will not give you chocolates because you might die.'

From behind Ombré, a man arrived. Neither boy nor dog had noticed him approaching.

'Tim, what are you doing there, son? Have you found yourself a new friend?'

Ombré jumped, startled. He turned round quickly to face the man. He was very tall and Ombré had to sit down again in order to look up high enough to see the man's face clearly.

'Hello, father. Yes. This is the Mister Dog I told you about last time we came to see mother. The one who did his wee on the gravestones.'

The man bent at the knees and squatted all the way down to Ombré's level. He looked him straight in the eye.

'Bad dog!' he said. Then he winked.

Ombré blinked rapidly.

'No, father, he is not a bad dog but he does need to learn some good manners. And I will teach him. I think he is already a very clever dog but I will show him how to behave properly.'

David smiled and looked across to his son.

'How will you manage that, Tim? He's not your dog, is he? He probably belongs to someone who works here at the cemetery. He must have an owner somewhere or other. He's a handsome fella, isn't he?'

The man leant back over to Ombré and patted him gently on the head. He reached over and pushed his big fingers into the fur on the back of his neck and began kneading the flesh. Ombré could have easily allowed himself to relax and enjoy the attention, but ever since his time on Alphonse's farm, and the misunderstanding with the blanket truck driver, he was understandably very wary of adult males. His fear manifested itself verbally.

~ *Attention!* Watch it! he yapped, quickly pulling away from the man.

'Frisky too!' laughed David. 'His owner *must* be around here somewhere, Tim – good looking dog like that.'

Ombré wasn't taking any chances by letting the man grab hold of him. He could smell a goodness in him – he was clearly nothing at all like Alphonse – but if he was anything at all like the boy, he might have shaken Ombré's paw clean off or hugged him until his ribs popped. He twisted his head back and tried to nibble the man's wrist but he was too quick. The man laughed again and started to weave and rotate his hand in front of Ombré's snout and jaws. Ombré tried to grab hold of the spinning hand, but the quicker he snapped, the faster the man gyrated it, smiling all the time.

'Father, please do not tease Mister Dog.'

'Sorry, Tim,' he replied. 'I was just having a little fun with your pal.'

Timothy's father stopped the game and let his hand fall in front of Ombré's face. A foolish move, thought Ombré. He seized his chance and quickly grabbed hold of the muscle on the man's thumb and chewed on it, savouring the flavours it held. The man made no attempt to remove his thumb, and instead turned back to face his son, who had begun talking again.

'He does not have an owner. He is here every time we come to visit mother. I have asked the men who work here and he does not belong to any of them. They called him that bloody dumb dog and said that he has been here for a week. And I said he was not dumb and one man said that was more than could be said for me. I think he was trying to be nasty to me. Was he, father?'

'Yes. Yes he was, son. But you are *not* dumb! I'm sorry people are like that to you, I really am, Tim. It's just that ... you know.'

'It is okay. It is not your fault that people are like that.'

'Good. That's it – don't let them bother you. Come on, son, give me five!'

'Give you five what, father?'

'Never mind, Tim, don't worry about it.'

'I am not worrying, father.'

'Okay. That's good.'

Whilst father and son spoke, Ombré had let go of the man's thumb and had started to walk away from them. He had been distracted, and was busy sniffing a nearby tree trunk with enthusiasm.

Oh là là, quel parfum!

He smelt something delightful floating on the air around the tree. A female must have passed through his territory when he was distracted and she had marked one of his trees. His nose had let him down inexcusably but, now that he had picked up the whiff, she smelt *très très bonne* indeed. How had a *fille* snuck in and left her calling card without his noticing? He must investi—

'Where are you going now, Mister Dog?'

Yes, a frisky *fille* had definitely left him a trail to follow.

'Father and I are going now so goodbye, Mister Dog. We will be coming to see mother again soon and if you are still here we can talk some more.'

Ombré was not listening. Now, where is she hiding? he thought. The boy spoke to the back of his head.

'I am sorry, Mister Dog, but I asked father if we can take you home with us and he said no.'

The boy caught up with Ombré and knelt down in front of him. He reached out with his open palm and wiggled his fingers. Once again, without any real conscious thought-process, Ombré's left paw lifted and put itself in the boy's hand. They shook amicably and Timothy stood up to leave,

'I am sorry, Mister Dog, but we can not take you. Father will not let me keep you.'

The words fell on ears that were concentrated elsewhere. Ombré turned quickly and set off to sniff the grass around the tree.

'He's got other things on his mind, I think,' said David. 'It looks as though he's found an interesting scent to track. Don't worry, Tim, he'll probably be here next time we come, so you can see him again.'

The man and boy walked away, father taking big strides, son walking with a rapid gait to keep up. Ombré barely noticed them leave. His mind truly was on other things.

Now then – that *fille*. Where is she? Behind this tree, perhaps? *Non*. This big stone? *Non*. How about *this* tree? *Non*. Perhaps the rose bush? *Aïe!* That hurt! She was proving very difficult to locate but Ombré was confident his nose would lead him to where she had been. He hoped she was still there. Hmmn, it smells as though it's coming from ... from the waste bin over ther—

Ombré suddenly stopped sniffing the air and froze.

~ 8 ~

What was he *doing*? What *was* he thinking, the foolish dog?

Ombré had allowed his hormones to do the thinking and not his brain. He needed to rectify that. And quickly. He knew nothing at all about the tall man or the small boy except that he would be happy to let the boy stroke him until his ears fell off. They had not been averse to his advances and they smelt more than acceptable. His instincts told him they could be trusted. And he had let them walk away.

~ *At-ten-dez moi!* Wait for me! Ombré shouted as he set off running across the park after them.

His legs took him across the cemetery so quickly he left a wake of scuffed grass and leaves behind him. He hurdled small gravestones and collections of flowers, and sprinted along the path towards the car park. He sidestepped a young couple pushing a wheelchair with an elderly man in it, and swerved past a large group of people who looked very preoccupied. He was sufficiently distracted by such a sombre spectacle that he almost ran straight into the side of a very long black car. He skidded to a halt just before he head-butted the door, his claws grating on the road.

He spied the boy and the man putting helmets on their heads and climbing onto a big motorbike.

~ *Attendez!* Wait!

They didn't hear him.

He ran faster and closer; just in time to hear the engine roar to life and power away. And then they were gone. He watched the motorbike leave and continue round a shallow bend. Then he heard it slow down and stop. Had they heard him? Were they waiting? Ombré's legs pumped and pumped like over-revved pistons and he chased after them round the corner, convinced this was his chance. Nothing could outrun him when he was this determined, and he was so sure he could catch them up that his tail wagged excitedly as he ran.

He spotted them again. On the front of the motorbike, he could see the man looking from right to left and right again. *Oui!* They had heard his calls.

~ *Attendez!* he shouted again.

The man looked right and left one more time and then the motorbike roared away from the junction, its own pistons too efficient for Ombré's.

~ *Non! Non! Non! Attendez!* he shouted and whined as he continued his chase along the tarmac.

When eventually he tired and slowed, the bike effortlessly increased the distance between them. Ombré carried on running even when he could no longer see the motorbike; it had disappeared along a winding lane high with hedgerows. All that was left of his failed pursuit was the smell of burnt fuel. It was heavy in his nostrils so he chased it further, in the general direction of the dissipating fumes. But he knew it was useless. He slowed his pace and came to a gradual halt, out of breath and out of luck. The muscles in his legs ached, his heart was beating crazily and his tongue hung out so far he almost stood on it. But the biggest pain was in his head. He had been a stupid French fool.

Ombré stood solemnly where he stopped and he panted heavily. His chest heaved and his legs shook from the exertion. He hung his head low, dejectedly, and tried hard to shake off the ideas that had started to form – of a new life. How could he have let them get away? Why did he let them slip through his paws? His body sagged.

Up until then, he had thought he was happy again. He believed he could persevere and prevail. He had almost convinced himself he didn't need any human guardians in his life, but the suddenness of losing the opportunity of finding a new family had made him aware that he had been kidding himself. Trying to make the most of what he didn't have. Of course he needed someone! Who was he trying to fool?

His thoughts were interrupted when a car horn blasted as it screeched to a halt behind him. He turned round and faced the car, unaware and uncaring that he was a dog's length from being flattened on the road. He looked up over the bonnet at the driver, with limp ears and a look that said he really didn't care. And he didn't. The driver shouted some offensive comments at Ombré, sounded his horn again and set off, swerving round the dog. Ombré paid no heed and stood on the spot until he had gone. Then he sulked slowly to the side.

He had nowhere else to go so he wandered slowly back to the cemetery. At least he would be in familiar surroundings there, and it was peaceful enough for him to ponder his loss. As he plodded back, several of the funeral-goers stopped him and bent down to caress him, but he wasn't in the mood for random socialising. The only thing he noted was that they looked as sad and lost as he felt.

The far side of the cemetery was quietest so he picked a spot behind one of the large gravestones that had some new flowers placed by it. Soon after, Ombré saw that it had started to rain upwards again, but he didn't feel like dancing, or drinking from the showers. He rested his heavy head on his paws and let out a long deep sigh. Stupid dog! *Imbécile!*

He lost himself in deep thoughts; brooding memories that took him back in time further than usual. He wished *maman* were there to console him. She would have known what to do. He slumbered in self-pity and inner loathing and drifted back to his early days with her, and of his times with the Morettis and Belle. Things then were so much better. He wished he could turn back the clocks to France, and still be with them all. Time was supposed to be a healer of all pain, but for Ombré, time was standing still. He sulked, and he chastised himself for his foolishness. Drifting in and out of memories, from puphood to present, from France to England and back again, Ombré took himself as far away as possible from the cruel reality of his predicament.

His daydreaming was interrupted an hour or so later when his ears suddenly twitched and picked up the sound of a familiar engine. They flicked up and open, and swivelled to locate the origin of the noise. It was getting louder. It was coming closer. He heard the deep growl of a large motorbike. Even though he was not fully awake – his mind still stuck somewhere deep in those wonderful French Alps – he realised exactly what the call of the engine meant.

Instantly alert, he was ready to run as fast as he could back to the car park. This time he would not let them escape. He catapulted quickly onto his paws but was shocked when, inexplicably, he almost strangled himself. Something pulled tightly around his throat. He had experienced that very same asphyxiating feeling when he was on Alphonse's farm, and he had no doubt what it was. He was held fast by the neck. While he was lamenting his time with Belle, someone had sneaked up behind him, caught him in his blind spot and had slipped a large choke chain over his neck.

'Got you now, you 'orrible little mutt,' said the groundsman. 'It's the doghouse for you, you little sod,' he added as he pulled at the leash.

Pulled hard backwards by the neck, Ombré turned to face a very big man in green work clothes. Instinctively, and rather foolishly, Ombré dug his heels in firmly and spun away from the man again, trying his best to run away and towards the car park. The man was too strong and he pulled Ombré up sharply by the leash, so high that both his front legs were clear of the ground. He snapped his head round and tried to grab the leash from the groundsman's hand but he moved too quickly. He twisted and pulled Ombré even higher. His neck was being stretched and his eyes were bulging. Out of the corner of one of them, he could see the boy over in the car park reaching down to pick something up from a bench –

Timothy had left his motorbike gloves behind. Could those gloves be the ticket to Ombré's new start? He strained hard on the leash and tried to call to the boy for help.

The groundsman took hold of the leash with both hands and lifted Ombré completely clear of the ground. If he didn't act fast, he wouldn't have a life left to live, let alone one to mess up quite so successfully. He kicked and writhed and spun, and powered his back legs wildly in the air. The man had a good strong hold but Ombré's desperation surprised him. He managed to spin so much as to unbalance the man and Ombré grabbed one of his thick hairy forearms between his jaws.

As he hung from the man's arm with his legs flailing, he clamped his lower jaw shut tightly. The groundsman cried out and released his other hand from the leash. He swung the free arm and hit Ombré hard in the ribs with his fist. Ombré yelped loudly in pain, letting go of the man's arm, but he carried on kicking and writhing desperately; still held high, his neck muscles close to tearing. He kicked and spun so much that the man couldn't hold him up in the air any longer, and he dropped him heavily to the ground.

The man lifted his free arm again, ready to pummel Ombré's body. Before he had chance to connect, Ombré lunged his head forwards and closed his jaws firmly around the man's arm again. He felt the skin pop, and the groundsman's grip relaxed. He let go of the leash completely and it dropped to the ground.

Without hesitation, Ombré darted towards the car park as though his life depended on it – which it did in a way.

The heavy choke chain was still hanging around his neck and the leash dangled awkwardly between his legs, slowing him down as he ran. His back legs repeatedly caught in the hand loop and he could not avoid tripping over it. He shot a quick look back to see if the man was chasing him but he wasn't. He was waving his arms and fists in the air screaming at Ombré, but he didn't care. Ombré bellowed back, as if to tell the man it had been his own stupid fault. He hadn't hurt the groundsman too badly; he was sure of that because he had no taste of blood in his mouth.

Ombré could see the boy, climbing back astride the motorbike. With that heavy chain around his neck, though, hindering him and fouling his legs, Ombré would never catch them. Could life be so kind and so cruel in the space of a few moments? In sheer desperation – he wasn't thinking rationally – he grabbed the leash tightly between his teeth, pulled at it and shook it viciously. All he succeeded in doing was wrenching his neck painfully and pulling the chain tighter around his own throat. He panicked and thrashed his head wildly from side to side again, trying to shake off his tethers. But it was useless. He looked up again and watched the motorbike begin to pull away, the little boy's arms wrapped around the man's waist. He looked down at the ground and felt totally lost. They disappeared slowly round the corner again and out of view. They were going home without him. Home, thought Ombré; I had one of those once.

He felt wretched. Ombré let his head fall low, his snout between his front legs, looking down at the long leash that had killed his chances. At least in that position, the heavy choke chain slackened its constriction around his neck. He lay down on the tarmac and sighed heavily. He had lost them ... again. For one brief moment, his life had meaning. Now it was senseless again. What had he done to deserve such harsh treatment?

Yet, within the flow of desperation ran a fine artery of hope. A memory flickered dimly in his mind. It faded in and out, but he could feel it coming slowly forward and into focus. One month ago, almost to the day, he had escaped from Alphonse's farm back in France. How had he done it? Think, dog, think! Stop whining and feeling sorry for yourself, and *think*!

~ 9 ~

There were four of them on the farm – Alphonse already had three other canines – so Ombré felt superfluous to the man's selfish requirements. There was no favouritism on his part; he treated them all the same. Like dogs! Alphonse was a most unpleasant man, a *paysan* of the harshest nature, and he harboured not one single gram of warmth towards Ombré or the others during the two months Ombré was there.

None of the dogs did a great deal to earn their keep, but nothing much was asked of them either. They spent most of their time locked up in the decrepit old barn, or tied up to various items of decaying farm equipment that littered the yard. Alphonse never let them off their ropes to exercise or to play; their daily food rations consisted of little more than rotting vegetables from the fields and Alphonse's leftovers mixed with tasteless crunchy biscuits. He let the dogs' drinking bowls run dry and they had no choice but to drink the fetid water from the old bathtub that was outside the barn. Most of the time, the water had a scummy film on it and it contained a cemetery of drowned insects. Sunk at the bottom, the skinny carcass of a dead bird had been there more than a week when Ombré first arrived; it was still there when he escaped two months later.

The dogs were each on a very long rope. Ombré's was just long enough to allow him to almost reach the extremities of the farmyard from his anchor on the tractor chassis. This could well have been a deliberate move on Alphonse's part, such was his callous nature to tease Ombré cruelly with what was beyond the farm. When Ombré strained hard enough on his leash, pulling it as far as he could without strangling himself, he found he could stretch it just far enough that the tip of his twitching snout was almost through the gateway of the farmyard. He lifted his snout and probed the cool breeze that fluttered around his nostrils. He could smell the difference in the air that lay beyond. It smelt fresh and inviting, but it was agonisingly beyond his reach. When Alphonse was out working in the fields on his shiny new tractor, Ombré pulled hard on his restraints and sat solemnly at the boundary to dream of the world outside. The beautiful world he had sampled with the Morettis.

As spring started to blossom slowly into summer, Alphonse began making the most of the longer evenings to tend his crops. Ombré would sit and stare at the beckoning horizon as the warm glow of the evening sun cast an ochre tint over the fields. As the sun set and his shadow grew taller and thinner, he couldn't help but feel that he would surely end his days on the farm. The dread of spending the rest of his life shackled to a tractor enveloped him with a sadness and despair that brought on the crying and the howling. He never knew for how long he lost himself in his self-pity, but he was always interrupted by the other hounds hurling scathing abuse and chiding him for his discontent. He was forced to pull on his rope and retreat for some peace and sadness in the dark solitude of the barn. But their droning voices followed him inside.

~ *Mon Dieu*, dog! Every night, you sit there, staring out into the fields, moaning and complaining, crying like a little puppy. Why don't you face it? You're here for good like the rest of us. Here until you die.

Another of the dogs joined in.

~ *Oui*. Just accept it, why don't you! Here until you die. And if Alphonse catches you trying to chew through your rope again, he'll kill you himself. And if he doesn't, we will, because every time you try to pull one of your escape stunts, we're all punished.

Ombré had learnt the hard way that to pester and annoy Alphonse too much resulted not only in harsh words, but more often in a heavy newspaper across the snout or a swift kick to the ribs and rump. Alphonse was frequently quite unstable on his legs after too much wine and *pastis*, so there was never excessive force in his physical attacks, but they left their mark on Ombré all the same, both physically and mentally. He was able to dodge some of Alphonse's wild swings and kicks because his aim was not always too good; Ombré managed to sidestep the flying boot, the empty bottle or the bucket of water. But sometimes, they found their target. For the rest of his life, if ever anyone raised a newspaper in front of him, even innocently to read, he would start to tremble, his back legs quivering uncontrollably. If the newspaper ever happened to be rolled up when raised, he even lost control of his bodily functions.

His three female cohabitants, however, were not as quick, they being of *troisième age* – well into their canine eighties, Ombré guessed – and they were too often on the receiving end of a punishment or hurled missile aimed at him. He never knew the names of the others or exactly how old they were, but he always thought of them as the three ugly sisters (they were actually sisters, and they were very ugly). Ombré's antics did not endear him to them too well.

He did learn, however, when was the perfect time to aggravate Alphonse, for it occasionally benefited *les dames* and him. If he timed it well, Alphonse would come storming out of the house, and the missile he would throw could be a stale half-baguette or a length of fatty *saucisson*, even a mouldy lump of cheese. The other dogs ate well those nights, and they deigned to accept it was perhaps worth the pain and punishment for the welcome change of diet.

Why ever did he let Alphonse take him 'home' with him in the first place? Ombré wondered. Since that day, Ombré had not once left the confines of the farmyard. Alphonse seemed amicable at first and it was he who had made the first move. One too many measures of *pastis* had influenced his uncharacteristic fervour. The *pastis* carried on flowing, but the tap on the fervour valve remained firmly closed from then on. During the days before he met Alphonse, Ombré had become a regular scrounger in Alphonse's local bar and was, by then, quite well known. He was ultra keen to find a new roof over his head and to share some human companionship, so when a slightly slurry Alphonse threw him a heavily salted pistachio nut, and then another, Ombré was sucked into his world. He should, instead, have trusted the first instincts of his nose, for Alphonse carried several suspect aromas that Ombré couldn't fathom or organise.

His ultimate escape from the farm to freedom came about with nothing more than a simple stroke of fortune. When the realisation hit him, he cursed himself for not having discovered it much sooner. He could have saved himself a lot of strife.

Alphonse had already replaced several of Ombré's half-chewed rope leashes after his continual escape attempts. The leather collars became thicker and the ropes heavier. After one almost successful escape attempt, Alphonse removed Ombré's leather collar and gnawed-at rope leash and tied him up with a huge metal link choke chain and leash. The sisters enjoyed this, and scoffed that it served him right.

~ Try getting out of that! challenged one.

~ No sunset sprints for you, young dog, mocked another.

~ It looks as though you'll outlive us on the farm, *n'est-ce pas*? confirmed the third.

True to the invitation, he did try. And he failed convincingly, to the endless pleasure of the old-timers, who rolled around the dusty earth on their backs, kicking their spindly legs in the air ecstatically. All he succeeded in doing was wearing down the points of his teeth as he ground away at the metal chain leash. The choke chain was so large and heavy it hurt Ombré's neck muscles and shoulders to hold his head high – something that *maman* had told him and his siblings always to do.

After too many near self-strangulations, Ombré accepted

defeat. He worked out that hanging his head low was the only way to relieve the loading, for at least his noose rested a little looser in that position. He began to spend more time skulking around and lying down, simply to relieve the strain on his muscles.

One rainy evening towards the end of May, he was feeling particularly sorry for himself, his mind wandering as it often did. He was thinking about *maman* again. It was more than four years since he last shared her company and warmth. If she had passed away, was she watching over him? He felt a strange presence, and a warm wave passing through him. Perhaps it was his own mind conjuring up a comforting scenario so that he could be with her again.

The other dogs were already asleep in the barn, snoring and breaking wind. Alphonse was inside the house doing the same. Ombré plodded aimlessly in small, slow circles in front of the barn, with his head low, keeping his collar and leash slack. He watched the troops of ants running hurriedly between the rain puddles that were beginning to form. He rubbed his nose in the softening dirt and pushed them around, just for something to do – he had to occupy his mind somehow. He began to drift away again. When was the last time he climbed a snow-clad mountain with monsieur Moretti? When was the last time he bounded through a towering field of wild flowers with Belle? When did he last eat a whole crunchy carrot, fresh from madame's garden? When was the—?

The choke chain fell over his head. The heavy noose simply fell forwards, clean over his ears and landed on the ground with a clunk. His first instinct was to bolt into the fields and run as far away from the farm and Alphonse as possible. And that's exactly what he did.

He didn't once look over his shoulder, and he didn't slow until the farm was no longer visible behind him. Then he slipped into a higher gear and pelted away from hell. He doubted the Devil would come looking for him. He ran so fast through the fields that they became a speeding blur. Crop after crop whooshed past his face.

He was free. Free as bird. And fly he did.

The wheat shivered in the cool rainy breeze as he ran. Along grassy tracks and muddy dirt tracks he sprinted, running at full speed because he could. His legs powered him along, his tongue hanging out to taste the delightful fresh air, his ears tucked back to improve his aerodynamics. Nothing could stop him.

He shouted loudly as he ran. They were cries of pure elation.

~ Liberté! Liberté!

The field track became a vehicle track ...

That became a lane ...

The lane changed to a road, and then a wider road – a deserted ribbon of tarmac ...

The countryside whizzed by and ...

~ 10 ~

... and as Ombré ran, faster and further along the road, the road became wider ...

and busier ...

And then ... only a few hundred metres ahead, he saw the young boy and his father on the motorbike. He was gaining on them. His powerful legs pushed him along faster and faster, barely touching the ground. This was his chance.

Back in the cemetery, the collar had not dropped over his head quite as easily as it had on Alphonse's farm; it was not as large or as heavy. In the end, Ombré succeeded by jumping up onto a bench and dropping his head very low over the edge. He stretched his neck downwards and pawed the collar, flexing and swivelling his ears forwards to encourage it over his head. Slowly, slowly, he wriggled it over his ears and it fell free.

Running faster than he had ever run before, he eventually caught up with the motorbike and then increased his pace a notch to overtake. His speed surprised him, but not as much as it surprised David. As he powered past, tongue flapping in the headwind, saliva splashing from his jowls, Ombré watched the man's helmeted face do several double takes. The boy's expression never changed.

~ *Arrêtez!* Stop! shouted Ombré.

They pulled over to the side of the road and stopped. Ombré's brakes were not quite as efficient as the motorbike's; he skidded to an eventual halt and pulled over too. Timothy climbed off the bike.

David flipped the side-stand down, dismounted and removed his helmet. The boy kept his on. Ombré was exhausted. Normally after exercise, he panted at around two hundred to the minute, but after his forty-kilometre-an-hour marathon, his heart was pounding rapidly and his chest was heaving so quickly he thought he might throw up – although that may not have persuaded the man and boy to take him home with them. The man looked both confused and amazed. The boy appeared unmoved by Ombré's gallant efforts. What would Ombré have to do to impress him? Timothy broke the silence and the quizzical looks.

'It is obvious that Mister Dog wants to come and live with us, father. I said we should have brought him.'

Ombré flopped down, grateful for a chance to recover. He tried several times to retract his tongue into his mouth but it proved too unwieldy and his lower jaw wouldn't stay closed. He looked up eagerly at them both and wagged his powerful tail to try to divert their attention from the giant slathering ribbon that hung from his chin.

Ombré's tail had always been a very important tool for him in terms of communication, and he used it daily to convey his emotions. Without it, he would have become semi-mute – like so many Jack Russells. He was not sure if the man and boy would understand the finer subtleties of a dog's swinging tail so, to be safe, he tried several types. As he was entering dauntingly new territory by asking them to take him home with them, he knew he ought to display his submissive tail first. He immediately stood up and folded it neatly behind him, tucking it away – wishing he had the same control over his tongue. He looked from man to boy and back again and accompanied this with one single little yap.

He then moved on to his hesitant wag, a nervous little toing to the right and froing to the left that was met warmly, especially when he let out two friendly yaps. Next, he tried an inquisitive tail flick, confident that he was gaining ground. The man and boy were talking between themselves, but they were still looking down at him, so he knew he had at least some of their attention. He hoped his show would not be without reward. He stole repeated glances over his shoulder to be sure his tail was doing as he told it and that it was not letting him down.

When he knew for sure that he had at least established their trust, he *finale*-d with the most confident wag he could manage. He was very careful, though, not to push it up too high, or to stiffen it, for he didn't want to imply any form of dominance on his part. Then he voiced his wishes again, convinced he had won them over.

~ No doubt about it, he told himself with a yap.

'No, Tim, I'm really sorry,' said David. 'That's my final decision. We can't take him home with us.'

'But, father,' replied Timothy from within his helmet. 'He has no home to go to and we can give him one.'

'We can't, Tim. Be reasonable now. It's not the right time, son. Don't you think we have enough to worry about? You have to try to understand. Things are pretty tough for me at the moment, you know. I'm struggling to make any sense of it all. It's all just so difficult.'

'I do understand. This is why we should take Mister Dog home with us. He would be good company for you.'

'We can't take him, Tim. I'm at work all day, and you're at school. I've just got too much on my plate.'

'Father, I think you are making excuses. And if you do have too much on your plate then this is another very good reason for taking Mister Dog with us. You can share your big portion with him. And I will share my fish fingers and mashed potatoes and mushy peas with him. But not my raspberry jam and ready salted crisp sandwiches. I will not share those with anybody or any dog.'

'Oh, Tim, Tim, that's not what I meant. It's just an express—'

'I have a good idea, father. You could take Mister Dog to work with you.'

'How *could* I, Tim? That's a silly idea. Now come on, please be reasonable. We can't take him home with us and that's final. Okay?'

'Father, how can you suggest that we leave Mister Dog here? He could be knocked over and killed by a car or worse.'

'Tim, what could be wor—? ... I didn't mean that we should just leave him here, Tim.'

'We will have to take him home at least for today because we can not leave him here.'

'No, true. But ... How ... how can we take him home? We're on the bike.'

'He will follow us of course. He has followed us all the way from the cemetery. If you go slowly he will be able to run next to us.'

'Well ... well, okay. But only for one night. One night! And tomorrow, I'll take him to the shelter. Understood?'

~ ~ ~ ~ ~

Ombré slept in the garage in the boot of the car. He could have slept absolutely anywhere after being forced to run alongside the motorbike all the way to their house.

When the man patted the boot of his car and said something encouraging, Ombré launched himself in. He turned round to face the man and thanked him for the offer of a bed for the night with an affectionate lick of his hand. Compared with how Ombré had been living recently, it was deluxe accommodation. Instinctively, he turned a couple of circles and lay down. He placed his chin on the lip of the boot and looked up over it to the man, who had a big grin on his face. He yapped his sincere thanks again. The grin widened. But then it suddenly disappeared.

'Sorry I can't have you in the house, boy, but I don't want you getting the wrong idea. But you'll be okay in here, won't you? You're lucky to have so much space, really – you certainly wouldn't be as comfortable in the boot of my car. I know it's silly keeping this big old estate, but it was Rosie's and ... and I just can't seem to bring myself to sell it. I ... I will one day, I suppose. Anyway, boy, enough of my ramblings, you get some sleep. You must be tired after all that running today.'

The man had made him very comfortable with a few old towels, and with a picnic blanket that had a very feminine odour to it, which tickled Ombré's nostrils. It was a very pleasant aroma, and he had noticed the same one clinging to the kitchen and to some clothing hanging up by the back door. He wondered where the smell had come from because, although he felt a strong female presence, he didn't see one. He was too fatigued to try to work it out.

David left the car boot open but he locked the garage door behind him. Ombré was a little concerned about being locked up all night, on his own again, and he cried softly to himself after they had left.

He stopped crying when it dawned on him where he truly was. He had a lovely pile of comfortable bedding and he was safe and secure in a warm, dry garage. Inside the house were two gentle humans who had taken him into their lives and had fed and watered him for no other reason than because they wanted to. They owed him nothing, yet already he owed them something that he could never repay. His dignity, his self-esteem, his life. What reason did he have to be upset? He pulled himself together, wiped sleep from his eyes with a paw and rolled onto one side, letting out a puff of contented air. He stretched out all four legs as far as he could and yawned. He ruffled a towel with his snout and pulled the blanket closer to him to make a big pillow. And then he drifted off to sleep, twitching and squeaking quietly, talking to himself in his dreams.

~ Well, dog, you have certainly landed on your paws here. Don't mess this one up like the others, eh! Best behaviour in the morning. No shouting during the night, no pushy behaviour, and definitely no casual flatulence at breakfast. Can you do that, dog? Can you?

His sleep was interrupted by a dull and regular thud-thud-thudding from behind him. Whatever could that be at that time of the night? He lifted his sleepy head and looked down his flank. His tail was thumping a steady beat against the inside of the car boot. He watched it for a while and then he pulled the feminine blanket closer still and fell back into a deep and happy sleep.

He needn't have worried about being all alone.

Timothy sneaked into the garage in the dead of night with a handful of salty biscuits for him. He placed them on his towels and immediately left again without saying a word. Ombré found this a little odd, and he wasn't particularly hungry anyway because David had already been in once with some little treats an hour or so earlier and had talked to Ombré for a while.

'There you go, boy,' David had said. 'These should keep you going. Just thought I'd check up on you, see if you are okay. But don't let Tim know I've been in, eh?'

David returned for a second time a few hours after the boy's first visit, with yet another delivery of treats. Ombré was confused by all the attention, especially when all he wanted to do was sleep. He would have the biscuits for breakfast.

'Just making sure you're still okay, boy,' said David in a whisper. 'But don't you get any ideas, now. I'm still going to have to take you to the shelter in the morning. We can't keep you, you do know that, don't you? I know Tim won't be pleased, but—'

Timothy entered the garage for a second time.

'Father, why are you in here at six of the clock in the morning?'

'I was just seeing if—'

'Do you like him?'

'Yes, of course I do, Tim. I like all dogs. It's my job.'

'Father, you are not being honest with me are you? I know you are telling me one of those little fibs again.'

'Of course I'm not, Tim. I was just checking on the dog. I thought he might be cold or something.'

'It is the twenty one of June today, father, and I had my shorts on. Why would Mister Dog be cold? Why are you hiding those biscuits behind your back?'

'What? Oh, these. I was jus—'

'Shall we keep him? I knew you would like him.'

'No, sorry, Tim. Like I said, "One night". And then I have to take him in to the shelter. We can't keep him. Come on now, son, let's get back to bed.'

'But you like him.'

'Yes, Tim, I do like him. I've already said that.'

'Good. Good night then, Mister Dog. Sleep tight and hope the dog fleas do not bite.'

'Tim, son,' said David. 'You can't keep just calling him Mister Dog, you know.'

'But why not, father? If we are not keeping him why does it matter what I call him?'

~ 11 ~

One night in the garage led to two.

Ombré pushed his campaign along with a zealous display of affection. He could see that monsieur David was an animal lover. He saw it in his eyes and felt it in his touch. And he had already realised that Timothy was like no other human he had ever met – and that when he stroked Ombré, it felt almost as good as when Belle used to nuzzle up against him. He wasn't sure who needed whom the most, but he accepted that they all needed one another very much. Ombré filled the small but unbridgeable distance that separated father and son.

Some time during the peaceful darkness of his second night in the garage, Timothy came in to see Ombré, as he had done on the previous night. He climbed into the boot of the car with him and asked Ombré to move to one side. He sat down in front of the dog and leant against the side of the boot with his knees tucked up under his chin, and he began stroking Ombré's back methodically, top to bottom. Ombré sat up alert and faced him, shuffling forwards slightly so that he was at Timothy's feet. Timothy reached behind Ombré's right ear and started to tickle it. If he carried on like that for too long, there was no chance Ombré would stay awake to listen to Timothy. He hoped tonight's visit would not last too long because he was very tired and he had been having a super dream that he wanted to continue. Timothy interrupted Ombré's reverie.

'I know father is still pretending we are not going to keep you but he is only saying that so he can say it was his choice to let you stay. So if you are going to be in our family I need to tell you about me my father and my mother. I know you will not be able to tell me about your life but I am sure your life is not very exciting because all you do is eat and sleep and go to the toilet a lot. I think I am a lot older than you so I will have lots more stories than you to tell. Father says you are about five or six. I had my tenth birthday on the first day of March but it was not a very good birthday because mother was not there.'

Timothy's fingers dug in rapturously behind Ombré's ear, and he felt his eyes growing uncontrollably heavy. Stay awake, dog, he told himself. Pay attention and don't be rude, you have to be on your best behaviour with these two. Ombré opened his eyes as widely as he could and looked up at Timothy inquisitively. He raised a paw and placed it lightly on the boy's slippered foot. Timothy reached down, put his palm between Ombré's front legs and started to caress his chest. His other hand remained behind Ombré's ear. Ombré moaned with pleasure – *Zut!* that felt good – a long guttural groan from deep within.

'You like it a lot when I tickle you behind your ears like this. I can see you do because your head is wobbling and nodding. Mother used to do this to father but his head did not wobble or nod but he made a little moaning noise like you. Are you trying to talk to me, Mister Dog? I know you can not speak my language but I imagine you talk a lot with your dog friends. I talk a lot too. Talking a lot is part of my illness. Father says my illness is not really an illness but I know he is only saying that not to upset me. But I am never ever upset. I wish I could be. Or happy or excited or angry. The only time I get angry or upset is when somebody touches me. I can touch animals and birds and dogs and they can touch me but if a person tries to touch me it scares me. Father says that it is not me that has the problem it is the other people.

'He says I have to learn to ignore them when they tease me or call me names. The names they call me do not bother me but I know it upsets father a lot. He says they are just jealous because I have lots of special gifts that they do not have. I asked him if he meant like the big *Encyclopaedia Britannica* set he and mother bought me for my eighth birthday but he said no it was another type of gift. He said it was a gift not to be given or received but one that I have always had and always will have. He said it was a gift that I could not really share with anyone else but this did not make much sense to me because mother always told me I should share my things. But father told me some gifts are so special that they are not for sharing. I asked him if he meant like my raspberry jam and ready salted crisp sandwiches. He explained that even if I can not give my special gifts away I could still sort of share them like mother had said. This confused me even more but father listed all the things I can do that other children can not do and he said that these are my gifts.'

Ombré's eyes closed heavily and his head drooped. He began to snore which woke him instantly with a jolt. He blinked rapidly and lifted his head to listen. His paw was still resting on Timothy's *Wallace and Gromit* slipper.

'I did not realise that these things were gifts because most of the other children at special school can do similar things. But father is wrong because there are lots of other things that some children can do that I can not. Like I still have my stabilisers on my bicycle. My balance is not very good and the boys on their mountain bikes make fun of me and call me Wobbly Timbo. They call me other names too like Tiny Tim and Timberlina. But they are only words and words can not hurt. Sticks and stones can hurt but not words. I really like words and I like learning languages too. I can speak a little bit of Spanish and Polish and Chinese but sometimes I mix them up in the same sentence. I understand tiny bits of Dutch but I can not speak it very well. When I play my Dutch CDs father says it sounds like they are speaking backwards with a cough sweet stuck in their throats. I told him he was being silly because it is not possible for a person to speak backwards but I told him that Chinese people do write backwards.

'My best favourite language is French because the French do not use apostrophes very much. I do not like apostrophes and I do not like the boy who delivers our newspapers. Apostrophes are untidy little things and they give me migraines. They are like millions of stupid little tadpoles all swimming around inside my head pushing on the backs of my eyes. Father uses them all the time. I mean apostrophes not tadpoles, Mister Dog. I always like things to be very tidy like when I feed the birds and they eat up all of the birdseed. I like birds a lot but not when they poo on my head. Father says it is lucky when a bird poos on your head so I asked why and he said it is lucky that hippopotamuses can not fly. I think he was trying to do a joke. But you are like me, Mister Dog, you do not understand jokes.'

Ombré was having trouble staying alert. He removed his paw and lay down at Timothy's feet. A risky move, for he knew he would soon drop off in that position, but his head was so heavy he had no choice. He lowered his chin onto one of Timothy's slippers and sighed. What a strange looking dog, he thought, as he rested his snout on Gromit's face.

'I have lots of language books in my bedroom and one hundred and thirty two books in total. I have a book called *Living With Your Dog* that I bought from the British Heart Foundation shop. I bought it because I want to learn about you. Father already knows a lot about dogs and animals because of his job. I have already learnt that the average bark of a dog is one quarter of a second long and the dogs who bark the most are Yorkshire Terriers and Beagles and they never shut up. And did you know there is a dog called a Bagel which is when a Bertie Bassett Hound is mixed with a noisy Beagle. My best favourite one is a Cockapoo because it sounds very rude and this is when a Poodle is mixed with a Cocker Spaniel. But I do not know how they mix two dogs together. What sort of mix are you, Mister Dog? I will ask father tomorrow. I think you are a Labra something but you are definitely not a Labradoodle.

'Father says I have more books than the local library but I do not. I know because I asked the librarian Missus Stansfield and she said she had a lot more than me. She is an old lady but is very helpful and I said she looked like that actor Robin Williams from the movie film *Mrs Doubtfire*. I do not watch many movie films but I watch history programmes and a lot of wildlife programmes. I really like the movie film *Rain Man* which is very good. I have watched it hundreds of times. My best favourite bit is when Dustin Hoffman reads the telephone directory. I read ours too and I think it is a very clever book. There are lots of numbers and interesting addresses in it but I like it best because all the names are very neatly organised and it is really easy to find where all the other families called Briggs live.'

Timothy delicately lifted Ombré's head up off his slipper and made him stand up. Ombré was feeling rather groggy, but did as he was asked. He watched Timothy shuffle around in the boot and looked on, somewhat puzzled, when he took in his hands one of the old towels monsieur David had put in the boot for him. He rolled it up neatly, put it behind him and lay down, using it as a pillow. Ombré took this as the signal that it was bedtime for both of them. There wasn't much space left in the boot with Timothy lying down, but Ombré managed to find a very comfortable spot alongside Timothy, with his chin resting on the boy's waist. Timothy reached down and caressed Ombré's back. Within seconds, the dog was asleep again and snoring loudly. Timothy carried on stroking and carried on talking.

'One day I think I might laugh at something or even just have a little smile. When mother laughed too much she said her ribs ached a lot and sometimes she had a very little wee in her knickers. Perhaps one day I will laugh at something but I hope I do not wee in my *Finding Nemo* underpants. I think I almost laughed once at special school but my teacher Miss Filipčič said it was not nice to laugh at Matthew Mollinson. He has a gift like me but it is not exactly the same. He twitches and shouts a lot and uses very bad language but he teaches me lots of good naughty words. When I laughed at Matthew Mollinson I felt my face go a little bit tighter and my cheek muscles tensed. My top cheeks not my bottom ones.

'Miss Filipčič is my best favourite teacher at special school and she is from Slovenia but she has lived in England for most of her life and for all of mine. Her first name is Ljubljana which is the capital city of Slovenia but it also means beloved. I told her there are lots of people with names of capital cities and we played a game of guessing names of people that are capital cities. I won easily and anyway she cheated because she said Sydney. Miss Filipčič has a little habit of saying things when she thinks nobody can hear her but I have very good hearing and I can. My balance is rubbish but my hearing is very good and when I fall off my bike I can always hear the big boys laughing at me. When Miss Filipčič does her talking too loud thing she is embarrassed that I have heard because her top cheeks go really red like a beetroot. I like it when that happens. Do dogs blush, Mister Dog?'

The question fell on ears that were closed for the night. Ombré's back leg was twitching in the sleep of dreams and he was snoring loudly.

'Miss Filipčič told me she was born in a place called Bohinj and she told me a story of why Bohinj is called Bohinj. I looked it up on one of my maps but Bohinj is a lake and not a place so she could not have been born there unless she is a fish or a mermaid. It is my best favourite story. I will tell you it, Mister Dog, if you stop snorting like a pig.'

Timothy stopped stroking Ombré, but let his hand rest on his back. He began to tell his best favourite story, more to the roof of the car than to the dog.

'When God was dividing the world into countries he was very very busy. And so he did not notice a small group of people in the corner who were waiting patiently for their country. And when God had finished giving all of the countries away and everybody else had gone home to their new countries he noticed these people still waiting quietly in the corner. He asked them why they had not gone home yet. They said they had no home yet because God had not given them one. He apologised and shook his head and said there were no more countries left. Then God rubbed his big grey beard and scratched his head and smiled. He said that because they had all waited so patiently and had not pushed and shoved like everybody else that he would give them a small piece of land that he had just remembered about. I liked that bit of the story because the people did not push and shove. I do not like people who push and shove. God told the people that this tiny little bit of land was a very beautiful place and he had kept it secret from everyone because he was planning to keep it for himself for his retirement. But because he is a big generous man and also because he is God he gave them a place called Bohinj. Miss Filipčič told me that Bohinj means the place of God in her dialect. I told Miss Filipčič I liked the story but I knew it was not really a true one because God did not divide the world into countries it was the explorers who did that. But I like listening to her stories.

'When Miss Filipčič tells me this story she always laughs a little bit because she says it makes her feel good. She says a laugh a day keeps the sad times away. I would like to be able to laugh with her. And one day I would like to cry too. I have seen mother and father cry. Once when I saw mother and father crying they told me they were crying with happiness. I have seen father cry a lot since mother went away but I know that is not happiness. I want to cry about mother because I think I should. I try to cry and sometimes I try to laugh but it never happens properly. I screw my face up and concentrate and try to think of things that make other people sad or happy or make them laugh. My best favourite funny joke is this but I never laugh at it. The two longest names of towns in the world are Llanfairpwllgwyngyllgogerychwyrndrobwllllantysiliogogogoch in Wales and Taumatawhakatangihangakoauauotamateaturipukakapikimaungahoronukupokaiwhenuakitanatahu in New Zealand. Can you spell them? The answer is t h e m.

'When father finally tells you that we are keeping you, Mister Dog, you will need to know we have rules for living in our house. You will have to obey them or father will take you to one of the animal shelters and you would not like that. So no barking during the night. No eating the food that I give to the birds and no begging from the table. I will share some of my food with you after we have finished eating but not my raspberry jam and ready salted crisp sandwiches. And no bottom pumping unless you are alone. Father does not like it at all so that is what I have to do. And no biting anyone either but I do not do that. I have asked father not to put you on a leash or to put a collar around your neck. I told him that when we found you at the cemetery you were a free animal and that it would not be fair to make you wear them. I said you are not a slave dog. So you must promise to behave and not bite the postman or the milkman. But you can bark a lot at the paperboy if you want because he is not a good person. He throws stones at the birds and bullies me and pushes me and punches me very hard on the arm and makes it go all dead. Do you promise? If you do bite anybody then father will take you away and they will give you a really really big injection that will make you sleep for ever and you will never wake up again. They only give that sort of really really big injection to very naughty dogs and bad people in America. If you see the man who killed mother you must not bite him but you must tell me and I will give him the biggest biggest injection ever ever ever in the world.

'You are not allowed up the stairs in the house when father is home. When he is not home you can come up the stairs but only in my room. And when father is in one of his very quiet moods you must not disturb him. I think he is thinking about mother then so it is much better to leave him alone to think.

'Mother was killed six months ago when she took some money from the hole in the wall doing some shopping for Christmas. It was in the evening and she was buying presents for us. I know this because the police found a book and some CDs in her bags. The book was a mathematics study book by K A Stroud for me and the CDs for father were of some horrible heavy metal music that he liked when he was a lot younger and when he had a lot more hair on his head. Mother did not give us the presents but the police did and they did not wrap them up very nicely. We did not have a real Christmas last year. I hope we have one this year. You can come too if you like.

'Father says that when you miss someone they always appear in your mind when you are not expecting it and you can hear their voice whispering in the trees and on the wind. When I close my eyes when I go to sleep I can see her face because I know not to close them too tightly now. I have some of those sticky stars and planets on my bedroom ceiling that glow in the dark and when I go to bed I can see her face smiling in the planets and floating between the stars. Father tells me it means I am missing her very much. I like missing her because I do not normally have these little feelings. Miss Filipčič at special school says that I must miss her a lot for me to feel a thing like that and she cried when I told her about my planets. Look, Mister Dog, can you see the birds outside? It is nearly daytime already so they must be hungry. I will go and feed them because you are a sleepy head. Sleep well, Mister Dog.'

~ 12 ~

Although he was still sleeping in the garage, Ombré was thoroughly relishing his stay with monsieur David and Timothy, even if they did both deprive him of any chance of a good night's sleep. The next evening, just before dark, David beckoned Ombré to follow him outside. He did as requested and trotted alongside him to the garage, as was becoming a habit. But Ombré was confused. He tilted his head and lifted a paw in query.

~ Bedtime already, monsieur? It's not even dark yet.

David opened the boot of the car but, worryingly, he didn't encourage Ombré to jump in for the night. When he reached inside and roughly gathered up his blanket and towels, Ombré's heart skipped. Automatically, his ears flattened as if weighted down with lead, and his tail headed south. He looked up at David and whimpered. Was he destined for the streets again? David filled his arms with Ombré's bedding and walked purposely out of the garage. Ombré didn't dare to follow him, and he stayed in the corner of the garage, trembling nervously.

A few seconds later, David poked his head back round the garage door and saw him shivering under the workbench.

'What are you whining for, "*Mister Dog*"?' he laughed. 'We're not getting rid of you, you big, soft mutt. Come on, let's get you inside where you belong.'

He crouched down and looked straight into a petrified Ombré's eyes and then set off again out of the garage, whistling two high notes as he exited. As a new arrival in England, Ombré was still trying hard to pick up the strange language and mannerisms of Timothy and David, but a whistle of that sort is universal. He slowly came out from under the bench and approached the garage door. He poked his snout round it nervously, stretching his neck and bending it round the doorframe. With his paw folded back in concentration, he studied David as he walked up the driveway towards the house, whistling a tune as he went. When Ombré saw he was not heading for the street, his heart jumped again. Everything stood up to attention – his tail, his ears, his snout. Even his eyebrows lifted when he fully comprehended what this meant.

His body eagerly followed his head out of the garage and he ran excitedly to David's heels. David looked down over his shoulder at him and beamed. Then he whistled the same two notes again and said, 'Come on then!' Ombré replied loudly with a tune of his own. He jumped up against David's leg, pulled the blanket from his grasp and pelted towards the house.

'That's more like it,' shouted David. 'Message finally got through, has it?'

He waited impatiently at the back of the house for David to arrive, his tail sweeping the dust and dirt off the steps.

They all sat down for dinner. Well, Ombré stood – he can't eat sitting down; can't reach his bowl. David and Timothy sat at the table and had their meal, chatting to each other, while Ombré gobbled eagerly at his own bowlful, not joining in the conviviality.

'Why can we not call him Mister Dog?' Timothy asked. 'I like it.'

'Well, Tim, "Mister" is a little impersonal, don't you think?'

'No, father, it is a very polite name. What about Dog?'

'No, son. Tell you what, why don't we choose something that he reminds you of? Or the way he behaves? Something a little more relevant.'

'Okay, father, what about June?'

'Why "June"?'

'Because we met him in June.'

'Well, okay ... but June is a girl's name, so that's no good.'

'Wednesday then.'

'No, Tim. I don't think "Wednesday" is a very suitable name.'

'Andrew is a very nice name.'

'Not for a dog, it isn't. Come on, Tim, be serious.'

'I am always serious, father. You know that.'

'Yes, okay, Timothy, but—'

'What about Saint Francis of Assisi?'

'What about him? You want to call a dog "Saint Francis of Assisi"? It's a bit long-winded, isn't it?'

'You told me Saint Francis of Assisi is the patron saint of animals.'

'Yes, he is, but—'

'What about Francis then?'

'Yes, "Francis" is much better. But your uncle's name is Francis.'

'What about Shadow?'

'Why "Shadow"?'

'Because he follows us around all the time.'

'No, I don't think so.'

'I like Wagger.'

'I don't.'

'Do you like Banana?'

'Tim, why would you call him "Banana"?'

'Because of the way he bends when he is excited and wags his tail.'

'No, sorry, Tim, I don't think that's a good idea either.'

'I have a good idea, father. Why do you not choose the name for Mister Dog? You say every name I choose is not a good one so you choose one for him.'

David looked down at the dog and smiled to himself.

~ ~ ~ ~ ~

The three of them made regular trips back to the cemetery. At first, this scared Ombr– ... scared 'Ozzy', for this was the new name David chose to burden him with. On their first visit, he refused to leave the car and hid under the blanket on the back seat. They left him in the car with a window open. Curiosity soon got the better of him and he jumped out and followed them.

Timothy was strolling around the park feeding the birds from a plastic container that he carried. (Ozzy once tried some of whatever was in Timothy's container; he certainly never pestered him a second time.) Timothy loved birds and he was forever feeding them. At home in the garden, there were little bird boxes in all the trees and on the fences.

David was crouched down on the grass at the other side of the cemetery, so Ozzy followed to investigate. He was placing some flowers against one of the squat stones that Ozzy used to sleep behind when he was Ombré. He was talking quietly to himself. Ozzy didn't like to interrupt, but he was so intrigued by monsieur's actions that he pushed in between his knee and arm to gain a better look. David lifted his arm a little to let him through and Ozzy sat down and looked up into his eyes. David then wrapped his arm round Ozzy's body and pulled him close. What were they doing there? thought Ozzy. He looked persistently into monsieur's eyes for an answer. He also wanted to know the reason for the small drops of water that trickled down monsieur's face and landed on the top of his head, so he placed a paw on David's knee. Monsieur wouldn't look down at him but, instead, he lowered his eyebrows and spoke softly to the grass in front of them.

Ozzy pulled himself gently free from David's embrace and stepped closer to the gravestone for a better look, sniffing it for clues, but it didn't help solve the mystery. Because monsieur appeared so lost in his private thoughts, Ozzy decided he ought to be patient and wait. He lay down on the grass and sniffed the scent of the flowers for a while.

Their shared peace was interrupted by a very loud shouting. Ozzy instantly recognised the voice and heavy odour of the groundsman he had bitten. Snapped out of his daydreaming, he jumped to his paws and hurtled back to the car as fast as he could. He jumped up, straight through the open window and onto the back seat. Peering sheepishly out through the window, he watched monsieur and the man exchange words and gesticulations in the distance, and then they parted company. David went to collect

Timothy and they returned purposefully to him at the car. Ozzy saw that monsieur had a frighteningly serious look on his face. He knew he was in big trouble. He had messed it up again. Ozzy climbed guiltily down behind the front seats and lay on the floor with his nose pushed under them. He didn't want to see, hear or smell what they were going to do with him. David ignored Ozzy and spoke instead to his son.

'Timothy,' he said. 'I have to tell you something very, very important and you must listen. Okay?'

'Yes, father.'

'I have just spoken to a cemetery worker and he told me that he was bitten by Ozzy on the day we took him home. He showed me the marks on his arm. They were only small marks, but that's not the point. Do you understand what I'm telling you, son? If this is true, then by law, we have to—'

'You can not kill Oswald. That is very cruel.'

'Tim, listen.'

'You can not kill him, father. How would you like it? Oswald is a very good dog. I am sure that he had a good reason to bite the man. I think it was because he was nasty to Oswald.'

'We are not going to kill him, Tim. But, good reason or not, a dog can't go around biting people like that. Now, I explained to the man that Ozzy was a stray, and as part of my job, I have taken him in and given him a home. He has agreed not to take matters any further, okay? But you must understand that if he does it again – if he *ever* bites anyone again, then ...'

'I understand. A dog must not bite anyone. But it is not fair. If I was a dog and somebody did a bad thing to me I would bite them too. It is not fair.'

'That's just the way it is, Tim. So, as long as you understand that, we'll be okay. Okay?'

'Yes, father.'

'Good.'

'Have you agreed to my suggestion that you should take Oswald to work with you to help you raise money for charity?'

'I'm thinking about it, Tim ... thinking about it. I'll have to discuss it with my bosses, but you might have a good idea there, son. A very good idea. But will you try to do one thing for me?'

'What, father?'

'Could you stop calling Ozzy, "Oswald"?'

'Why, father? Ozzy is a very silly name for a dog. Oswald is a much better name and I think he looks much more like an Oswald than an Ozzy. He is an intelligent thinker like Oswald the Owl not a stupid old heavy metal singer.'

'Yes, I'm sure he is. Anyway, come on, Tim, we did agree, didn't we? Can you please try to call Oswald, "Ozzy" from now on?'

~ ~ ~ ~ ~

Ombré/Ozzy/Oswald knew he had fate to thank once again for steering him into monsieur David's and Timothy's lives. He quickly grew very fond of his new guardians, but each in a different way. As days turned to weeks, David and he grew very close. When Timothy had retired to bed in the evenings, they sat together on the terrace or, if it was a cooler evening, they leant side by side against the sofa watching television. Ozzy felt a sadness and a hollow emptiness in monsieur. David draped his arm round Ozzy's shoulder and stroked the side of his neck and his chest. Ozzy relished the soft caresses, and if monsieur ever stopped too soon, Ozzy would look up to him, prodding him with an insistent paw or probing his armpit with his snout. He felt monsieur didn't have too much experience of stroking dogs, because sometimes his was a caress very different from others he had enjoyed with the Morettis. He pulled Ozzy in close to his side and held him very tightly for a long time without actually doing any real stroking. With David's arm wrapped around him, Ozzy placed a paw up on his thigh, and he felt ever so close to monsieur that way. Yet sometimes, he seemed so far away.

His relationship with Timothy was on a different level, and he learnt a lot with him. It didn't take Ozzy long to understand that

Timothy was unlike any human he had ever met, and once he had accepted that he was unique, their relationship and friendship grew. Timothy had only one little habit that annoyed Ozzy: he enjoyed folding his ears inside out all the time. That aside, he was a wonderful boy, and Ozzy knew he would stand by him no matter what the cost.

~ 13 ~

David worked as a Fund-raising Manager for an animal charity called PAWS – the People's Animal Welfare Society. He toured the country, meeting people and potential donors who wanted to give to the cause. These included individuals, small groups, large groups, and friendly old ladies who were very generous with their life savings.

Ozzy became the first ever charity dog worker amid the human employees. PAWS ran hospitals, animal shelters, veterinary practices and charity shops; it had several hundred doctors and nurses working for it all over the UK, with hundreds more voluntary staff as essential back-up. Ozzy's role was unique.

The two of them travelled far and wide, and met some remarkable people and animals. Ozzy was privileged to be introduced to those kindly humans who wanted to help the needy animals, and he was not ignorant of the fact that he had been through some of the same experiences as many of the dogs he chatted with. Had his circumstances been less generous, and had Timothy not persuaded his father to take him home, then it could so easily have been him in one of the hospitals or shelters.

They spent a lot of their time visiting the potential donors at their homes, or escorting them around the hospitals and the practices. They made presentations to clubs, groups and organisations. Ozzy always sat at the front of the presentations with David – sometimes up on a little stage. They were quite a pair. Within six months of their hiring Ozzy, the PAWS management took the decision to employ dog mascots in other areas too. Timothy's pioneering system was working well and donations had increased noticeably in David's area.

There were soon eleven additional dog mascots working with their respective fund-raising officers. In most of the other regions, there were two officers and mascots, but David and Ozzy worked their area as an inseparably close-knit pair – man and his one best friend.

For London and the south, there were two cheeky little Pugs called Zig and Zag, who, like Ozzy, had seen hard times. They were rescued from a tied-up bin liner in a canal by a fisherman. Happily, they both made a full recovery – one to tell the tale, the other to wag it. For the middle part of England, it was Flip and Flop. They were real characters and entertained everyone with their comic canine capers. For Wales and the area around Liverpool, it was such a big catchment area with a high concentration of hospitals, shelters and shops that there were three officers and mascots. Wag, Scally and Arkid knew the area well and consistently boosted donations. At first, Ozzy could not understand their dog-speak at all – the regional twang was incomprehensible to him; but at least he was finally getting to grips with English dog-speak in general. The two mascots who covered Ireland were brothers, Bilbo and Frodo. After two years with the charity, Ozzy never understood them properly. He didn't much care for the two Scottish mascots (the other dogs called them 'mcscots'); they were unpredictable little white terriers with poor social skills. Jekyll was of fairly even temperament, but Hyde was another matter altogether – two-faced little devil. He curled his lips and snarled at Ozzy, and displayed open disdain for his French ancestry.

~ ~ ~ ~ ~

Life at home was a dog's dream come true. Ozzy soon discovered that David was similar to his first ever guardian, monsieur Moretti, in that he was always doing something odd in his garage. They had a common love for fiddling and tinkering with things and they would have made great friends. Ozzy noticed that monsieur David spent a great deal of time removing parts from his motorbikes and then putting them back together again. But how he concentrated at all with that horrible loud music blaring away was something Ozzy never understood. Timothy refused to go into the garage when his father was listening to it, and Ozzy too withdrew to the peace and quiet of the lounge to protect his sensitive ears. He much preferred something classical, the likes of which madame Moretti had listened to in the Alps. Perhaps rather predictably, he was rather fond of a little Bach or, just as appropriately, some of Wolfgang Mozart's timeless masterpieces, to which his head would nod and sway from side to side – when he could stay awake long enough.

One evening, David called Timothy and Ozzy into the garage. He had a mischievous look in his eyes.

'It's finished, Tim,' he said. 'Come and have a look.'

'What is finished, father?'

'Come and have a look and you'll see.'

'Are you listening to that horrible noisy Black Sabbath heavy metal music again, father?'

'No, I've turned it off for you. And it's not noise, Tim. That, my boy, is quality. Not like that rubbish they make nowadays.'

'Why do you not listen to some of my music, father? You know I have some very good CDs. I have *Sounds of the Sea* and *Dances of the Dolphins* and *Forest Chants* and *The Sounds of Nature* and lots of pan pipes.'

'Okay, Tim, thanks. Maybe another time. Here, come and see what I've made.'

Ozzy ambled jauntily between man and boy, and followed them into the garage. He craned his neck high to see what monsieur wanted to show them. He had constructed something very odd-looking that rested on the front of his motorbike and sidecar but Ozzy couldn't quite see high enough to work out what. He had already been warned it would spell big trouble for him if he put his claws on the precious shiny paintwork of monsieur's machines, so he jumped up against David's legs and twisted his head round to see. Still he couldn't work it out.

David stroked Ozzy's head with one hand, and with the other, he waved over the full length of the sidecar and looked at Timothy and him with a satisfied grin. Then he said something Ozzy recognised from his Moretti days.

'*Et voilà!*'

Ozzy was confused. He looked across at Timothy to wonder if perhaps he had any idea.

'What is it, father?' said Timothy.

'It's a harness for Ozzy, of course! So he can come out on the bike with us.'

Hearing his name mentioned, Ozzy looked straight up into David's face and noticed he had a glint in his eye. It worried him. Ozzy's eyes opened wide in a mix of curiosity and concern. Timothy's eyes held no clues, and it would be some time before Ozzy discovered the reason behind monsieur's excitement.

'Father, are you planning to take Oswald out on the back of your motorbike?'

'Yes, of course. He can be a real biker dog! But it's not for the bike. It attaches to the front of the sidecar, so Ozzy can sit right up front. You'll be in the sidecar as normal.'

'Have you been watching my *Wallace and Gromit* DVD again, father? Will you not get into trouble with the policemen?'

'Well ... well, I'm not really sure, son. But it will be great fun. And it could be a superb marketing idea for PAWS.'

'Do you think Oswald will like it?'

'I'm sure he will. You just wait, Tim!'

'Do I have to wait here in the garage?'

'No, Tim, of course you don't. Why don't you and Ozzy go back inside now and watch television? There's a wildlife programme on tonight, I think. I'll just finish up in here.'

'Okay, father. Come on, Oswald.'

Ozzy was still attempting to work out what they were discussing when David put his palm on the dog's head and pushed him gently to the ground. Timothy called to him, patting his thighs with both hands and they returned to the house to sit down in front of the television.

'Father worries me you know, Oswald,' Timothy said. 'All these funny things he does to occupy his time. I think it is because mother is gone and he feels like a part of him is missing. I do not know which part it is but I know it must be a big part because he is very sad. I hope he gets that part back. I am very glad you are here for him. Father loves you a lot you know. I do not really understand love so I will have to just like you a lot for the moment if that is okay? Father says love is a very special feeling between two people and that it sends a big bubble of air through your tummy. Miss Filipčič at special school says it too. Sometimes I get a funny feeling in my tummy when I eat too many Mars bars or Snickers in one go but I do not think that is the same thing. Can dogs feel what love is, Oswald? I think you must be able to because I can see it in your eyes and your tail that you are very happy. Father says I will know what love really is when it hits me for the first time and I asked him if love is so wonderful why would it hit me?

'Oswald, the wildlife programme is starting and we do not have our special glasses on. Bollards. Oops I swore then, Oswald, did you hear me? You must not tell father because he says I am not allowed to use bad language. I said bollards but I know that is not the real swear word for it because Matthew Mollinson told me the real one. Wait here and I will go and get the special glasses. I will get you a pair too. I have seven pairs of them. One for each day of the week. They are very clever glasses and when you watch a wildlife programme through them you feel as if you are really with the birds and the animals which is brilliant.'

Timothy and Ozzy settled down on the carpet, both of them lying down and facing the television, and they watched their programme. Timothy's arm lay across Ozzy's back.

An oily David soon entered the lounge.

'Timothy?' he asked. 'Why is Ozzy wearing a pair of glasses?'

'These are my special glasses, father. You know that. The ones for watching nature documentstories. Oswald and I are watching the programme together.'

'Okay, son. Tim ... remember it's actually a document*ary*, not a document*story*, but yes, I see. Of course. Your special glasses. Which day's has Ozzy got on?'

'Wednesday. I know it is Friday today but I only have one Friday pair and I am wearing those ones and we can not both wear them at the same time can we, father? We could swap them over at the adverts but we are watching BBC1. But it is okay because we first met Oswald on a Wednesday so he can wear them.'

'That's fine, Tim. I'm sure Ozzy won't mind. Son, you've had those special glasses for a fair few years now. Don't you think it's time to get rid of them? You do know, don't you, that there are no actual lenses in them.'

'Father, you worry me sometimes. That is why they are so special of course.'

'But, Tim ... Yes, of course. You two enjoy the programme. I'll just go and have a shower and clean myself up.'

'Okay, father. Would you like me to make a cup of tea for you later? Oswald and I are too busy watching the documentstory at the moment but I can make you one when it has finished.'

'No!' answered David a little too quickly. 'No, Tim, it's fine. I'll do it after my shower. You watch your programme, eh. Can I make you a hot drink too, son?'

David had not yet dared ask Timothy to make him a hot drink again – not since he had taken one into the garage for him the previous week. Timothy registered his father's reluctance, and told Ozzy the tale.

'I made father my first cup of tea ever last week but he did not really like it. I watched him drink it all but I could see he was not enjoying it so I asked him why. Father told me I should not have put a tea bag and coffee in the same cup at the same time and also that I am supposed to boil the water first and not just take it from the hot tap. Father made me a cup of tea to show me how to do it properly and it tasted much better and it did not taste of coffee at all. But he still will not let me make him one will you, father? Yes I would please like a hot drink, father.'

'Of course, son. No problem. Tea, or is it boiled water and lemon tonight?'

'Tea please, father. Could you also please bring a five centimetre length of cucumber for Oswald? And please can you cut it lengthways in two equal halves and scoop out all the soggy seeds. He does not like the soggy seeds.'

'That's one pretty strange dog we've inherited there, Tim. Eating cucum—'

'I do not think it is any more strange than you eating banana sandwiches with brown sauce, father.'

~ 14 ~

It was a pleasantly warm autumn evening, a few months after David had moved Ozzy indoors, and they had just finished another family barbecue. Ozzy had eaten very well as usual, and his heavy stomach dropped gratefully to the ground where he stretched out and relaxed at David's feet. He and Timothy were talking above; Ozzy slipped into a pleasant daydream about one of his favourite Alpine strolls with Belle.

'Will Miss Filipčič be coming here for dinner one evening, father?'

'What? Why do you ask that, Tim?' asked David, confused by his son's unexpected question. 'What makes you thin—?'

'I thought that is what adults do when they like each other.'

'Well, it is, but what makes you think that your teacher and I like each other?'

'It is obvious, father.'

'It is? Is it? Why?'

'Because you come to collect me from special school much more now. I thought the reason is that you like Miss Filipčič a lot.'

'No, that's not the reason at all, son. I come because I have more free time from work at the moment, and ... Did she say she liked me or something, Tim? Miss ... Miss Filipčič?'

'She said you do good things for the animals. And you are a good father.'

'Really?'

'Yes, father. And I told her you are a good cooker as well as a good father so I asked her if she would like to come here one evening for a meal.'

'You didn't, did you, Tim? Tell me you didn't.'

'I can not tell you I did not, father, because it would be one of those fibs that you tell sometimes and I can not tell fibs. I asked her to come for dinner because I said that you needed some adult company.'

'Tim ... Tim, I do appreciate your intentions, but you can't simply go asking people around for dinner like that. It's not for you to do. That sort of thing has to come from adults.'

'But adults take so long about everything. They are always so worried about other things and they never do what they want. I told Miss Filipčič that it would only be for dinner anyway and not for all that rumpy pumpy stuff that you and mother used to do a lot.'

'Tim! What have you been saying? Has that Matthew Mollinson from school been teaching you—?'

'But she can not come for a meal or rumpy pumpy stuff tonight anyway because she is going to the cinema. But she said she would try to come on her way.'

'She said *what*?'

'I thought that because Miss Filipčič has no husband and because we have no mother any more that she could come around.'

'Oh, Tim. If only it was as simple as that. We can't just replace your mother.'

'I know, father, but you are allowed to have a new woman friend. She is a very nice person and she said she would like to see my book collection too. And the four of us can get to know each other.'

'Son, I know you mean well, but, it wouldn't ... It just doesn't feel right. It's only been ... since your mother ...'

'Miss Filipčič knows all about mother and how she was killed. I have told her everything because I like her and I trust her. We talk a lot. We talk about special school and about books and about your work and she tells me her Bohinj story a lot. And we talk about Oswald too. And when I said that it would be just for dinner and not for all that rumpy pumpy stuff she laughed. And then she said something quietly in a whisper that I think I was not supposed to hear but I did. So I asked what she meant and her face turned very red like it does sometimes.'

'What—? What—? What did she ... what did Miss Filipčič say, Timothy? Just out of interest.'

'It did not make any sense at all. She talks in silly riddles like you do sometimes.'

'Okay, but what *exactly* did she say, son?'

'She said something about the time being may be. But that did not make any sense so I asked her to explain what she meant but then she suddenly wanted to tell me her Bohinj story again.'

'Oh, right. Right. I ... I see. Tim, do me a favour, will you? Would you mind clearing up? I'm just going to ... I'll just grab a quick shower in case Miss Filipčič calls. Thanks, son.'

David jumped up quickly from the bench and, unaware that Ozzy was still dozing on his feet under the table, gave him a rather rude awakening. Ozzy felt the dull kick under his ribs. He leapt to his paws and ran out from under the table to see what all the commotion was about. He ran round the table and voiced his questions to monsieur but he completely ignored them. How very uncharacteristic of him, thought Ozzy; he didn't even apologise for kicking me. David turned on his heels and dashed towards the house, barking orders back at Timothy as he ran. Timothy didn't have time to tell him that the sliding doors into the kitchen were still closed.

~ ~ ~ ~ ~

Ozzy was pleasantly surprised when a female human called at their home a while later. Monsieur and he opened the front door to her. The intoxicating fragrance fired so powerfully up his nostrils that he initially thought she was the owner of all those delightful aromas he had discovered over the previous months. They all gathered in the kitchen and stood around the breakfast bar.

Monsieur had assumed a very strange mood, Ozzy remarked. Timothy noticed it too.

'Father, why are you stuttering like Harry Jackson at special school does?'

Ozzy approached Miss Filipčič and lifted his head to introduce himself. She reached down to stroke him so he licked and nibbled her fingers a little. He was very reluctant to let go of the two tastiest fingers, but she removed them and patted his head. He moved round a fraction and began to sniff her where he knew he would be able to deduce if she was trustworthy and if he liked her, but, within seconds, he felt someone grab hold of his tail and pull him backwards.

'Oz-Ozzy! S-stop it. S-stop that now!'

'Father, are you okay? Do you need a glass of water?'

'N-no, Tim. I-I'm f-fine, son.'

Ozzy turned quickly, grabbed hold of David's wrist and, with a playful but insistent growl, told David to unhand him immediately.

~ Hey! Let go, monsieur! What's your problem? I'm just saying hello to mademoiselle, that's all.

~ ~ ~ ~ ~

Ozzy was very happy to welcome mademoiselle Ljana into the household and they saw a lot more of her during the following weeks and months. He noticed that when she visited, her presence had a relaxing effect on monsieur. Something heavy had been lifted. He felt it and smelt it on monsieur and all over the house. It was as though someone had thrown open a huge window and had let in rays of glorious daylight.

Ozzy found the overload of contrasting smells confusing at first, but it soon became obvious to him that the feminine bouquets belonged to two different people. When he was sure monsieur wasn't watching, he was able to carry out a full formal inspection tour of mademoiselle Ljana, and he soon established that hers was definitely a new odour in the household. His snout told him to trust and welcome her.

For Ozzy, the only downside to her regular visits was that monsieur had developed a terrible habit of singing loudly in the shower while his deafening music blared throughout the house. The only escape Ozzy and Timothy could find was when they all took trips out on monsieur's motorbike. At least there, he couldn't play that dreadful din. Or sing.

They had some terrific times out on the bike and sidecar: Timothy spread out in the sidecar and Ozzy secured on the front in his harness. He loved it. On their first little sortie, his eyes were streaming by the time they arrived home. It took David some time to wipe all Ozzy's saliva from the paintwork, but he didn't complain too much. The next time they took a ride out, Timothy put a set of his swimming goggles on Ozzy's head to protect his eyes from the wind. And monsieur bought him a little blue bandanna, but he refused to wear it. He preferred to chew it and throw it around the lounge instead.

At the weekends, they became the centre of attention at the motorcycle meetings and get-togethers. Unfortunately, Timothy's prediction came true and they also attracted the interest of the local constabulary, so that was the end of that, and Ozzy was forced to sit inside the sidecar. He soon found this was much better, though, because he could sit comfortably with Timothy behind the glass screen without having to wear his silly goggles. He must have looked frightfully ridiculous with them on but, as a dog, Ozzy was more than used to making a complete and utter fool of himself. He quite enjoyed it actually. Nothing pleased him more than to bring a smile to his guardians' faces, or laughter to their eyes. Like all dogs, he was a born performer – and *mon Dieu*, did he put on an epic show for the Morettis when he was still a pup in the Alps! However, they were not always quite the willing spectators he believed them to be.

~ 15 ~

Any recollection of his days before the Moretti family adopted the cheeky little ball of fur that was to become Ombré has become increasingly flawed over time. The memories come and go in faded and jerky patches, so he is very happy when he can remember so far back, and even more pleased when he can recall his days with *maman*. He never met his father; *maman* didn't paint a very appealing picture of him at all. His times with *maman*, however, were precious. He was only seven or eight weeks old when he last saw her and he wasn't ready to be abducted and removed from the warmth of her attentions. Heavens! He had only learnt to cock a leg a few days previously. His first clumsy steps to maturity and then he was dognapped. He still had so much to learn from her. She didn't even have time to give him or his siblings a name.

It was chaotic in their little den with so much pushing and shoving and fighting for food. It was every dog for itself. Every so often during those early weeks, a giant sweaty hand reached into the den and brusquely plucked one or more of the tiny pups out. It was very scary and he cried, and whined, and weed a lot. At first, he tried to bite his way out of the grasp, but *maman* told them all that the big hand was that of the human and they had to learn how to socialise with it.

Soon the human began to treat them with a little more respect, and even fed them extra meals, which was a pleasant change, because there was only so much milk a hungry pup could stomach. The human tickled and stroked him affectionately, and he got to quite liking that – rather a lot, if the truth be known. Sometimes, he enjoyed it so much he tried to extend his out-of-cage trips. He especially relished the sweet caressing behind his ears and along his back; he could have taken that for hours at a time – and often did.

One morning, the big human hand reached in and took him out of the den as was usual. It carried him to the table, undoubtedly for more of the daily poking and fiddling, and some extended ear tickling. He cheekily nibbled at the human's fingertips, looking back to the den and squealing in delight to *maman* and his other siblings.

~ *Allez*, see you all later. I'm off to have my tummy rubbed for a while. *À bientôt!*

The big hand put him directly into a little metal cage and closed the door. He never saw *maman* again.

~ ~ ~ ~ ~

Those first days away from *maman* and those dark lonely nights in the Moretti household were a terrifying experience; one he would not have wished on his worst enemy – not even on a cat!

When he was let out of the little travel cage and aired to his new environment, he immediately recognised the two people as those who had visited him at *maman*'s place. He had warmed to them instantly because they spoke softly, held him delicately and tickled him in all the right places. He had tentatively tried the face-licking routine to test their reaction, but they didn't like it. They smelt good, a thousand and one aromas, and he licked their hands and fingers clean, savoured every one of them.

But he was scared, and he missed *maman* and his kin. He whined and cried like a baby for the first few nights. He sulked, hid under things and behind them, and complained all night long about being left on his own. Whenever any one of them came near him and lifted him up, he inadvertently showered them with little warm dribbles. He tried to apologise but his voice was still so feeble. And he left 'deposits' inside the chalet. Each time he had a 'little accident', monsieur or madame Moretti lifted him up and bundled him outside – he had not fully learnt that he must do his necessaries outdoors. Most of the time, he simply forgot; other times he was caught out by the sudden need. And sometimes it was just *too* cold for him to even consider venturing outside. But what really confused his young, inexperienced brain was why madame took such great pleasure in pushing his snout in the various smelly piles that she discovered around the place.

This all confused him greatly. Why had they brought him home in the first place if they insisted on rubbing his nose in things and throwing him outside all the time? Why *did* they take him from *maman* if they didn't want him inside their home? His young developing mind made a decision that gave him enough justification to set off back to the den to find her. He was a determined little pup, and he waddled purposefully out of the front door and down the drive, head held high, stubborn as can be. A long way to go, but resolute all the same.

He never made it far.

Once or twice, he reached the edge of the property before his tiny frame was halted. He felt air underneath his body as he was lifted clear of the ground, but he carried on walking anyway, his little legs spinning regardless. His guardians even had the audacity to laugh at him. They turned him to face them, said something incomprehensible and carried him back into the chalet, dodging his little jets of wee.

One day not too distant, and purely by chance, he happened to be outside when the call of nature took hold. He found a comfortably private spot, but no sooner had he finished than he realised monsieur had been secretly watching him. Alain crouched down and thrust a tiny biscuit of sorts into the little pup's face. It smelt good so he ate it. Alain gave him another one, and he ate that one too, only vaguely aware that monsieur was patting him on the back and stroking his little head rapidly. He was saying something too, but the greedy pup was too busy gulping down the unexpected treats. Although not through any careful planning on the young pup's part, they had several repeats of this, and slowly he began to fathom their human logic. He took it to mean 'outside good' but 'inside bad'. They eventually reached an accord. He tried to do his rounds outdoors all the time – unless he really, really had to go and they had not left a door open ... or if it was raining too heavily.

~ ~ ~ ~ ~

Perhaps he had committed another unintentional *faux pas*, but before long, he was being hauled in and out of the local vet's on a regular basis, where a friendly but intrusive man did things to him with all manner of evil instruments. He pushed and pulled, pummelled and probed. He folded the young dog's ears forwards and backwards, and enjoyed kneading the flesh of his scruff. On one visit, the man surprised him from behind and inserted something very cold where he shouldn't have inserted something very cold. In his most commanding squeak, he yapped at the vet to stop, turned round quickly and gripped one of his fingers. It had a strange rubbery taste that he didn't like at all.

His regular sorties to the end of the drive carried on for a while, but grew less frequent. Although he was growing fast and his legs were powering him further and further away from the chalet each time, he accepted it was simply a habit. Did he really want to leave?

Then his escape attempts stopped altogether. Life in the mountains improved. With his decision to stay, he assumed a few more canine duties and carried them out with dedicated conscientiousness. He sprawled at the front door and surveyed comings and goings, and vetted any callers. This was the entrance to his new family den, and *maman* had told them to always protect your pack's territory. Whenever the Morettis and he came back from a day out, he was always first through the door, making sure that there were no intruders and it was safe for them to enter. He led the way, checking every room first, upstairs included. When leaving the chalet, he was always the first outside, first to jump into the car, again to check it was safe. It was his eternal duty to be minesweeper and safe-path finder. Except when they visited the vet's practice, when he delegated the duty to monsieur and let him go in first. In doing so, he discovered that his powerful little legs could propel him backwards just as fast as they could forwards.

But there was never an escape for him. Alain always cornered him as he cowered and whimpered under a chair or table. He put up a valiant fight, but because his paws were so nervously sweaty, he had no real grip. Alain pulled him out of his hidey-holes by the scruff, or sometimes by his tail or back legs if he had dived in headfirst. He was easy prey with his face buried in a corner and his rear end sticking up in the air. Monsieur ignored his protests and carried him into the room where the man with the long blue coat, who smelt too clean to trust, interfered with him.

~ ~ ~ ~ ~

His home was a huge chalet halfway up a mountainside, close to the picturesque Alpine village of Abondance. He arrived there in the dewy spring and, once he had finally settled in and decided to stay, he could not have wished for a more promising continuation of his eventful life. Their chalet was one of a dozen in a scattered group a few kilometres from the village down in the valley. It had plenty of space for a young pup to stretch his legs and explore. The view was magnificent. All around were majestic forests, lofty peaks and high mountain ranges. If only he had taken more time to appreciate the scenery instead of being such an impudent little tyke.

His guardians took a very long time to select a name for him – around the same time it took him to eat a generously good-sized bone. They proposed dozens of possibilities, all of which they shouted, whispered, or called to him as he lay by the fireplace fighting with his bone. They wanted to see if any particular one would solicit a response. Some did; others didn't. To some, he raised an eyebrow, to others he twitched an ear. To the rest he preferred to concentrate on his feast. Amongst them were suggestions from the young twins: Bijou (Jewel), Chiot (Puppy) and Titus, which was not very apt for a dog the size of Alain's walking boot. Madame Isabella, as was her religiously biased whim, had put forward Fresco, Église and Abbaye, all of which Alain turned his nose up. Had *le chiot* understood what was going on, he would undoubtedly have done the same. Alain wanted to call his new best buddy Peroni after his favourite beer, but Isabella gave him such a glaring look it scared both Alain and *le petit chiot*. The search continued into the evening and voices were raised – including that of the pup by the fireplace who, with all the shouting, was unable to concentrate on his bone. Would they ever agree on a name?

~ 16 ~

What the adults eventually settled upon had a rather melodic ring to it, and it rolled off the family's tongues easily. They were unanimously keen on it – finally! – so the pup by the fireplace briefly stopped chewing and gave a short wag of his tail and a couple of little yaps to seal his approval. Although he was unaware of the significance of his christening – it was just another word they shouted at him across the lounge – it was *un petit jeu de mots* of the Spanish '*hombre*', and the French, '*ombre*', for 'shade', because Ombré liked to play 'chase the shady patch' a lot.

He was a cheeky little animal during his upbringing – difficult to believe, *n'est-ce pas*? – but still he learnt a great deal in those early years, most of it from Alain, who had assumed the role of Alpha One Male in their pack. Isabella spent a fair amount of time away from home with work, whereas Alain worked mostly from home and was always around the chalet. Ombré tried hundreds of times to test monsieur's authority but was reprimanded on each one. The lofty position of top dog was taken, so he had to settle for second in command.

There was one particularly major thing Ombré could not get to grips with for a very long time, and that was coming back when called – his recall was anything but total. Even so, they never used a leash or collar on him. In most other disciplines, he was a model dog and was well rewarded for his aptitude, but coming back (or not, as the case was) was not his specialist subject. Otherwise, he was a good little pup. He never stayed out overnight and he never mixed with the wrong crowd. Well, that's not quite true. On one or several occasions, he did stay out all night with friends, but he was always back safely before his guardians rose the next morning.

Although he was still only small, by the time he reached three or four months, he had become a bit of a handful. Perhaps it was the changing weather playing with his emotions and hormones. High summer was tapping on the shutters, and the evenings were much longer, which meant he had more hours in the day before bedtime. This meant he had more time to explore, more time to play, and more time to get into trouble. He was proficient at all three. He cleaned and sharpened his teeth on the chairs and table legs and he chewed on the black cables that were attached to various items in the chalet, even though he found the taste of plastic to be rather unpleasant. He wasn't always a quick learner, and when he did manage to chew all the way through the cable that attached to the big square box the family sat in front of in the evenings, he learnt his lesson the hard way.

They had a few more trips to the vet's, but this didn't worry young Ombré too much any more, not now that he had an understanding with the man in the blue coat.

He could feel his body changing and he was growing up rapidly. He began to feel strange stirrings, a longing for something. He felt something rushing through his body, as though he had been injected with an energy boost. It was a confusing time. There were new smells in the chalet settlement and down in the village. Smells that had to be explored. He began taking a keen interest in *les filles*, so he was often late for dinner, which got him into endless trouble with madame. His mind was in turmoil and he needed advice. He became arrogant, cheekier, and he was convinced he could take on a higher level of responsibility in the pack. The Alpha One spot was definitely up for grabs again, or so he thought. He started to spend much more time outdoors exploring and satisfying the inherent wanderlust that was making his paws itch.

He found himself missing *maman* again and thought of setting out to find her. He missed the pack life, and yes, he missed his brothers and sisters too. He sneaked out after dinner, and wandered, looking for any sign or smell of his old family. He had no real idea what he expected to find or where he hoped to find it, but he couldn't control it. It was something he had to do, even if it did lead to repercussions.

It appeared to annoy madame whenever he brought a new friend home, and he caused his guardians endless trouble with the villagers and neighbours on those occasions when he turned up with a local *fille*. Monsieur asserted his authority and intimidated Ombré by producing a collar and leash that he dangled in front of the dog's face menacingly. He threatened that if Ombré carried on with his boisterousness and nocturnal jaunts he would have no choice but to make him wear them.

But it was hard for him to keep up with the rules, for they were forever changing and it depended on who was making them. Asking for seconds at the dinner table was strictly forbidden; except on certain days when madame made a special meal. He always used to be allowed upstairs and into the bedrooms, but madame now deemed that out of bounds. Previously, he was allowed up on the sofa; then he wasn't – unless monsieur wanted a good cuddle. The adults made and changed the rules and the girls twisted them.

Madame proposed her own solution to Ombré's growing pains and problems by looming over him with menace, opening and closing her index- and middle fingers rapidly. She did this a lot, and she gave him such a fierce stare that it petrified him. Curiously, he noticed, it appeared to worry monsieur too; each time she did it, he flinched and gave Ombré a mournful look.

The chickens were not to be eaten, except by the Morettis. Ombré was allowed to chase them for fun, but not to kill them – but the chance never once arose, as they were far too quick on their rubbery feet. The sheep was not on the menu either, confirmed by a sharp rap or two on his snout. He did eat well though; usually two to three meals a day, and although an enforced semi-vegetarian diet was not precisely what nature had intended for

Ombré, it was during this time that he developed his penchant for carrots. He absolutely adored raw carrot – the crunchier the better! (He had to wait until he was four and a half for Timothy to introduce him to the delights of cucumber.) As time passed, Ombré even learnt to pick his own carrots from the little allotment behind the chalet – quite the little gardener he was. Madame didn't agree.

Ombré was able to supplement his diet elsewhere on a regular basis. Down in the village, market day was great for titbits and leftovers; especially when he tagged along with his good friend Sherpa, a wizened old Pyrenean Mountain Dog who had moved to the Alps last year. They were both very popular among the villagers.

In those early days, monsieur often attempted to supplement Ombré's diet for him too. But Ombré easily out-fooled him. He learnt never to trust anything circular or white that appeared in his bowl. These additives normally materialised straight after a visit to see the man in the blue coat, so he always knew when to check if monsieur had buried one in his food. He always gave himself away because they were the only times he stood over Ombré and watched him eat – every morsel. Or so he thought. Ombré learnt to hide them in his mouth and look up at monsieur with an innocent 'I'm-a-good-dog' expression on his face. Then he would sneak outside and drop the chalky tablet or jelly pill with all the others, or he would give them to the goat.

At family mealtimes, although Ombré knew it both impolite and forbidden to ask for food, he was actively encouraged to do so by the twins. His usual mealtime position was under the dinner table, where at least he could share some of the aromas. Otherwise, he would maintain a respectable distance and put a sheen on the wooden floor with his tail. When the girls thought their parents were not watching, they slipped him goodies under the table. Neither of the twins liked carrots so he was always on hand to vacuum up any stray slices or gratings that 'accidentally' fell to the floor – as long as madame hadn't overcooked them, in which case, he left them to stick to the soles of monsieur's slippers. Likewise, the girls despised sprouts, whereas Ombré loved them, so he always disposed of the evidence for them. He never understood why he always had the lounge to himself afterwards. The adults often treated him when their own meals were over, and he slowly became a connoisseur of tender mountain hams and cheeses, and Isabella's awfully good *tartiflette*.

As time progressed, madame calmed down and monsieur relaxed. Monsieur threw out the dreaded collar and leash, and madame stopped doing that nasty snippy-snip-snip thing with her fingers. This enabled Ombré to relax too, and it had the effect of reducing his wanderlust. It *had* been a very hot summer for them all, so that probably didn't help matters.

From then on, things improved in the Moretti chalet. Ombré met a lovely *fille* down in the village. A real beauty, jet-black thick fur and a true diva in his love-struck eyes. She was a small mountain dog of sorts, but a strange breed that young Ombré hadn't come across before and didn't recognise. She had the most curious but appealing of attributes. Ombré wouldn't normally have gone for a *fille* with a tufty little beard, but he had to make an exception, for Belle wore it so well, as she did her delightful bouquet. He had already picked up her aromatic trail a few days before they first met, and her *Eau de Montagne* was so deliciously potent that his nostrils thought they had finally arrived in paradise. Her unique *parfum* was bettered only by her beauty.

She had the darkest, most sparkly eyes Ombré had ever seen and they made him go weak at the haunches. She was a little bit closer to the ground than he was, slimmer, and a good bit older. Wise and intelligent with it too. She knew a lot about life, and she shared many tales with him. Her sultry dog-speak melted Ombré's muscles and soothed his mind so much that he used to close his eyes to concentrate. The problem was, Belle thought he was nodding off, and she would jab him with a paw to wake him. What began as puppy love matured, and his feelings for Belle deepened.

Their time together passed quickly and before Ombré knew it, it was his first human birthday – what could be called his 'manniversary'. He turned one in March …

… and then time passed so quickly he was two …

… showing no signs of slowing down, it sped by and he became three …

His first and second manniversaries had both been great successes, and he knew his third one would easily equal them. It promised to be a memorable day indeed. He had great plans to share it with Belle; he had a special present for her. But before that, and before even his first manniversary, he and the Morettis shared their first truly wonderful family celebration: Christmas, and all the festive fun that came with it.

~ 17 ~

Alpine summer had turned to autumn. As autumn blended into winter, the days became shorter and temperatures dropped. The family began to wrap up when they ventured out walking, but the change in weather didn't worry Ombré, who already had a very good winter coat.

After one particularly long expedition up along the Swiss border, they returned home for a good meal. They were all exhausted, and while the family dozed in front of the television, Ombré sprawled in front of the fire, spread out like an animal hide, letting the heat warm him through. Outside, it was a chilly evening.

The Morettis eventually filtered up to bed with gaping yawns – yawns easily matched by Ombré's, but he stayed by the fire awhile, the crackling embers and he sharing pleasant thoughts. Eventually, mesmerised by the orange glow, he nodded off in front of the fire. He didn't make it to his bed until much later on during the night.

In the dark heart of the night, Ombré woke to see monsieur sneaking down the stairs. He watched him tiptoe through the lounge. Ombré was still on his hearthrug at the time and monsieur stepped carefully over him to the fireplace, trying not to wake him. Half asleep, Ombré watched him through one eye as he hung three big socks on the fireplace. Then he turned and walked over to Ombré's bed and put a fourth one just behind it. When monsieur had sneaked back upstairs Ombré, understandably intrigued, ventured away from the fire and to his basket.

His own heavy snoring and burping woke him up before dawn the next morning. He wiped the sleep from his eyes. He stood up and stretched, kicking his left leg, then his right leg, out behind him to wake up his muscles. He made his way over to the window and, yawning like a snapping alligator, jumped up against the window ledge for a look outside.

Alors, he thought, what shall I do today? A good long walk in the mountains again? Or maybe chase the chickens for a while? He knew it was the weekend again because madame was home, so it would be his turn to go to fetch the bread from the *boulangerie*. Perhaps he could call in and see Belle on the way. With his snout, he pushed the curtains to one side for a better look. He thought he might lie by the fire all day instead, because it would probably be a bit cold outsi–

~ *Sacrebleu!* What's that?

His eyes bulged with shock, his tail jumped skywards, and his ears swivelled backwards so much they touched each other. He jumped down from the window ledge and pelted through the lounge. He shot across the hallway and screeched to a halt at the foot of the stairs, ready to bound up them.

~ *Zut!* he reminded himself. I'm not allowed upstairs now!

But this is urgent, he decided, and catapulted up the stairs two at a time. He barged open the door of the master bedroom and ran straight in. He jumped up onto the bed and yapped at monsieur and madame. He knew they were there because he could see two lumps under the covers, so he shouted even louder and pawed the quilt. The two lumps slowly began to stir. They both sat up in bed looking very annoyed about something, but Ombré had other things to worry about. He bounced around, shaking his rear end from side to side, and told them to get up. Monsieur shouted at him.

'Ombré – down!'

Madame joined in the shouting contest.

'*Qu'est-ce que–?*'

Ombré interrupted her.

~ *Allez!* Quick! Come downstairs and look!

He threw himself off the bed and skidded out of the room on the bedside rug. Turning back to face them through the doorway, he shouted to them again.

~ Well, come on you two. Hurry up!

'What's got into him?' yawned Alain, rubbing his eyes.

The twins arrived in the hallway. Ombré bolted past them to the top of the stairs and descended them in three leaps, shouting back up to them as he landed.

~ Come on! *Allez!*

Eventually the humans heeded his call and joined him downstairs. He was running back and forth from the window to the front door, as though on elastic. He jumped up against the door, shouting excitedly, scratching it with his claws and trying to open it himself. The family caught up with him and peered down at him as if he were barking mad. The girls squealed as they caught a glimpse through the window.

'*Regarde, papa, il neige.* It's snowing.'

'*Oui, oui, oui! Il neige, papa, il neige. Super!*'

Alain looked down at Ombré and shook his head slowly, smirking to himself. Then he slowly moved forwards to open the door.

'Ah, that's it, is it, Ombré? You've never seen snow before, have you. *Allez.* Well go on then, out you go.'

Isabella took Alain by the hand and kissed him on his mouth. This confused and annoyed Ombré. Why was she always allowed to share monsieur's flavours and tastes when he never was?

'*Joyeux Noël, mon chéri,*' she said to her husband. 'Merry Christmas.'

Ombré helped monsieur open the door with his snout and barged past him, desperate to get outside and investigate his discovery. The girls were close behind him, still in their nightdresses, but Isabella pulled them quickly back inside.

~ *Oui*, shouted Ombré. I'm first! I found it!

Madame agreed with his justification and waved a finger at the girls.

'*Allez, les filles*, go and get dressed first,' she said. '*Et* ... haven't you forgotten something, *non*? *Bon anniversaire, Virginie. Bon anniversaire, Angelique. Et Joyeux Noël.*'

Ombré dashed out into the fresh morning air and was suddenly hit, not by the biting cold, but by a tidal wave of confusion and fear. He skidded to a halt on the very lip of the top step. He turned round to monsieur for some back-up and yapped.

~ I'm not sure I like this. What is it? What *is* all that white stuff?

'*Allez*, go on,' Alain assured him. 'Go and explore it then, big, brave dog. What are you waiting for? Christmas?'

Ombré sat down and faced him, looking up for guidance. He lifted a paw in confusion and voiced his concerns.

~ What's happened? The house has sunk and all the steps have disappeared! I used to jump down them. Where've they gone? And where's the path? I'm scared. I don't like this.

Ombré's fear was immediately dispelled when he realised that monsieur sensed and understood his nervousness. He approached Ombré and crouched down. He was so relieved monsieur understood that he stepped forwards to welcome his reassuring touch and advice. He looked up, voiced his gratitude and allowed monsieur to pick him up for a cuddle. He tried to give him a kiss like madame did, just to say *Merci*, but before he could even flick out his tongue, Alain threw him off the patio into the scary white stuff. Ombré sank up to his shoulders.

'*Voilà*,' said Alain. 'That'll teach you to wake us at seven o'clock on Christmas morning. Well, go on, go and play.'

Whatever the stuff was, it was frightfully cold. Ombré's undercarriage was freezing. Once he had caught his breath back, however, it took him just a few seconds to discover the snow to be immense fun to play in. The strangest thing about it was that it was both very soft and incredibly hard. When he tried to run in it, he sank. When he tried to eat it, it disappeared in his mouth and he was left chomping on water, snapping his jaws together like an idiot. Yet, when the girls threw balls of it at him it really hurt. And when he tried to find the snowballs they had thrown, they too had disappeared. It was superb fun ... except for when monsieur threw a snowball; he launched them very hard indeed. Ombré was busy working out his revenge strategy when madame called them all back in for breakfast. They would return for more fun and games later, but the humans couldn't run around in the snow on empty stomachs. Ombré wasn't at all hungry, as he had dined rather well during the night.

When they returned inside, Ombré shook himself clean of snow and noticed monsieur standing by his basket with a severely wrinkled frown across his forehead, not unlike D'Artagnon the Shar-pei from in the village. He was holding a sock and he was tapping a foot on the wooden floor. He called Ombré over with a curled index finger and told him to sit down. Without warning, monsieur rapped Ombré on the snout with the empty sock as though he had done something wrong and then, with a smile on his face, he opened it up and rolled it over Ombré's snout all the way up to his eyes. Some of his habits were becoming very odd indeed, thought the dog. But Ombré was most grateful actually, because in the toe of the sock was a small biscuit that he hadn't been able to reach during his nocturnal feast.

Ombré never did know what monsieur actually did to earn *his* keep, but he usually found him buried in his workshop in the garage, making all manner of contraptions. One such thrown together piece of equipment was made of a little old rucksack, some lengths of plastic tubing and a tangled mess of straps, bungees and buckles. Alain called it his *bagàdos*, from 'baguette' and '*sac à dos*' (rucksack), and it was this invention that he forced Ombré to wear most weekends.

Although it was fast approaching mid-morning, Ombré hadn't yet been sent into the village for the bread, which he was quite surprised about. He presumed the excitement of the snow and the snowball fights had taken priority. Monsieur was too lazy to go into the village at the weekends, so he always sent Ombré down to the *boulangerie*. He didn't mind, as it was usually a pleasant morning run, an opportunity to stretch his legs and warm up for a decent walk later in the day. It took him around fifteen minutes down the mountain and a bit more back up – unless he called in at Belle's. Running down to the village was eventless, but once madame *la boulangère* had loaded up the *bagàdos* with baguettes and croissants, he always drew curious looks from any early-morning tourists and walkers. The locals were used to him, but to the tourists, a dog dressed up as a sci-fi rocket launcher had them reaching for their cameras.

Alain had also fabricated a little back pouch for him so he could occasionally call in at the butcher's during the week to collect fresh meats, dried sausage and cured hams. Ombré soon discovered that by rolling over on the ground or brushing against a tree, he was able to dislodge the pouch and treat himself to a splendid breakfast, so he was never asked to go shopping at the *boucher*'s again. It never stopped him from visiting, however, because monsieur *le boucher* had a lovely pet *fille*, who just happened to be Ombré's lithe little beauty, his gorgeous Belle. But monsieur *le boucher* did not approve of their relationship and he made it very clear that Ombré was not welcome.

He wasn't at all in the mood for going down to the village on that snowy Christmas morning. He knew it would take him an age to collect the bread because the snow was as deep as he was tall; but as always he set about his duties conscientiously. He nosed into the utility room and unhooked his *bagàdos*. Normally, monsieur would fit the *bagàdos* to him, but if ever he was still sleeping, Ombré had to lug it awkwardly down the valley and madame la *boulangère* would fit it for him. He carried it over to monsieur, sat down and put on his best sad dog look. Alain took it from Ombré's mouth and carried it straight back into the utility room. It works every time, Ombré congratulated himself. The big marble eyes and angled head routine.

'There's no point going today, Ombré, you silly dog,' Alain told him. 'It's Christmas Day. The *boulangerie* will be closed. Come on, everyone! Let's get the sledges out.'

The girls cheered.

~ Whatever you say, *chef*; Ombré wagged his agreement.

They had a wonderful day together in the snow. He learnt to sledge – Ombré the Olympic. He shot down the slopes on a sledge with the girls, while Alain and Isabella had their own. Ombré and the twins were by far the fastest and always reached the bottom ahead of the slow adults. What they weren't so proficient at was stopping. As they sped, out of control, towards the pond at the bottom of the hill, Ombré braced himself in anticipation of the freezing cold bath to come. But instead of the ducking he expected, they slid and spun across its surface, which was very confusing for him and his puppy logic. Then the girls taught him to ice skate as well. He also learnt two more lessons that day. First, it is entirely possible for a dog to do the splits – with both sets of legs! And second, ice is definitely harder than his lower jaw.

~ 18 ~

By the time Ombré had reached two, and was approaching three, his friendship with Belle had matured to something very special. They were inseparable; nothing could come between them – not even monsieur *le boucher* and his razor-sharp meat cleaver.

The pair loved their walks together up in the mountains. When they took their evening strolls, they usually settled down for a breather at the top of the mountain viewpoint – Belle didn't have Ombré's stamina – and they lay shoulder to shoulder, staring out over the unrivalled scenery, with Lac Leman in the background. To appreciate the views better, Belle sometimes hopped up and placed her front paws onto Ombré's shoulders, craning forwards to sniff the mountain breezes and all that was carried on them; her mouth agape, tongue pulling in any flavours floating in the air. She was the best mosquito-catcher Ombré had ever seen. He didn't mind being her footstool one bit.

Occasionally they didn't say much, content in the shared silence of eternal chums. Other times, they chatted as if they had only just met, telling each other little snippets about themselves and their lives, with their paws touching – Belle liked to lay her paw over the top of Ombré's. Like most *filles*, Belle was right-pawed so she always positioned herself to his left side. This led to a silly little game they played where she would put her right paw on top of his left one, and he would quickly pull his out and drop it heavily onto hers, and so on. Things sped up to a blur until Belle usually ended the game by grabbing Ombré's paw between her jaws and chewing his toes.

They play fought a lot too. Ombré managed to convince Belle that he always let her win, but she was a tough little thing, and her jaws were a lot stronger than his were. It gave him a great excuse to lie back and relax with his legs in the air, enjoying the devoted attentions of Belle – though on occasion, Ombré was convinced that she mistook his thighs for dinner. He would voice his pain jokingly to her.

~ *Aïe!*

~ *Ah, zut!* Don't be such a Poodle.

Ombré always took this retort as a signal that she wanted to play rough, so he jumped up and bowled her over with a glancing snout to her flank. And then he took his revenge and chewed on her legs until his jaws ached. The play fighting usually ended with a spell of nuzzling and mutual preening. After all, that's what friends are for.

~ ~ ~ ~ ~

And so it was, on the very first day of March, his third manniversary – in dog years, his twenty-first birthday – that Ombré sprinted eagerly down to the village. He had never taken Belle up to his secret lake before, but he felt this was the perfect time to venture up there together. It was his and monsieur's favourite trek, and they had done it so many times. When monsieur first took him up there, Ombré the pup found the steep climb very hard going, but these days, it was Ombré who had to wait for monsieur, puffing and panting up the mountain like an old dog. Madame was not as serious a walker as monsieur, and the twins never showed much interest in being dragged up a mountain by their father and his faithful hound only to have to trudge back down it again later.

The hike usually took them around two and a half hours, or three if they were both heavily laden down with Alain's fishing gear. Alain carried the rods, net, tackle box and chair, and Ombré was loaded up with the bait because Alain didn't like to carry the live maggots so close to his body. He had adapted a neat little harness and container for Ombré that sat squarely on his back, but unlike with the pouch for the fresh meats from the butcher's, this was one delicacy Ombré didn't try too hard to sample.

The lake was high up in the mountains, resting serenely at 2,000 metres, so they could do the walk only in the warmer months once the snow had taken its annual leave. At the top, the turquoise-watered lake was protected by and sheltered below a massive amphitheatre of ragged rock that pierced the sky defiantly. Around the lake was a spongily lush, grassy plateau, perfect for Ombré to practise his Victory Runs, or roll around on, or fall asleep on, depending upon how much he had wolfed down for lunch.

After the long pull up to the lake, he took the opportunity to dive into its rejuvenating waters and perfect his doggy-paddle. He had great fun diving underwater; he loved to see how far he could go on one breath, and what was the largest stone he could retrieve from the shallows. He didn't venture too deep, however, as it became very cold only a little way down, and the water blackened, which frightened him.

They played a game up at the lake, one that most dogs teach their guardians. Ombré discovered that if he presented monsieur with a stick and forced it into his hand, he could persuade him to eventually throw it. Once Ombré had successfully retrieved it and pushed it back into his hand, he usually invited monsieur to throw it again. He would run a good distance from Alain, continually looking back over his shoulder to ensure he was still holding on to the stick until he got as far away as possible. This ensured that monsieur would have to put some real effort into it and not just a weak throw. He had an excellent throwing arm but he was often reluctant to employ it. When satisfied, Ombré turned round, reared up on his hind legs and shouted the well-known rules.

~ Throw it now! As *far* as you can!

Monsieur soon got the basic hang of it, and it was up at the lake that Ombré and he honed their techniques. Ombré soon accepted, however, that he would have to contend with monsieur's inexperience and ineptitude. He often spotted the stick hurtling in some other random direction to that which had been agreed, so he had to totally change course to retrieve it. Most annoying! And sometimes monsieur just pretended to throw the stick across the pastures or into the lake. But Ombré wasn't stupid enough to dive into those chilly waters for a stick or stone that monsieur still held on to behind his back – well, not too often anyway. He was most confused, however, when monsieur turned up one day with a boomerang.

Alain soon tired of the game, the sleep-inducing effects of lunch and beer were usually too much for him; his energy levels depleted in reverse proportion to his Peroni levels. He sat down and dozed in his fold-up chair. Once or twice, when he was snoring the afternoon away, Ombré noticed his fishing rods twitched and bent.

Ombré amused himself and ran around the plateau and scree slopes, chasing a few marmots or teasing the slothful salamanders with his snout. Sometimes he continued up to the very top and along the narrow ridge to meet the other walkers, and to soak up the views. He couldn't wait for Belle to meet his marmot friends and for her to see the views. When he tired of running amok, he would flop out in the afternoon sun for an hour or so, before they commenced their descent home for another fishless dinner.

After a spell of unexpectedly warm weather and an early thaw, monsieur and he had made an early trip up to the lake in the last days of February. It was up there on the ridge that Ombré had his idea to finally take Belle up to his secret lake for a manniversary treat. He was very excited.

After a hearty birthday breakfast, he ran down into the village to collect her. As he was banned from the butcher's nowadays, he stood on the opposite side of the road and called for her. She appeared from the back of the shop, looking radiant as ever, and with a mischievously bright sparkle in her eyes. She had an impatient look on her face and Ombré had the feeling she was keen to tell him something. Whatever it was, he had an even better surprise for her. He called a jovial *Bonjour* to her across the road. My, she looked excited – probably because she knew it was his manniversary. She shouted *Bonjour* back and jogged gracefully across to meet him, her silver whiskers glistening in the sunlight. The driver of the tourist coach didn't have time to brake as she disappeared under his wheels.

~ 19 ~

Monsieur *le boucher* blamed the Morettis and their good-for-nothing dog for the tragic accident. As if losing Belle weren't enough, Ombré was, yet again, put under strict orders to keep well away from the butcher's premises. He tried to obey, but he couldn't help it. It was as though a magnet drew him back to the spot where she was taken from him. No matter how much his guardians waved a finger at him or rapped him on the snout, he couldn't stop himself from returning.

At first, he visited daily in the hope that Belle would return. Maybe he could turn back the time and make the coach driver brake, or call across to Belle to wait until it had passed. He concealed himself on the other side of the road behind the bus shelter, watching, waiting, hoping, crying. He felt her presence, but he never saw her. She never again peered out from the window of the upstairs flat.

A month after her departure, Ombré was back at the scene again. It was raining very heavily. He was sitting in a puddle, paw deep in water, with his nose and ears hung low and loose, shivering but not caring. He was too depressed to make an effort. His eyebrows were so laden with raindrops that they ran down his snout and dripped into the puddle. There was a deep glassy film of water on the road. On its rippled surface, Ombré saw Belle's form lain out, floating on the water, drifting slowly out of his life. He tried to think about why she had been so keen that fateful day. Had she somehow found out he was taking her up to the secret lake?

Had Sherpa told her? He tried to conjure up her voice but, every time a car drove past, it was whisked away in the drenching wake. She had gone.

He had been there for around an hour, reliving the accident in his head when monsieur *le boucher* spied him. He rushed out of the shop doorway, waving a menacing weapon. He ran across the road, splashing heavily through the puddle where Belle's image rippled, and he lunged at Ombré. Ombré ducked clear and scarpered. *Le boucher* set off after him and chased him all the way through the village as far as the *boulangerie*, where Ombré darted inside and begged madame *la boulangère* to help him. The butcher burst into the shop after him, still waving the cleaver, but when he saw madame *la boulangère* crouched low at Ombré's side, stroking his sodden, trembling body, he lowered it begrudgingly. *La boulangère* shouted something at him, he shouted back and then he stormed out of the shop, slamming the door behind him.

Ombré lifted his paws up onto madame *la boulangère*'s knee and gave her a big sloppy kiss on her face. After drying herself and Ombré off with a towel, she thrust a mini-croissant between his jaws and opened the door to let him out.

Once he had checked his route was clear, he walked slowly through the village and back towards home, in no real rush to get there ... or anywhere. He had to let her go. He simply had to. He must try to shake the image of her beautiful laughing eyes from his mind – for they sparkled no more. At least she had gone quickly. They were desperately hard times for Ombré. His days were devoid of interest and his nights were empty of happy dreams. His guardians knew he was pining badly, but they could do nothing.

Two weeks later, they left the Alps. Six weeks after she had gone from him, Ombré left Belle behind for ever.

~ ~ ~ ~ ~

It was a cool spring morning in the middle of April. Inside the chalet, Ombré stood up, stretched and yawned, and went for a quick drink to freshen his night breath. Then he nipped outside to do his usuals. There was no sign of movement from the humans so he knew it was the weekend. He collected his *bagàdos* from the utility room and set off down to the village.

It was market day on Saturday, so it took him longer to fetch the bread than it did on Sundays. He had to say hello to some of his friends and their guardians; he would divert to see the cheese woman, who always gave him a few big chunks; he would be chased by the fruit 'n' veg man for trying to steal a carrot or two, and then he would go to the *boulangerie*. The queue for the bread was always longer at the weekends – undoubtedly why monsieur sent him down – but he waited his turn in line like a good dog. Madame *la boulangère* carefully loaded up his *bagàdos* with the usual four baguettes and a bag of croissants, stuffed his favourite savoury weekend treat into his open jaws and bade him a *bon weekend*.

That particular Saturday, he went again to the *boucherie* and sat across the road, staring blankly at the tiny patch of innocent-looking road where it had all happened. After a while, Sherpa arrived. He approached, had a quick sniff and a leg-cock to say hello and then started up a conversation.

~ What are you doing sitting there – and with that ridiculous contraption on? Come on, Ombré, there's no use punishing yourself. It wasn't your fault. *Allez, mon ami*, let's take a stroll and catch up; haven't seen you for a while.

By the time they said goodbye and Ombré had left the village, the sun was already high in the sky. He set off back up the track at full speed, thinking that if he didn't hurry, they would be having the croissants for lunch not breakfast. As he ran quickly up the hill, his mind wandered back to when he first met old Sherpa.

Big hairy lump that he was, it was no wonder he suffered from terribly whiffy D.O. His doggy-odour problem aside, he was a great friend and always had an answer to Ombré's endless queries. Sherpa was one of the most intelligent dogs Ombré had ever met, easily on a par with Bazou. He loved to talk, and every day he amazed Ombré with his knowledge. He once saw Sherpa chomping away urgently on some dandelions as though he were frightened someone or some dog might steal them. Ombré had tried some himself on one occasion, but they made him vomit violently.

~ Precisely, *mon ami*, Sherpa assured him matter-of-factly. That's the whole idea, you see. I've got a poorly tummy. I'm filling my face with this horrible stuff so I'll throw up later, and hopefully cure myself.

~ Wow! Where do you learn all this stuff, Sherpa?

~ When you've been around as long as I have, you can't help but pick up a few tricks.

~ Does it always work?

~ Not always, *non*. But if it does, be really careful where you are when it starts to do the trick. It really annoys madame when I vomit half-chewed dandelions all over the kitchen floor. But take great care, I warn you, because if you eat too much of the stuff, it can kill you. Forget chocolate, Ombré – dandelions are little yellow devils if you overdo them. And as for daffodils – well ... trust me.

~ I do, Sherpa. I do. Can you tell me some more, please? Please, please, please!

~ Woah! Slow down, Ombré – you can't learn it all at once. You gotta learn some of it by making your own mistakes as you go along.

~ *Allez*, please!

~ Okay, just a couple more – anything to shut you up. If your guardians' kids ever encourage you to chase a grape around the lounge – I don't know why they do that; must be a human thing. But anyway, play along by all means. Amuse them, but don't ever eat it. Ever! You'll regret it, I tell you! And if they ever try to get you involved in that ridiculous human tradition of kissing under the mistletoe at Christmas, then *your* best move, Ombré, is to run and hide. And stay hidden. Don't let that stuff anywhere near you.

~ Why not, Sherpa? I like it when they kiss me – even if they won't let me kiss them back.

~ Why *not*? Are you listening? Because it's poisonous, that's why.

~ Oh, right. Sorry.

~ Right, I think that's enough education for now, okay? I've got a list of these as long as my bushy old tail, but *petit à petit*, that's the best way to learn. Tell you what, we'll go for a stroll one day in the mountains and I'll point out what's good and what's bad. Okay, *mon ami*?

~ I'd like that a lot! *Merci*, Sherpa.

The two dogs – little and large, young and old – often went out walking for a session of questions and answers. Sherpa walked for hours and hours on end. Even strolling, he covered ground with such a speed that Ombré had to jog just to keep up. He was twice as high as Ombré was, and Ombré easily fitted underneath his lolloping gait – which came in handy when it was raining; though he had to try not to breathe in the tangy air too deeply.

The first time Ombré met Sherpa, he had the shock of his life. Ombré was having a bit of harmless fun in a pasture full of sheep and their youngsters, chasing them from corner to corner, when suddenly, he was picked up by his tail and flung through the air. When he recovered and stood up again, facing him was a huge rabid inbred sheep. He shouted obscenities at it, presuming it would be frightfully scared and would run away in panic. Imagine Ombré's surprise when that particular sheep stood its ground and answered him back in fluent dog-speak. Its voice was so deep and threatening, Ombré's tail instantly disappeared between his legs, and he cowered like a frightened lamb, which was highly appropriate under the circumstances.

~ You harm just one of my sheep, you little runt, and I'll run you through the shearer, I will.

Ombré immediately apologised to the mutant sheep and, even though Sherpa was unlikely to have felt threatened, Ombré lay down on his back to signal his respect and that he meant no harm. Nervously, Ombré asked Sherpa how a sheep could converse in dog-speak. Sherpa approached him and loomed high above, growling deeply and gutturally, and he told Ombré he wasn't a sheep, stupid hound! He was a dog bred to look like a sheep so that idiots like him couldn't spot the difference.

Still young and blissfully innocent, Ombré was amazed.

~ What – you mean a dog mated with a sheep and produced you?

~ *Non!* You fool. *Mon Dieu!*

~ You mean it was the other way around? *Zut!*

~ *Sacrebleu*, dog! Were you born stupid or do you just get it from your guardians?

Sherpa sat Ombré down on the grass and explained. Ombré wasn't sure whether to believe him. It could all easily have been a lie because he couldn't see Sherpa's face or eyes at all, as they were covered in a thick foliage of fur. And as he couldn't see Sherpa's tail either, Ombré had to take his word for it that he was, quite literally, a sheepdog.

~ That's weird.

~ No more weird than a half-breed Labrador on stilts.

When Ombré finally reached home, the chalet was in chaos, and breakfast was evidently the last thing on anyone's mind. There were cardboard boxes scattered all over the place. Outside the chalet, there was a large box van with its rear door open. Monsieur had emptied the whole garage into the garden. Ombré ran to him with the bread. He wasn't pleased with Ombré's tardiness.

'Where've you been until this time, Ombré? It's after eleven. We gave up on you.'

Ombré made a tour of the grounds and of the chalet. Madame had emptied the contents of the kitchen and was putting it all in boxes. The girls were in the lounge putting things in big banana boxes. What *was* going on? He pestered madame and the twins but they refused to pay him any attention. He ran back out to see monsieur. It took him a while to find him, hidden under a moving mountain of fishing gear. Little by little, the chalet's contents were packed and loaded into the back of the big van.

He ran from room to room, person to person, trying to discover what was happening. Then suddenly, he realised the enormity of it. His treasure! He had several chews and bones scattered about the chalet, and the Morettis were obviously searching to steal them. He had spent a long time hiding them in places where he knew they would never find them. Even he sometimes forgot where he had hidden them – under the doormat by the back door; behind the sofa, and in madame's walking boots (she rarely used them, so this was a very good spot). He sometimes stashed a half-eaten chop on the chicken's nest – that way, he could go back afterwards and it would still be warm. He dashed to check. The chickens had gone but there was his booty, still buried in the straw. To play it safe, he collected up all his chews and bones, and hid them behind the stock of firewood at the back of the chalet; his guardians wouldn't need to go there until wintertime.

He had one more bone that he knew of, so he ran quickly to retrieve it before it was too late. It was a huge specimen and he had camouflaged it well in the middle of madame's roses. He was relieved to find it still in place. He thought: well, if everyone is going to ignore me, I'll just take my bone and go for a walk.

Up on the hill, he spotted Sherpa again, still out on his daily tramp. He ran after him and offered to share his bone. Sherpa wasn't fooled.

~ Come on, spit it out. What's on your mind, Ombré? You wouldn't be sharing that wonderful thing with me if you didn't want something in return, now would you.

~ Why are my guardians so determined to find my bones, Sherpa? And why is the chalet all empty and hollow?

~ *Ah oui*. Your turn now, eh? That's what happened to me too if you remember.

~ What? *What* happened to you?

~ Your guardians are moving house – that's what. Off to pastures new. I was a Pyrenean, remember, before I was shipped over here to these dogforsaken Alps.

~ There's nothing wrong with the Alps. But ... but, this is their home. I've lived here all my life ... for more than twenty years.

They ... they can't go. They can't leave me here. What will I do all on my own? I won't be able to reach the cupboards to get my food out. I—

~ They're not going to leave you here, you dumb fool. They'll take you with them, of course.

~ But ... but *where*?

~ That's anybody's guess, I'm afraid. And you'll be the last to find out. You'll know when you get there and not before. Selfish bunch, those humans.

~ But the Alps are my home, Sherpa.

~ Not any more, pal. Not any more.

~ But— but—

~ Now come, come. Be a dog about it. Don't go all sucking-your-blanket on me now, Ombré. Let's think about this a minute, eh? A new start ... a new life. I was too old to be shipped halfway across the country from the Pyrenees, but you'll make new friends in no time. Sprightly little devil like you.

~ But ...

~ And it will probably do you some good as well – you know, to get away. It'll help you get over your loss ... the accident. You gotta move on, pal. Can't keep dwelling on all that's been and gone. What *you've* got to do, Ombré, is just *be*, and *go*. I'll miss you, I will. Hmmn, I wonder where you'll end up? North, I reckon – that's the way the wind blows.

~ 20 ~

He missed the Alps at first – the mountains, the endless pastures, the snow, and the untainted air. He sulked for a while but, as Sherpa had predicted, he soon grew acclimatised to their new home in northern France. Yet, even after a whole year away from her, he still missed Belle as if it were only yesterday. But time stands still for no dog, so Ombré resolved to make the most of his new life. Eventually, he grew to love the region – beautiful in its own way. He still thought about her every day, but Sherpa was right on that subject too. He had to move on. The fashion in which Ombré chose to 'move on', however, was surely not what Sherpa had in mind.

He was out for his usual weekend romp with the Morettis, this time in the endless expanses of the Barenne National Park, a thirty-minute drive from home. It was there, deep in the dappled forest, that he met Noisette: the first *fille* in a year to stir up any real emotion in his brooding mind. The Barenne Park covered a massive area and a dog could never tire of its allure. A flat land dotted with hundreds of tiny lakes and ponds, a spider's web of walking trails and paths, and covered with dense woodlands in which Ombré could easily hide and disappear.

Sitting on the deck of an open-backed jeep, Noisette exuded canine charm. She was almost regal in her pose as the beaten up old vehicle trundled along the track. Never would she equal Belle, but she came in a very close second. Nosiette's scent pulled Ombré along behind, as if his snout had been hooked by a fishing line. He tailed the jeep, bouncing along on his clipping tiptoes and strutting his stuff. He puffed out his chest, showing off his white patch, hoping to impress her. The flatbed was not moving too fast, but it took a lot of running and several attempts before he was able to finally jump aboard.

He sat bolt upright facing Noisette, and maintained a statuesque pose, with straight back and legs tucked neatly under. Behind, his tail was swishing from side to side, sweeping the jeep's deck clear of discarded bottle tops and cigarette butts. Noisette appeared to like him, so he stood and approached her to say *Bonjour* properly.

The jeep slammed to a halt, the driver's door was flung open and a man ran to the back, shouting at Ombré, a furious look on his wiry face. He picked up a big rubber boot from the flatbed and swung it at Ombré, catching him full on the shoulder. Before he had time to recover or steady himself, the man grabbed him by the scruff with his spade hands, and doghandled him brusquely from the jeep, throwing Ombré some distance to the ground.

He landed heavily and cried out in pain. He was about to run back at the man to give him a real piece of his mind when the big brute launched the other boot at him, catching him on his ribs this time. Ombré let out a yelp and retreated quickly into the trees. From his hiding place, he watched the man collect the boots, return to the jeep and caress Noisette.

~ Hey, that was supposed to be my job! shouted Ombré.

Noisette's over-protective guardian climbed back into the driving seat and the vehicle spun off in a swirling plume of orange dust. As the jeep departed in the misty cloud, Ombré caught one last vision of Noisette and he knew from her look that she was deeply saddened by their missed opportunity to get to know each other. Or perhaps she had dust in her eyes.

C'est la vie, he thought, and set off resignedly back along the forest track to round up the Morettis. He knew they would be trailing behind somewhere as usual, not too far away. But when he looked around him, he didn't recognise that part of the forest at all and he began to worry that he may have strayed a little too far while chasing and riding on the jeep. He cocked his head to one side and flipped open his good ear to establish their whereabouts. He could hear birdsong, and leaves rustling in the early evening breeze. He could pick out human voices from here and there and a multitude of other sounds that vibrated his eardrums, but he couldn't hear any of the usual Moretti sounds. They must be waiting for him back at the car, he presumed, so he set off back in that general direction as quickly as he could.

He reached a crossroads of forest tracks, none of which looked particularly familiar. A young deer darted across the track and, with a graceful kick, entered the undergrowth on the other side. It stopped and turned round to look at him, quizzical, unfazed. They looked at each other for a moment and then the deer started, and disappeared into the trees. Normally, Ombré would have given chase immediately – deer were such softies and always made for a good pursuit – but not that day.

His instincts told him to take the track straight on. He ran fast. When he looked further along the tree-lined avenue, it ran on and on. So, he ran – on and on.

His shadow started to lengthen and he realised dusk was not far away. He increased his pace and sped through another crossroads. Then the track turned a sharp right. He felt the Whippet in him take control and he banked heavily into the turn spraying leaves and gravel out of the curve as he rounded it. He ran without slowing. He reached another crossroads and then a junction, heading all the time where his instincts told him. The track abruptly ended at a rocky escarpment.

Without even taking the time to curse his own incompetent instincts, he turned and ran back; up and down every track that his aching legs would carry him. But still he recognised nothing. The smells were confusing: the trees, the animals, the birds, and the lingering temptations of half-eaten picnics. Desperate now, he sprinted along another route to reach a wide crossing of tracks. He sat down in the middle for a much-needed breather and let his tongue loll freely. His legs were tired and shaking, and his ribs were very painful. From the corner of his eye, he spotted a young deer in the trees to his right. It was the same one.

~ *Non!* he cried. *Non!*

The deer heard him, gave a startled look and disappeared – fear on four legs.

Then as if by magic, a vehicle approached from the distance. As it came closer, Ombré saw the familiar shape of the Morettis' car and the welcoming sound of its engine. Thank goodness! I've found them at last, he breathed with a sigh of relief. The car already had its lights on, illuminating the track, and monsieur was driving very slowly; looking for him.

He became a little hysterical as the Morettis arrived, and he jumped up and down as they drove slowly level with him. He threw his paws up onto the car door and stretched his head up to the half-open window to greet monsieur before he'd even had chance to stop the car. He shouted excitedly.

~ Don't worry, girls, I've found you n—

The girls were not in the car; neither was monsieur nor madame. When he thrust his head upwards, the wide-eyed face of a woman stared back at him through the glass. She accelerated rapidly, sending Ombré sprawling onto the track. He landed heavily, hit his head on a log and the world turned fuzzy.

When he woke, he lay still on the grass verge where he had landed. The forest was dark and silent. The first thing he did was to cry.

~ 21 ~

It was his fourth manniversary but Ombré had nothing to celebrate. Was his birthday jinx following him and punishing him again? Would it ever end?

The darkness of night pressed heavily on his sagging shoulders. With his night vision and a guiding moon, Ombré continued to scour the forest for his guardians. He no longer ran; he was too exhausted for that. He searched for hours, as did the Morettis, but never would they find one another again. His family pack disintegrated in the vastness of the forest. He was alone and he knew it. When he stumbled upon an old stone cabin, he staggered inside and collapsed, allowing the night to swallow him up in its chilly embrace.

He spent the following week roaming the inhospitable streets of northern France. It went from bad to worse and back again for Ombré, and trouble followed him as if attached to him on a collar and leash. In search of food, he strayed eventually into the suburbs of a city and spent a night or two in a public park. He had never been to a city before: the noise, the pollution, and the mass of humans and vehicles petrified him. So many people, yet nobody cared. They had no time for him. Even the city dogs were too preoccupied to give him any time or advice.

It was there that he was captured by the dog police and thrown in prison. Ombré didn't know it was forbidden to sleep in the park overnight – an itinerant dog has to find somewhere to rest his head. They threw him brusquely into the back of the van with three other vagrants and ignored his pleas. He was given no chance to explain, no one to win over with big marble eyes and a furrowed brow.

The prison was an awful place. Ombré saw terrible things, despicable goings-on, and he witnessed events that would make the hairs on a dog's back stand on end. Underpaw dealings, wanton fighting, unprovoked attacks on other inmates, and even on the wardens. Conditions were appalling. Hygiene was a disgrace, with soiled waste left in the cells.

The daily exercise regime was almost non-existent. The dogs were allowed only one hour a day in a large, fenced compound, but it was not a place where Ombré could relax or take time to think. The pound was where most of the fights occurred, with some dogs ganging up on others: the new blood, the meek ones fresh in off the streets – like Ombré! It was easy to predict the ones who would be picked on, and the ones who would do the picking. He saw one particular attack on a Corgi who came in on the same day. Three long-timers circled him like a pack of wolves, and when they had finished with him, he ... he ... – it still haunts Ombré to picture it.

The ringleaders and troublemakers strutted around the place as though they owned it, puffing out massive chests and showing off their muscles with a powerful swagger. These huge beasts towered over the rest of the dogs and shoved them around with their fat, twitching snouts and slathering jaws, raising heavy legs onto their victims' shoulders, pushing them into the dirt. Other ruffians were short but wide, incredibly stocky, and walked like Komodo dragons, thudding their heavy paws onto the dusty earth, making it shudder. They wore big studded collars and had ostentatious-sounding names like *Titan*, *Rambo* and *Tueur* (Killer), and they paraded around the exercise yard, sneering nastily and telling every dog what depravation they were going to commit next.

Then there was the Chihuahua gang, who made up for lack of size by being the most vicious little creatures a dog would hope never to meet. Nobody tangled with them. Alone the four brothers were simply irksome and intolerable; together they were a force to be avoided – especially in the exercise yard, where they gathered and tormented the other inmates. The ringleader was Taco. His three siblings, Nacho, Fajita and Burrito, were unfailingly loyal. Ombré kept his distance from them, ignored their taunts as best as he could and resisted any urge to remind them to enjoy their brief little spell at the top while it lasted, because theirs would not be long lives. There is an old saying in the dog world: 'Long snout, long life – short snout, short life'. Ombré knew the Chihuahua Gang would not reign evil for ever.

Dogs were three or four to a cell, so it was no surprise that territorial disputes broke out. Night-times were the worst, and after lights-out, many a cry and wail echoed along the corridors. The more timid dogs cowered in the corners of their cells, crying and whining. Ombré did his fair share of crying too. Across the corridor, a pair of soulless staring eyes watched him intently. Ombré curled up into as small a ball as possible and closed his eyes tightly to hide. But even through his eyelids the stare penetrated and threatened. It taunted him: *You're dog meat.*

A dog in a place like that can all too often have his dignity and self-pride stripped clean off his back, and there is nothing he would not do to survive. But not so with one particular dog who Ombré met during his incarceration. He was sharing his cell with one of the more established prisoners, but he didn't acknowledge Ombré at first; he preferred to stare at him continually, looking him up and down. This petrified Ombré, so he avoided any eye contact and stayed tucked in his corner. His other cellmates – though he would hardly call them friends, uneducated pair they were – told him that the big dog was sizing him up and assessing his potential.

~ Potential for what? Ombré queried in a whisper.

They sneered at him knowingly between themselves and whispered.

~ You'll see, soon enough.

Ombré sat in the corner and his thighs trembled and shook. His paws sweated. The other dog must have heard their comments, because he lifted his head from his slumber and fixed them all a stare that struck silence and fear into the cell. They all cowered and looked down at the ground.

The dog approached Ombré for the first time one afternoon during the exercise period and, at first, he thought he was being singled out for a mauling but, *grace à Dieu*, he had misjudged his cellmate's intentions. He was a mature, silken Husky known as Bazou and had been locked up for several months. No other dog ever touched him. He had 'a reputation', 'a name', and the others knew he should not be tackled. If another dog was ever foolish enough to make full eye contact with him, 'the look' was all it took for the opponent to retreat – Bazou's eyes were different colours and one was pink. Rumour had it that he had served time in the military. The other dogs also claimed that Bazou had once ripped a burglar's buttock clean off with one bite.

For some reason, Bazou tolerated Ombré and took him under his wing, so to speak. He told Ombré he had warmed to him because he found him somehow aloof, above the rest of the brainless mutts. He said it was refreshing to see, because Bazou was becoming old and weary, drained, and tired of life. It was not his first time inside; he was a repeat offender. He had tried to reform, had attended obedience classes and had even seen a dog-shrink – but he bit the man's arm quite severely. He was a snow dog, he grumbled, born for running across arctic plates and ice fields, not to be cooped up in small houses and city apartments. It was the stress and the boredom that brought on his acts of aggression.

He told Ombré about other dogs he knew in the prison, those in similar circumstances to him. Some had received what he called the big jab as punishment. Ombré asked what he meant by 'The Big Jab' but Bazou wouldn't tell him, assuring Ombré that something like that would never happen to him. Ombré was intrigued and pressed him on the subject – curiosity might well have killed the cat, but as a dog, he thought he would be safe. Bazou gave him the eye, so Ombré quickly changed the subject.

~ Bazou? Why do some of the inmates pick on the other dogs? And why does Taco have such an interest in me?

~ It's because they're all bored in here and they have to find some way – any way – to relieve their tension. It's just a habit-thing really, a way of asserting their superiority in the 'pack'. It's even worse with the cross-breeds. Nasty little creatures they are. I once saw four of them gang up on a Saluki, you know. Three of them cornered him while the other one savaged him. He was never the same again was old Gangly. Very sad.

Bazou continued.

~ No, it's a sad state of affairs all this rabid violence. That's how King Charles met his end – tried to steal the throne from the wrong dog.

~ Yes, I heard that story.

~ Well, it's true! And if you ever see that big old English mutt Stafford the Bull sneaking up on you, then a word or two of advice. Run like you've never run before. And if you can't run, then fight; but make sure you fight rough.

The wardens clapped their hands and whistled to signal the end of the exercise period. Bazou and Ombré stood to join the file back indoors. Just before entering the building, Bazou suddenly took hold of Ombré firmly by his scruff and pulled him to one side. Ombré panicked. What had he done? Was Bazou going to rip his face off for his impudence? But he let go and spoke quickly, allowing Ombré to once again breathe.

~ Hey, youngster! *Un dernier mot*, a final word. If we don't see each other for a while, you take care of yourself, okay. You'll be out of here in no time if you play by the rules. And once you're out, don't *ever* come back in here again. Do you hear me? *Never!* Now, I'm going to tell you something. A secret. And if you ever tell any dog this, I'll rip your leg off and eat it in front of you. You hear? *You hear!*

Ombré nodded, swallowed and stuttered.

~ But of course we'll see each other again, Bazou. We're good friends now, aren't we?

~ *Oui*, we are. But anyway, my reputation in here – it's all exaggerated, you know. Blown totally out of proportion. But who am I to spoil their fantasies, eh? And it means I get an easy life. I have absolutely no idea why, but it seems I can put the fear of Dog into the other mutts just by looking at them; so, that's what I do. See! I reckon I'm pretty good at it too. But that burglar thing ... well—

A warden kicked Bazou's backside and propelled him along the corridor before he could continue with his story. He was ushered into a little side room by two solemn wardens. Ombré wondered where he could be going. He hoped he wouldn't be too long because he wanted to hear the burglar story, and he still had dozens of other questions for him about prison life. He decided he would approach him in their cell later in the evening.

Bazou never returned.

~ 22 ~

Ombré kept to himself and stayed always alert. But above all, when the humans ever came to visit, he tidied himself up, had a good wash and groom, and put on his best behaviour, as *maman* had taught him. He wanted to charm.

There was something he didn't like about the French couple who collected him a few days later. It must have been canine instinct, but they didn't smell very trustworthy – one or two smell receptors told him that something wasn't as it should have been. He decided to pay attention to his instincts. Moreover, the man tried to put a collar and leash on him. When he tried to hook the collar over his neck in the reception room, Ombré made a break for it, out of the building. He ran as fast as he could, as far as he could, and away from the potential dangers of city life.

Having escaped, it would be a week or more before he was taken in by Alphonse. He spent those days and nights roaming from village to village. He knew he had to get away, keep moving, because he could so easily have been captured again and thrown back inside.

So, imagine his shock when, just six months later, comfortably settled in his new home in England, monsieur David took him to his first PAWS animal shelter. He had already visited several hospitals and practices, but nothing could have steeled him for what he knew lay on the other side of the car park that day – his body stiffened and froze as if it were made of ice.

Ozzy instantly recognised the ominous style of the building and he could hear the crass shouting of the inmates echoing within its walls. He smelt a familiar stagnancy, and the memory of the depravity he witnessed back in France petrified him. He began to tremble and shake. He dived down off the back seat of the car and tried to hide behind the front seats. What had he done wrong? He had been a good dog, he was a good worker, a trusted employee. He had abided by all of the household rules and, not since the minor altercation at the cemetery had he fought with anyone. Not even the paperboy, who he would have very much liked to, ever since he smacked Ozzy hard on the nose with the rolled-up weekend supplements.

'Come on, Ozzy. What's wrong?' asked David. 'Come on out from down there. It's only a rescue centre, you dozy dog. No one's going to hurt you.'

David reached down, took Ozzy's rear in his hands and gently pulled. Ozzy whimpered from under the seat.

~ No, monsieur, please, don't pull me out. Let go of me.

'Now come on, boy.'

Ozzy growled.

'Hey! Ozzy! We'll have none of that! Don't you growl at me.'

~ I am *not* going in there!

Although Ozzy had no justification to presume monsieur David would put him back in prison, the memories were still too fresh in his mind to shut them out. He could see in monsieur's eyes that he meant him no harm, and he didn't smell a trick, but he couldn't risk it.

'Well, have it your own way, you stubborn fool,' said David. 'You stay in the car then. It's not the kennels for God's sake; I'm not going to leave you. We're not going on holiday! Chance would be a fine thing. Right, I'm off – I have work to do. You stay here and sulk. I'll leave the window down for you for when you change your mind.'

David let go of Ozzy, retreated and closed the car door. Ozzy watched him cross the car park and walk into the sinister building. As he did so, he turned to Ozzy, patted his thigh and whistled those two beckoning notes again.

~ No way! Ozzy yapped. I will never ever set a paw in one of those places again. Ever!

Ozzy followed David in after almost two minutes. He had left the door to the building ajar and, with a paw folded nervously, Ozzy nosed it open and sidled inside. When David saw him skulking along the corridor, he grinned and summoned Ozzy to him. He bounded up and nuzzled against his leg, apologising for his irrational behaviour. David took Ozzy's snout in his hand, closed it to a loose fist and jiggled it from side to side.

'Daft mutt,' he laughed.

The building was bustling. Wardens patrolled the aisles, there were dogs chatting to one another, and there were plenty of humans talking to the resident animals in their quarters. Some of the dogs shouted so loudly Ozzy wondered if they were trying to hold conversations with canine chums in the other wings of the building. Within a few short minutes, Ozzy's mood changed and he buried the ghosts of prison.

What a wonderful place! It was not the prison he had expected at all. It was a halfway house, a low-security holding for animals who had committed no crime. They were all between jobs, passing from one guardian to the next, hoping for a new home.

They met a prospective donor, and together they toured the establishment. After an hour or so, they returned to their respective cars. David shook hands with the donor and Ozzy held out a paw for her – a middle-aged woman with a tongue-tingling taste of yesterday's fried bacon and brown sauce on her hands. She shook it firmly.

'That's a very special dog you have there, David,' she volunteered. 'And he's *so* cute when he shakes hands like that. And he must be a clever little fellow, too – I see he's left-handed. *He*'s not on your books, is he?'

'No, luckily for him, Mrs Townley. He already has a good home. Don't you, Ozzy? Most male dogs do tend to be left-pawed you know. Females are generally right-pawed. But yes, he is pretty sharp, I must admit. Too sharp for his own good sometimes.'

'Yes, I'm sure he is. I can imagine. One more question, though. Something that troubles me a little.'

'Yes, of course. Sorry if I haven't covered everyth—'

'Oh, but you have, dear. You have. You can expect my cheque within the week. It's just that ...'

'Go ahead.'

'Why on earth did you call him Ozzy?'

~ ~ ~ ~ ~

Their PAWS presentations went from strength to strength. David provided Ozzy with an old foldaway table to sit on while he talked to the groups so Ozzy could see the people better, and they could see him. He was able to survey the audience much better, and his lofty position enabled him to participate more in proceedings – to earn his keep. He was very well provided for, especially at the presentations for the women's groups. They enjoyed queuing up to feed and tickle him. Ozzy loved the attention. In between courses, he rolled onto his back and basked in their attentive touch, which usually brought a chuckle. He felt like royalty. David looked down at him and shook his head.

'You're nothing but a flirt, you. I wish I got that much attention.'

The buffets were amazing. Fresh meats: hams, beef, chicken; and a wonderful assortment of rubbery cheeses. There were crisps and carrots by the table load, and whatever those delicious little pieces of sausage meat in some kind of edible flaky paper were, Ozzy couldn't get enough of them. But with the good came the very bad – what in the name of *Dieu* were those sandwiches full of that disgusting yellow-and-white mush with little green leaves and stalks?

It was at one of these gatherings that Ozzy tried his first cup of tea. Well, it wasn't a *cup* of tea, it was a saucer, but tea all the same. He liked it, but would have preferred a dash more milk. And perhaps if one of the women among the group had let him know it would blister his sensitive tongue. One kindly lady saw his predicament and helped him out because, as a dog, Ozzy had not learnt the art of blowing.

At another visit to a kindly group of women, these ones quite elderly, David's presentation was put on temporary hold when events took an unscheduled turn. Before he had chance to begin, a large, very loud woman called for everybody's attention and began to talk very deliberately.

'So, ladies, the minutes for today are as follows. There's the trip on the Manchester Ship Canal to organise, and the flower-arranging display to schedule in. We have the jumble sale next week, and we mustn't forget the collection for Mrs Keelty's husband's, err ... "delicate" operation.'

During the hour that followed, and whenever there was the briefest of pauses, David made to start their presentation, only to be stalled by a raised palm.

'Patience, Mr Briggs, please. We're almost there.'

Finally, they finished. David jumped to his feet and began to introduce himself. Ozzy sat up straight, in the middle of his table and faced the women, trying his best to look the part.

'Mr Briggs! *Please!* One moment,' barked the speaker. 'Now, ladies ... *before* Mr Briggs commences, shall we all stand for "Jerusalem". Mrs Fretwell, if you please.'

The speaker glanced over to an unseen someone hidden behind the huge piano and nodded her head once. Ozzy was shocked when he heard the wooden thing suddenly begin to play musical notes. He looked up at David for an explanation but he was too preoccupied shuffling his papers around the desk. Ozzy turned back to face the crowd, who had begun to sing. Sitting high up on his table, Ozzy had the most wondrous view of a room full of English reincarnations of Edith Piaf in fluffy tweed and tartan singing their hearts out.

And did those feet in ancient time
Walk upon England's mountains green?
And was the Holy Lamb of God
On England's pleasant pastures seen?
...

What could Ozzy do but join in?

The following week, company bosses called them into head office to praise their continuing efforts. Ozzy strolled down the corridors, skipping lightly on his paws, his head held high. Office employees came to say hello and stroke his proud head and tickle his tummy. David was given a new company car with a much bigger boot, which meant Ozzy had more room to spread out – he no longer used the cramped rear seats; the boot was all his! And PAWS issued him with a specially designed mascot's highchair to sit on at future presentations. The makeshift foldaway table was folded away one last time. Quite literally, Ozzy was going up in the world. He could not put a paw wrong. Until the incident with the paperboy.

~ 23 ~

His fifth and sixth manniversaries had come and gone without pomp. David and Timothy were unaware of Ozzy's actual canine birthday and, personally, he had ceased to put any importance on them any more. Ozzy turned forty and began to feel it – in his legs, in his mind, and in his whiskers, which began to lose some of their colour.

He was, however, very curious to notice that there was another celebration of sorts in the household on the same day as his manniversaries – the Briggs residence was full of cards with lots of colourful pictures on them. Ozzy watched eagerly as monsieur gave Timothy various boxes and packages all wrapped up in bright paper. Mademoiselle Ljana too gave him some parcels. Whatever the reason, Ozzy was very excited to see Timothy being spoilt, so he helped him open all his packages.

David was seeing Ljana on a regular basis by then and Ozzy was happy to note that he smiled a lot more than in the early days. On the downside, it meant that he and Ozzy had noticeably fewer cuddles on the couch because mademoiselle filled his old role. He wasn't jealous; quite the contrary. He didn't sulk in a corner or snap at her ankles as some Poodles he knew would have done. It was good that monsieur had found a suitable mate. They still made regular trips to Ozzy's old park at the weekends and they sat by monsieur's favourite stone for a while. And Ozzy finally made his peace with the big man in the work suit; they shook paws to seal their friendship.

As spring fused into summer, Ljana began to accompany them on their family walks; she loved the outdoor life as much as Ozzy did. They took lengthy hikes on the fells, especially up at Queen's Tower, which was a beautiful spot with stunning views over the countryside and as far as the coast. She even accompanied them on the motorbike and sidecar. She usually rode with monsieur, her arms wrapped very tightly around his waist, and Timothy sat behind Ozzy in the sidecar with his goggles on.

They travelled up, down and across the country on quiet, windy roads and little-used back lanes, joining the dots between scenic spots, snack caravans and biker haunts. They even journeyed as far as Scotland one weekend, but Ozzy stayed in the sidecar in case there were any more of those vicious white terriers lurking. They spent a great deal of weekend time at a very picturesque place by a lazy river, where there was a small mobile café at the riverside, and where they regularly met friends of monsieur who also had motorcycles. Ljana and Timothy usually took sandwiches and sat on the grass by the river's edge, but Ozzy and monsieur much preferred a bacon bun for lunch at the café. Ozzy and he usually had a cup of tea too; Ozzy drank his from a little bowl that the owners of the café kept for him.

~ ~ ~ ~ ~

One evening after a super day out and an even more super bacon sandwich, they retired to the lounge to relax and watch television. Ozzy sprawled out on his rug in the middle of the floor with Timothy, who laid his arm across Ozzy's back, massaging the root of his tail. They watched Timothy's favourite nature programme; David and Ljana were in deep conversation. Ozzy heard both his names mentioned several times but, because Timothy was now brushing his fingers lightly behind his ears, it was impossible to concentrate.

'David?' asked Ljana. 'I've been thinking – maybe we should go away for a holiday. We could go abroad. France, perhaps, and we could take the motorbike and sidecar with us. You know Timothy wants to go there to practise the language. And you were telling me about all those motorbike circuits that are supposed to be beautiful. I'm sure Oswald would be okay in kennels for a week or two, wouldn't he?'

'Yeah, that's a great idea. But we wouldn't need to worry about the kennels for Ozzy. Mick, the vet from the hospital, said he could always find a little space for him if we ever go away for a few days. You know Aussie Mick, don't you? – the one with the purple Kawasaki Ninja.'

'Do I?'

'Yeah, course you do. Hmmn, we could do that route in the Languedoc that Mick was raving about. The Circuit de Salagou. It sounds fantastic. He did it with his wife and said it was one of the best they've ever done. Two hundred kilometres of silky smooth tarmac, loads of little villages en route, and hardly any cars. Or caravans! And he said there's a gorgeous turquoise lake down there too, with a wild landscape around it. Mick said it belongs on another planet.'

Timothy stopped fondling Ozzy's ears, which woke him up. He stood up and went to sit down next to his father. Ozzy spun round and eavesdropped.

'If we go to France, father, you will have to learn to speak French better. You will have to make an effort. Your accent is really rubbish and you know that the French people can not speak English very well.'

'More like they won't. Bloody French! But I will, son, don't worry. Just think about it. Two hundred kilometres of ...' David drifted off into his thoughts. 'But the problem is ... it's just that Ozzy and I are really busy at work now and it would be impossible to take time away. No, sorry, folks, but I think it might have to wait until next year.'

'Yes that is probably a much better idea, father, and it will give you chance to learn some more French. You are very good at swearing but you are rubbish at French. And it will give us time to get Oswald a dog passport.'

'I don't really think we would take Ozzy with us, Tim. As I said to Ljana, Doctor Mick can look after him for us.'

Timothy hopped back off the couch, joined Ozzy on his rug again and started to tell him all about France. The adults stood up and went into the kitchen. As they both exited, Ozzy noticed mademoiselle looked very disappointed about something.

Timothy could still talk the hind leg off a dog, and often did. He delved into his pocket and placed something in the palm of his hand for Ozzy. It smelt sugary so Ozzy plucked it from him.

'Here, Oswald, try one of these. You might like them as much as I do. They are one of my best favourite sweets. I prefer Midget Gems and blackcurrant and liquorice but you can not have those because they will stick between your teeth and you will be chewing them for weeks. I do not like the black Midget Gems but father says I must not ask the man at the sweet shop to take them out for me because it is not polite. Here have a Polo.'

Ten seconds passed.

'You are so greedy, Oswald. You have finished yours already but you are not supposed to chew it. You have to play the game properly and let it melt on its own and see how long you can keep it in your mouth before it breaks. The best way is not to suck.'

Timothy was in a very generous mood, thought Ozzy. As soon as he had cracked and chomped one sweet, Timothy gave him another. And then another.

'Here have another one and do not chew it this time remember. My record for one Polo is eleven minutes and eight seconds. Ljana is very good and her record is twelve minutes and fifty three seconds. Father is rubbish like you and he crunches his all the time. Oh, Oswald, you have done it again. You are worse than father. And you should not chew with your mouth open because mother said it is bad manners. Never mind though at least your breath will smell much better now and Matthew Mollinson from special school will not call you dog breath any more. If you are not going to play the game properly I am going to go to bed now to watch mother floating in my stars. Remember tomorrow is Sunday and we need to be up early to give the birds their food before the paperboy comes and scares them all away.'

~ ~ ~ ~ ~

The August morning was a beautiful one – to begin with. Timothy and Ozzy were in the garden. Timothy was feeding the birds and stocking up their feeders and Ozzy was hiding under the bushes and checking on his bone stash. The paperboy was very late, the bulky weekend supplements taking him longer than usual to roll up and ram through the letterboxes carelessly. He appeared through the front gate with a smaller boy Ozzy had never seen or smelt before.

'Well, look here,' the paperboy shouted. 'If it isn't Tiny Tim 'n' his even tinier little mutt. Feedin' your little bird friends again, are you? No wonder you get on so well with little birds 'n' little dogs, eh, Timbo, is it? You're all tiny – 'n' you've all got tiny little brains. Why don't you get a real dog like ours? Our dog's much bigger 'n' better than yours, 'n' I bet he's a lot cleverer than yours 'n' all.'

The paperboy nudged his friend, Lee, and they both laughed. Timothy put the lid back on his bucket of bird feed and approached the boys. Ozzy followed, close at his heels.

Timothy said: 'Did you know, Gavin, that in the brain of one dog there are more brain cells than there are dogs in the whole world? I read it in one of my books and I bet you did not know that did you? But it is probably not true any more because that book was written in the year two thousand and six.'

'What are you goin' on about? Was that a sentence or just mumbo jumbo, cos I didn't get a single word? An' anyway, I know more than *you* do, weirdo. Like how to ride a bike properly. I stopped usin' my stabilisers when I was only six. How old're *you* now, Tumbly Tim? Nine is it?'

'No I am not nine, Gavin, I am twelve years and five months and thirty days old today.'

'We don't care how old you are! An' we don't care about your dog or your poxy little birds.'

The paperboy looked to his friend again and nudged him a second time. Ozzy could see from their mannerisms that they were planning something sinister. Whatever it was, Ozzy didn't like their actions, the threatening tone of voice and the nasty look on the paperboy's face, so he gave him a nasty look of his own, curling his lip and revealing his teeth. The paperboy looked down at him and spat on his head.

'What a shot!' he boasted. 'Just like Clint Eastwood in *Josey Wales*. We don't care about you, Timbo, cos you're nothin' but a waste of space. Your mum 'n' dad should've sent you back when you were born. Eh, Lee? Like they should've with your dog. But it's too late now, innit, cos mummy-wummy's dead now. She can't change her mind now, can she?'

'What is a mummy wummy, Gavin?'

'She's somethin' *you* don't have any more.'

The smaller boy spoke.

'Come on, Gav, let's give him the— ... Go on, it'll be dead funny.'

Ozzy growled at both boys and stood up. Timothy told him to sit and stay. He put his palm on Ozzy's head and held him steady.

'Good dog, Oswald.'

'Oswald! *Oswald!* Told you, Lee, eh? Said it was called Oswald, didn't I? Stupid name for a dog, innit. Ours is called Zeus. But what can you expect, eh? Stupid dog, stupid name. Whose idea was that then? Yours or your dad's? Bet it was yours. Mind you, could've been your dad's, eh? Eh, Lee? Doctor fuckin' Do-Little – talkin' to the animals 'n' all that.'

The paperboy prodded Timothy with a finger.

'Please do not poke me, Gavin,' asked Timothy. 'I do not like to be touched and it hurts.'

'I know that, Timbo! That's why I do it, idiot!'

'And actually Oswald has two names. I call him Oswald but father calls him Ozzy.'

'Typical, that is. Two names for his dog. Schizo dog, schizo Timmy.'

He prodded Timothy again, this time hard in the chest. Ozzy

growled audibly and moved forwards to warn the paperboy he was ready for any trouble. Timothy pushed on his head to stop his advance.

'Ooh, I'm *really* scared now,' said the paperboy. 'Your little mutt's growlin' at me. I might wet myself if I'm not careful, eh, Lee? I bet *you* still wet yourself all the time, don't you, Tim?'

Timothy ignored the cruel comment. 'Oswald. Good dog. Please sit. Good dog. Gavin, stop pushing my chest with your finger. I do not like it. It hurts. Please stop it. Stop touching me. Stop it. Stop it. Stop it.'

'Shut up mumblin', will you. Jesus – everyone round here's a fruitcake. You should all be locked up. Shit, I almost forgot then. We nearly forgot to give Tim his present, Lee.'

'It is not my birthday today, Gavin,' said Timothy. 'My birthday is on the first day of March. It is on the first day of March every year.'

'Course it is, you mong! Christ! We know it's not your birthday, but we got you a little pressie anyway. But first I'm gonna tell you a little story. I think you'll like it – it was in the paper 'n' everythin', 'n' the bloke got done for it by the police.

'Right, well, there was this bloke 'n' he was a bit weird, like you, 'n' he lived in a big messy house all on his own. This bloke had lots of bird tables 'n' stuff in his garden like you do, 'n' he used to feed them all the time. But then he must've gone a bit mad, cos he put loads of really strong glue on his bird tables 'n' then covered them with loads of birdseed. Then when all the stupid little birds landed for their food they couldn't take off again, could they, Lee? So this bloke just cut their legs off with a pair of scissors. An' all the birds took off again, like, but they'd never be able to land ever again would they, Lee? Cool, eh?'

Timothy drew his arms up close to his chest and began to tremble. Ozzy heard him exhale a pained moan, and he could smell Timothy was scared. He felt the low growl rumbling up from deep in his throat.

'Yeah, we thought you'd like it, didn't we, Lee? It's a true story, you know. My big brother Keiran showed us it in the paper. So we tried it ourselves, Lee 'n' me, like, in the back garden with some glue 'n' a Stanley knife. It worked a treat 'n' all. Look, we collected them all up specially for you. Here, Lee, pass me them legs.'

Ozzy watched the smaller boy dig into his pocket and pass a plastic bag to the paperboy. He opened it up, emptied its contents into his hand and held them out to Timothy. Ozzy couldn't see what was in his hands, but he knew something bad was about to happen. He could taste the tension and he could feel Timothy's anguish. His tail was as erect as a ship's mast, and it quivered nervously; the hair on his back stiffened like a wire brush.

'Here you are, Tim, mate – have these. Happy *birthday*.'

Timothy let go of Ozzy's head and rushed forwards before he could react. He pushed the paperboy hard in the chest with both hands. The paperboy stumbled backwards and hit the wall hard with his back. Ozzy heard his head smack against the stone, and whatever he was holding fell and scattered on the ground. Timothy bent down and started to pick the birds' legs up one by one.

The paperboy cried out and pulled himself away from the wall, rubbing the back of his head. There was blood on his hand.

'*You little shit!* You bust my head. That's it now – you're gonna die. Come here, you little shit!'

When the paperboy ran at Timothy, Ozzy's primordial instinct took control and he launched himself. Before the boy's foot connected with Timothy's crouched body, Ozzy sank his teeth into a fleshy calf. The boy yelled in pain as Ozzy shook his head violently from left to right. He heard his high-pitched scream but he refused to let go. He gripped the boy's leg as tightly as he could so he could not kick Timothy. He could taste the blood in his mouth. The boy kicked his leg wildly to try to shake Ozzy off, but he held on. He felt the boy raining his fists down onto his head and body, flailing his arms wildly. He tried to kick Ozzy with his free leg and they both tumbled to the ground in a heap. As the boy and Ozzy continued their struggle, he caught sight of monsieur running at him with a fearsome look in his eye, screaming his name at the very top of his voice. Ozzy knew things were about to get much worse.

~ 24 ~

The flavour of blood stayed in Ozzy's mouth for hours afterwards; it lingered between his teeth and stuck to his tongue. He drank several bowls of water but he could not get rid of that vile taste. Ozzy knew he had made a big mistake. But by disobeying one rule, he had followed another. He had done the right thing but he knew he would be punished. Would he be deprived of carrots or cucumber for a few days? He waited and he waited but no punishment came. There were no raps on the snout, no harsh words, and his rations stayed the same. The only real change Ozzy noticed was that the adults and Timothy had several conversations in which he heard both his names being used again and again, and monsieur was the one who raised his voice the most.

A few days later, the paperboy and his parents arrived at the house. Monsieur went outside with mademoiselle, and Ozzy watched the adults argue for a long time. Monsieur didn't let them inside the house – luckily for them! – but he could see the paperboy had a bandage around his leg. Ozzy stood next to Timothy at the front window with his paws up against the window ledge and he growled through the glass.

'Do not worry, Oswald,' Timothy said as he caressed Ozzy's scruff. 'I will not let them take you away. You are a good dog. You did the right thing. Father knows it too but those stupid horrible people want to make you go to sleep for a very long time. I am confused. I know I told you that you must not bite the paperboy but I am glad you did. But I do not know if I should be glad or sad. Father is very angry but he is sad too so I think I should be sad as well.'

Ozzy wasn't punished at all. In fact, he noticed, monsieur was even more affectionate than ever before. For the next few evenings, they resumed their cuddles by the sofa. He hoped mademoiselle wasn't jealous. He looked around the room at them all and tried hard to work out what was going on inside their heads.

~ I wonder what they're thinking, he muttered quietly to himself. If only they could talk.

~ ~ ~ ~ ~

Ozzy was surprised by the early morning arrival of monsieur in the hallway where he slept. It was a September day, and dawn itself had only just woken up – too early for the humans usually to be out of bed, yet monsieur was already fully dressed when he crept quietly down the stairs. He knelt down at Ozzy's basket, put his mouth very close to the dog's ear and asked if he would like to join him for an early-morning walk.

Of course he would! Ozzy bolted to his paws, stretched and shook, and ran to the front door expectantly, his tail equally as eager as he was to set off.

~ Come on, hurry up! Open the door, I'm bursting!

Lethargically, and with a sorrowful look in his eyes that Ozzy had never seen before, monsieur joined him at the door and opened it a little. He looked preoccupied ... worried. But why? Ozzy turned and sat down at David's feet with a quizzical look on his furrowed brow. He looked up at his guardian and voiced his concern. David put a finger quickly to his mouth.

'Ozzy, shush. Good dog. Shhh.'

David pulled the front door fully open and Ozzy darted out, unable to conceal his excitement or keep his voice down.

~ Are we going in the car? Or straight into the woods? Just let me do my morning chores first and get my stick, and then I'll be right with you, boss.

He glanced behind him, but monsieur hadn't even come out of the house. In fact, he had closed the door again. How curious, thought Ozzy briefly; he must have forgotten something. Perhaps his bag of nibbles and biscuits they usually took? Mustn't forget that! Ozzy had more-pressing matters to take care of, so he thought little of it. He'll be out soon, he told himself, as he nipped round the back of the house to water the bushes. Then he ran to the side of the garage and collected one of his favourite sticks to put in the car; he was in the mood for a good game of Throw.

There was still no sign of monsieur when Ozzy dropped his stick by the car, so he returned to the front door. It was still firmly closed. He mounted the two steps, put his snout against the bottom of the door and sniffed hard. He threw his paws up against the wood and called for him. Monsieur had told him to be quiet and not to wake Timothy and mademoiselle, but he had to attract his attention somehow. They were wasting good exercise time. He cocked an ear because he could hear three voices inside the hallway – Timothy and mademoiselle must have been up after all. He called for them to open the door, pawing it insistently, but they ignored him. What *were* they doing in there?

He ran round to the lounge window; he knew he would be able to see them through it. He jumped up to the window ledge and pushed his nose against the glass. He saw them clearly through the open lounge door in the hallway. Timothy and mademoiselle were still in their nightclothes, sitting on the stairs. Why did they look so sad?

He strained to hear but the glass distorted their voices. He scratched on the window to alert them to his presence but only monsieur noticed him. He reached for the lounge door and pulled it slowly closed.

Ozzy ran back to the front door and jumped up against the letterbox. He strained an ear again and pushed his snout against the letterbox, opening it ever so slightly. He could hear their muffled voices. What *was* going on? He heard Timothy talking first, and then monsieur replying.

‘Father, where are you going so early in the morning?’

‘I’m ... I’m just going out for a quick walk with Ozz— with Oswald. I’ve got piles of work to do today, so I won’t get chance to take him out later, son.’

David had never been good at hiding things from his son.

‘Father, please do not tell me big fibs. You are not taking him for a walk are you?’

‘Yes ... I am, Tim. I’m—’

‘I know you are taking him to have the injection. I know he is going to have a long sleep.’

No matter how much he had tried to hide the inevitable from himself, David had no choice but to admit the truth to Timothy.

‘Yes, okay. Yes, son. I am. I have no ... we have no choice, Tim. I’m sorry.’

‘It is not your fault, father. I know Oswald has been a naughty dog. But, father?’

‘Yes, Tim?’

‘Will it be a big injection or one of those really really big injections?’

The question surprised David, and he was lost for words. Ljana sat on the stair above Timothy. She lowered her gaze from David and spoke over the back of Timothy’s shoulder in a very quiet voice.

‘It will be a special injection, Tim. One that will make him sleep for a long time. But when he wakes up, he will be in a lovely place where there will be lots of other dogs for him to play with. It will be a place like Bohinj that God chose specially for good people ... and good dogs too.’

‘How long will he be asleep for, Ljana?’ asked Timothy, turning to look up at her. Then he turned back to his father and asked: ‘Will I be able to visit him in this place, father?’

David wished his son would stop asking him so many questions; he was finding it difficult to remain strong. His palms were sweating, his stomach was churning and he needed some fresh air. What could he say?

'No, Tim ... you won't. But when you're in your bed at night, you can look up at your stars and planets, and you'll be able to see Oswald's face next to your mother's. They will be together.'

'Father, I know you and Ljana are only saying this to try and make me feel better. I know you are telling me some more of those big fibs. I am twelve years and six months and fifteen days old today, father. I am not a little boy any more and I know what is really happening. Oswald will never wake up again will he? If I will be able to see him next to mother then that must mean he is dead. But at least it will mean that mother has some good company which is good. One day I think we will be with mother too and we will all be together again. You can come too, Ljana, if you like. Can I please go and say goodbye to Oswald, father?'

The first tear left David's eye. He wiped it consciously away with a finger.

'No, son. No ... I don't think that's a very good idea. Look, Tim, I have to go now. I'll ... I'll see you later, okay, and we'll have a good talk. I'll say goodbye to Ozz— to Oswald for you. Okay?'

'But I would really like to see him to tell him goodbye.'

'I know you would, Tim, but—'

'Please let me, father. I did not have the chance with mother.'

David screwed his face up and tried in vain to stem the flow of his tears. Ljana wanted to help David deal with things but, at Timothy's mention of his mother, she felt she ought not to interfere. She wiped her own stray tears from her cheeks.

'Okay, Tim, okay,' mumbled David. 'I'm sorry. Of course you can, son. You go and say goodbye to Oswald and then I *really* do have to go.'

Timothy opened the door and walked out with a purposeful stride, leaving David and Ljana to look at each other through watery eyes. David cupped his face in his hands and squeezed his eyes shut. He lowered his hands, wiped his face with the back of one, and let out a huge sigh. He gave Timothy a sheepishly brief glance, guilty that he could not do more. Outside, sitting on the doorstep, Ozzy was waiting patiently – unlike his tail, which was twitching ferociously. He was even more excited now; now that he realised they were all going out for a walk together.

~ Finally! What's been keeping you all? Are we going now?

With the door still open, Ozzy stole a quick glance inside the house and he could see monsieur and mademoiselle holding each other tightly. What *is* going on this morning? he thought again. He tried to push between Timothy's legs to get a better look, but Timothy closed them quickly, trapping Ozzy by the shoulders. Timothy bent down and picked Ozzy up in his arms. Fidgeting to gain a look over the boy's shoulder, Ozzy stole a final look inside. When the first morning rays of sun touched mademoiselle's features, Ozzy noticed some glistening little streams of water trickling down her face, like the ones that monsieur had back at Ozzy's old park. He tried to wriggle free and push inside to see what was wrong with her but Timothy walked away from the door and sat down on the garden bench. Confused, Ozzy had no choice but to accept Timothy's unexpected display of affection. He didn't speak a single word to Ozzy; Timothy simply sat him across his lap and held him close to his chest for several long minutes.

David came out of the house with a brave look on his face, Ljana's hand on his shoulder.

'Come on, son, it's time for us to go. Let Oswald go now, please. I'll see you later on, Tim. Okay?'

'Yes, father.'

With as much faked positivity as he could muster, David called to Ozzy.

'Come on, Ozzy! Fetch your stick, boy. Let's go.'

Ozzy chased after David as he walked quickly to the car and opened the boot. He picked up Ozzy's stick and threw it temptingly inside. Ozzy flung himself in after it and grasped it in his mouth. Before he had chance to turn round to show off his prize, monsieur closed the boot, almost trapping his tail. He was normally very careful not to do that, but that morning he was ever so distracted.

David walked to the front of the car, got in and closed the door. In the boot, Ozzy looked at Timothy, then at Ljana, and twitched his ears in bewilderment. So ... back to plan A, is it? he thought. Just me and monsieur then.

David started the engine and began to pull away. Suddenly, Timothy appeared at the driver's side of the car and banged on the window. David wound it down for his son.

'Father, I almost forgot. When you say goodbye to Oswald will you ask him something for me please?'

'Of course I will, Tim. What?'

'Ask him to say hello to mother from me. And tell him thank you.'

Holding back his tears once again, David said he would do as Timothy asked. But he was a little confused. 'But "thank you" for what, son?'

'For making us a family again, father.'

Gripping the steering wheel tightly, David nodded slowly to his son and, without another word, drove slowly out of the garden.

Timothy walked back to the front of the house to sit with Ljana on the steps and began talking quietly.

'Ljana?'

'Yes, Tim?'

'Can I ask you something please?'

'Of course you can. What is it?'

'I am not properly sure really. It was a little thing that father once said to me about love and caring and things like that and I want to check it with you.'

'Okay.'

'Well when father just told me that I would never ever be able to see Oswald again I got a really funny feeling in my tummy and I have definitely not eaten too many Mars bars or Snickers this morning.'

~ ~ ~ ~ ~

Ozzy stood up in the boot, darting from side to side, window to window, peering out to see where they were headed. Normally, monsieur and he would look at each other through the rear-view mirror, but today monsieur wouldn't make any eye contact with him. He occasionally glanced in the mirror, but it was only ever a fleeting look, and he quickly looked away when Ozzy caught his eye.

When they eventually arrived at the PAWS hospital, Ozzy was very confused. He had been keen to venture out into the woods or up onto the fells, not to work, so he planted his paws up on the back of the rear seats and yapped at David to ask why they were there. He didn't answer so Ozzy yapped a little louder.

~ What are we doing here? It's a bit early to start work, isn't it?

David remained in the driver's seat, his hands gripping the steering wheel, and he stared straight ahead through the windscreen. Ozzy concentrated his own stare, hard into the back of David's head to try to make him turn round. Or at least look in the rear-view mirror. But he wouldn't. Ozzy yapped at him again.

~ Well, come on! Open the boot, will you, I'm desperate again.

Finally, Ozzy attracted David's attention and he looked back at him through the mirror. They stared at each other for a long time, neither of them blinking nor breaking the gaze. Ozzy was very good at the staring game – Bazou had taught him well – and he rarely ever lost. But David held his eye a lot longer than normal and it was Ozzy who blinked first.

Ozzy looked at David again, trying his best this time not to blink, holding his eyelids up as long as he could. He was determined to beat him.

David blinked first. He wiped his fingers across both his eyes then scrunched his hands up into balls and rubbed them. Then he hit the steering wheel hard with both hands and shouted at Ozzy through the mirror.

'Shit, Ozzy. Will you stop looking at me like that. For Christ's sake, dog!'

Ozzy jumped. He had never known monsieur behave like that before. It scared him, and he trembled. David shouted again.

'Stop staring at me like that, will you! Don't you think this is hard enough as it is? Bloody hell, why did you have to go and bite the paperboy? Why, why, why?'

Ozzy was shaking, his front legs wobbling like jelly, and he could feel his ears twitching nervously. He whimpered in fear.

~ Why are you shouting at me, boss? I've done nothing wrong.

David's anger was over; he spoke now in a soft voice.

'Oh, Ozzy, why did you do it? I know he deserved it, the little brat, but ... you know I've no choice. I know you were only looking after Tim, and that little sod is going to get off scot-free. Too young to prosecute. It's not right. Oh, what's the point? It's too late now. I have to do it, Ozzy. Don't you see?'

Ozzy wanted to get closer to monsieur to find out what was disturbing him so much, but he knew he wasn't allowed in the front of the car. Monsieur's eyes were glazed. Eyes never lie and Ozzy knew something terrible was troubling him. He could see it, he could sense it, and he could smell it. Monsieur was scared. He tipped his head to one side and wondered what the problem could be.

'Ozzy, no. Stop that. Don't make it any harder for me. Christ, dog, don't you get it? Don't you understand why we're here? Shit!'

He slammed his hands on the steering wheel again. The horn was deafening inside the car.

Somebody arrived at the main door of the hospital, and Ozzy recognised him as monsieur's doctor friend with the big noisy motorbike; the one that monsieur liked to stroke almost as much as he did Ozzy. He walked over to their car and tapped on monsieur's window.

'G'day, Dave. How're ya goin', mate?'

'Not good, Mick. Not good at all. It's not right.'

'Nah, I know it isn't. He's a good kid, that dog of yours.'

'Do we really have to do this, Mick?'

'You know we do, mate. You got no choice. That's twice now he's bitten someone.'

'I know, I know. But—'

'Of course that little swine deserved it, but ... Come on, Dave, let's get it over with before we open up for the day. You know he won't feel a thing.'

'I can't, Mick. I can't do it. I just ...'

'Do you want me to take him in? You can wait here in the car.'

'No! No. Give me a minute, eh, Mick? I'll bring him inside in a sec. It's my responsibility. I need to be there. We'll do it. I know we have to, but not yet, eh? Look, I'll take him for one last walk ... one last run, and then I'll bring him in. I just need to see him running once more. I need to say goodbye properly. D'you see what I mean, Mick?'

'Course I do, mate. All right, Dave. You and Ozzy go and have a good old run, and then we'll do what we've got to do. Yeah? Okay? But don't leave it too long, mate. Catch you later.'

Mick put his hand on David's shoulder and squeezed it. Then he turned and walked back into the hospital. What *is* going on today? Ozzy wondered. He was truly bursting; if monsieur didn't let him out of the car soon, he would not be responsible for his actions. David turned to look at him over his shoulder and smiled.

'Come on then, boy! How's about a quick trip up to the Tower? Still got the legs for it have you?'

David's tone of voice and the look in his eyes told Ozzy that whatever had been troubling him troubled him no more, so he voiced his agreement and wagged his tail.

~ *On y va!* Let's go!

~ ~ ~ ~ ~

They soon arrived up at Queen's Tower and it was deserted. Ozzy was out of the boot like a bullet from a gun and he sprinted to the bushes. After he had sprayed the heather a few times, monsieur called him over and asked him to jump back into the boot. This puzzled the dog.

~ What? Already? That's not much of a run. Oh, I see – you want me to get my stick first. Okay, where is it? Let's play!

Ozzy jumped back into the car and quickly retrieved his stick. He turned round, sat down and faced David expectantly, with his stick held firmly between his teeth. But monsieur evidently wasn't ready to play yet – still half asleep by the looks of it – and he leant in and gently removed it from Ozzy's jaws. David looked into his dog's eyes and told him to be patient.

'Later, Ozzy. Later. I need to tell you something first.'

He reached further into the boot, grabbed Ozzy behind his haunches and pulled him forwards. Then he put his head down against Ozzy's and whispered in his ear.

'I'm sorry, Ozzy. I'm really sorry, but I have no choice. I have to do this. One last run, and then ... Timothy asked me to say goodbye, and ... and he asked me to say thank you. From me too. I'm so very sorry, Ozzy, I really am.'

David drew Ozzy up to his chest and squeezed him hard, lifting him from the boot. He squeezed so hard it made Ozzy yelp.

~ Woah! Easy there! You'll break my ribs if you're not careful.

'Christ, I wish there was some other way, Ozzy. You're a little diamond, you know. I'm gonna miss you, boy. You'll never know how much.'

David held him tightly and his legs dangled uselessly. He was trapped in the embrace, and his ribs were being squashed. He had no other means of escape so he licked David's face enthusiastically. David's mood suddenly changed and his face lit up. He put Ozzy on the ground, smiled mischievously and picked up the stick. He launched it far into the heather bushes.

'Fetch it, boy! Go on.'

Ozzy voiced his approval.

~ That's more like it!

Finally, their game commenced. They played a few rounds, and were having great fun. Ozzy was relieved to note that monsieur was now fully awake and bursting with his usual energy. Every time he returned the stick, Ozzy told monsieur what a great time he was having, and for him to throw it higher, further. David obliged. On one throw, Ozzy was very impressed when monsieur found a strength he never knew he had. Lazy monsieur Moretti had never been able to throw it that far.

Ozzy watched his stick soar high through the air, and saw it land heavily in the thick bracken at the bottom of the hill. It was an impressive throw, and as he set off after it, he congratulated David with a series of enthusiastic yaps over his shoulder.

It took him a while to find the stick, hidden so deeply in the thick undergrowth. He clasped it in his jaws and ran quickly back up the steep hill. When he had made it almost to the top, he had to pause to catch his breath. He dropped the stick and called out to monsieur.

~ Not so far next time! I'm six and a half now, remember. Not as fit as I used to be. Are you trying to kill me or something?

He picked up his trophy again and bounded over the brow of the hill. When he reached the car park, monsieur wasn't there. Neither was the car.

~ 25 ~

A cloud of dust was still swirling in the car park so Ozzy knew monsieur couldn't have gone far. Was he so long in the bushes? Was there something urgent that monsieur had rushed off to do? Maybe one of the dogs at the centre was ill? Was Timothy in trouble? The paperboy was bullying him again! Oh, *mon Dieu!* Quick, dog – you'd better catch him up before it's too late.

~ *Allez!*

Ozzy ran to the far side of the car park and up onto the brow of the hill. He immediately caught sight of monsieur's car in the far distance, disappearing rapidly down the snaking country lane. From the high grass verge, he launched himself across the road. As he sailed through the air he realised he still had his stick in his mouth. Before he had chance to let go, he was hit by a car.

The car stopped quickly and the retired couple got out of it. On very shaky legs. They looked for the dog behind and underneath the car, but it wasn't there. They looked on the grass verge, and they squinted back along the road.

'It's not under here,' said Richard.

'Well, he must be somewhere, *chéri*,' replied Françoise. 'He can't just disappear.'

'I know that, Fran, I know. But it's not here! It must be much further back down the road. I wasn't driving *that* fast, was I, dear?'

Ozzy jumped up.

'*Rich*ard, look. He is on the back seat!'

'Well, I'll be damn—'

'Yes, you will indeed. You nearly killed the poor thing. Have a look ... see if he is okay.'

Had it not been a convertible sports car with a low bonnet, Ozzy would surely not have survived without injury, so he was extremely grateful to Richard and Françoise for their selection of vehicle. But as he flew over their windscreen, he didn't have the opportunity to thank them. When he finally woke, he was understandably disorientated. Where am I? Where is monsieur? Why do I have a stick wedged in my jaws?

Richard removed the stick from Ozzy's mouth and inspected him. He was still incredibly dizzy so he allowed the stranger to touch and fondle him without protest. His mind wasn't yet focused and it failed to dawn on him that monsieur had disappeared for ever. Richard stroked him, ran his hands up and down his flanks and fiddled with his legs. He looked into Ozzy's eyes and Ozzy looked into Richard's. Who are *you*? thought Ozzy. Why are you staring at me like that? Richard placed a couple of fingers on the tip of Ozzy's snout for a moment and then wiped them clean on his shirt. Ozzy sneezed.

'Well, I can't be sure, dear, but it looks okay to me. There are no odd lumps, its legs are not broken and it's wagging its tail.'

He put out his open palm. Ozzy lifted his left paw and placed it in the man's hand, more out of habit than anything else. The man turned to the woman and spoke again.

'Well, it must be okay, Fran, if it shakes hands like that. Now then, do you have a collar or a nametag? Oh, you don't have one. How curious.'

After more stroking and touching, Richard and Françoise took Ozzy to a place not dissimilar to some of the ones he had visited with monsieur David, where a large woman in a white coat proceeded to fondle him with concern. Thinking about monsieur David, Ozzy's mind jolted awake and he realised that Timothy could still be in trouble. But what could he do about it? He had no idea where he was, his head was still groggy, his ribs were bruised and his legs felt like lead.

After a few days, they took him to a very sinister-looking building. When they arrived, Ozzy knew instantly what it was. He dug his heels into the back seat of the car and begged them not to do that to him.

~ No! Not again! I can't go through all that again. Taco might be in there. *Please!*

'*Rich*ard?' said Françoise. 'Surely he can't know it is the animal rescue, can he? He is petrified, the little thing. Could ... should ... shall we keep him? I think he wants to stay with us, *chéri*.'

'Well ... do we need another dog, darling?'

~ *Please!* Ozzy begged with fear-filled eyes. Let's get out of this place.

'It is not the case of do we *need* another dog, *Rich*ard ... it is do we want another dog. And my answer is "*Oui*". It has been more than a year now since poor old Napoleon passed on, and I think we could do with another little face in the home. And look at him, for goodness sake.'

'Well, I suppose ...'

'Good. That is that settled then. I was secretly hoping we wouldn't find his real owners. I wanted to keep him all the time, but I know you are such an English fusspot, wanting to do the "right thing" all the time. So, let us do the right thing and take this dog home.'

'Okay, we'll keep it.'

'*Him*.'

The man reversed the car away from the animal shelter and they left together. A new family unit had been formed. Ozzy was relieved and his tail reappeared as though on a return-spring. As they drove away, Ozzy registered the eagerness of the woman to keep him, but the reluctance of the man to do so. He hoped he wasn't going to be a problem. Ozzy had grown comfortable being Number Two in both his previous packs, and he had no desire to take over any controls at his age. He was almost fifty, and middle age was tapping him on the withers. His whiskers and chest-white were changing colour rapidly now – not to grey but to a distinguished silver.

The woman spoke and interrupted his thoughts.

'Well, we are going to have to think of a name for him.'

'Yes, of course. Do you have any suggestions, darling? What could we call it?'

'First of all, *Rich*ard, you can stop calling it "*it*". It is a he, for goodness sake.'

'Oh is it— is *he*? I hadn't paid much attention.'

'Well, I had no choice, *chéri*. When you hit him in your little toy car and threw him over my head, I could not help but notice he is a boy dog.'

'Oh, I see. Yes. Quite. So, what shall we call *him* then? How about Lucky? That's quite appropriate.'

'No, I don't think so, *Rich*ard. "Lucky" is so ... so ... so Englishly boring. And he is anything but that, aren't you, *mon petit*? No, we'll have to come up with something better than that, *chéri*.'

~ ~ ~ ~ ~

Nelson met Rascal some six months after he moved in with Richard and Françoise. They have been inseparable ever since. The first time Rascal introduced himself, he did so by landing on Nelson from a great height. Nelson was innocently minding his own business in the fields, sniffing a certain delicate whiff, when he felt an uninvited presence and bad breath land heavily on his shoulders, prostrating him onto a large cowpat.

Rascal was rude, impudent and disrespectful of his elders. He was an irritable little devil of a terrier and juvenile beyond his four years. A prime example of the undisciplined cross-breed – but crossed with *what*? wondered Nelson. Who had done the dastardly deed to produce such an odd-looking creature? Although he was only a youngster then, around three years Nelson's junior, he looked at least a hundred. With his wild shaggy hair and thick bushy eyebrows, he appeared to be wearing a much larger dog's coat.

But first impressions do not always last, and Rascal became the closest dog friend Nelson ever had. Opposites they were, but something had pulled them together. Gravity, perhaps? What Nelson first thought of as Rascal's failings and undesirable characteristics would eventually become the strong points and charm that Nelson grew to admire and respect. It just took him a while to change his opinion. Rascal's breath never improved, though.

When he first landed on Nelson's back, Rascal closed his jaws tightly around Nelson's scruff and nipped his flesh. Nelson jerked his head back quickly, throwing Rascal off balance so that he let go, landing on his back. He righted himself and then shouted relentlessly in Nelson's ear, in one of the highest pitched voices Nelson had ever heard – so much so that he had to drop low to see whether it was a dog or a *fille*.

As well as his rapid-fire voice, Nelson noticed that Rascal had a strangely odd canine accent, definitely not from the region. He had a curiously quirky manner of communicating and was in ever such a hurry to get his point across. Nelson had to concentrate very hard to understand his dog-speak. The canine term would be a 'yappie'. And he did yap ... and yap.

Nelson chastised Rascal for his unprovoked attack.

~ Who are you and what do you want? You don't just go sneaking up on a dog like that. Not even a polite circle or an introductory sniff first?

~ Sor-ry, ole dog. Thought you might fancy a bit of a run-aroun' or somethin'. You're fairly new to the neighbourhood, so I thought I'd introduce myself. But if you wanna be an unsociable old mutt, that's fine.

Nelson started to protest at his use of 'mutt', but Rascal interrupted him by lifting his leg and squirting just centimetres from Nelson's hind leg.

~ Charming. Most charming. Which obedience school did *you* get kicked out of?

~ Two of 'em actually, workin' on my third. 'Bout you – which geriatrics' kennel d'you escape from?

Nelson wasn't in any mood to be harangued so he lifted his own leg in reply. Then he raised his snout in assumed superiority and turned away from Rascal.

~ Name's Rascal, by the way. See y'aroun' then, gramps.

~ I very much doubt it, *mon ami*, snapped Nelson, slotting in a simple snippet of his long-lost French dog-speak to let Rascal know that he was not one of his uncouth kind.

~ *Allez, à bientôt!* Rascal yapped back as he shot across the field.

Nelson was dumbfounded. How did that little runt know French? How could that be possible?

~ ~ ~ ~ ~

Nelson and Rascal bumped into each other a lot during the days that followed – quite literally; with Nelson coming off worst in every collision. Nelson did his utmost to remain belligerently unapproachable. Stubborn, set in his aging ways, yes, but he wanted to take his time. To sniff Rascal properly, and to formulate a just opinion, which was extremely difficult when Rascal insisted on yapping at his heels all the time, jumping on his back and snapping at his rear.

He should have known Rascal would never let him have an easy time, not with his mixed genes dictating things. Nelson could see him preparing his bull-charges fifty metres or so away. He crouched down in the grass, tongue hanging out, panting two hundred to the minute, and then he ran at Nelson as fast as he could on his stocky little legs. Nelson should have learnt his lesson from the dozens of times Rascal did this, but he thought, No, he's bound to stop before he runs into me. Surely, he will sideswipe and skid to a halt. But no, not once. Nelson's walks were never relaxed affairs any more.

Most times, Nelson took monsieur Richard and madame Françoise with him on his strolls, but sometimes he preferred to go alone. Monsieur had tried only once to make him wear a collar and leash, but Nelson stood his ground. He had the cheek to try to put them on him without even asking and, quite out of character, Nelson snapped threateningly at him.

When Richard tried to slip the collar around Nelson's neck, he darted to the other side of the room and began to tremble and shake in the corner. He was very scared and he didn't know how to handle the situation. His whole body vibrated, his legs shook uncontrollably and he cowered low. They were both lovely people yet they were attempting to chain him up. It brought back haunting memories.

Richard registered the dog's fear and put down the collar and leash, out of his reach, to let Nelson know he had postponed the threat. He called Nelson to him softly. Eventually – Nelson was still unsure if it was just a cruel baiting and a false lull – with tail between his legs, he slowly approached. Richard stroked Nelson's head gently and offered soothing words, designed to calm him. But Nelson was unconvinced, and he feared that monsieur would try again another time. As Richard stroked him, Nelson lifted up his paw and placed it on the man's knee. He pawed at Richard's leg insistently, alternating his frightened eyes between Richard and the armchair in the far corner of the room where the collar and leash lay. Richard did not fully register Nelson's apprehension. Instead, he spoke to his wife.

'What a strange reaction, Fran. I think our new dog is perhaps a little potty. Must have had a bump on the head when we hit him in the TVR.'

'When *you* hit him, *chéri*. No, he is trying to tell us something.'

'Don't be ridiculous, darling, he's a dog.'

'Yes, I know he is a dog, dear, but he is ... I always said there was something different about him.'

'Indeed! He's quite possibly loopy.'

'Nonsense. Look at his eyes. He is trying to tell us something! What is it, Nelson, what *are* you thinking? What is going on inside there?'

'Not a great deal if you ask me, Fran. You're both as daft as each other. I think I'll leave you two to have your little chinwag. We'll try him another time with the lead – when he's not so excitable. Do you really think it's wise taking him on holiday with us? I don't want to be arrested at customs for transporting a mad dog and an owner who thinks it can talk. Maybe the kennels would be a better option. I ask you, darling – the next thing you'll tell me is that he's trying to tell us he doesn't want to wear a collar and lead, or something equally ludicrous. I'll be outside if you need me; I'm going to mow the lawn.'

Richard stood up quickly. Nelson was startled by the sudden move and he reacted instinctively. He feared that monsieur was going to get the collar and leash again. He ran to the armchair and jumped up onto it. Before they could reprimand him for climbing on the furniture, he picked up the offending items and ran out of the lounge with them in his mouth.

Richard and Françoise chased him through the house.

Nelson sprinted into the garden and stood in the middle of the lawn with the collar and leash glued in his mouth. One of the few places he was allowed to do his necessaries in the garden was behind the big plastic container on wheels; Nelson had noticed that his guardians put things they didn't want into it. Personally, he rather liked it; there was always a tempting hotchpotch of interesting smells coming from it. He ran to the wheelie bin with the collar and leash still clamped between his jaws, and he dropped them both by the side of it.

He yapped once at his guardians.

He then picked up the collar – *only* the collar; he left the leash by the bin – and trotted over to Richard with it dangling between his jaws. He jumped up against Richard's legs with both paws and wagged his tail enthusiastically. With his tail swinging back and forth, he thrust his head upwards and pushed the collar into Richard's hand.

Standing next to her husband, Françoise watched Nelson's antics. Her eyes were wide and her head was turning slowly from side to side. She had a hand held to her mouth and was chuckling. She looked at Richard.

'Pick your chin up from the floor, *chéri*. What is the matter, has a cat had your tongue?'

~ 26 ~

Nelson's collar was the brightest of reds, like those of so many black dogs he had seen since arriving in England. Richard and Françoise decided to have him chipped too. He very much approved of his new collar and thought it very sophisticated. It was another weapon in his armoury for wooing the English *filles*, and he wondered why he hadn't accepted to wear one sooner. It had a shiny metal disc attached to it, and what he liked most was that the disc sat very neatly and squarely on his chest; almost hiding his now-silvering white patch. It had a very pleasant metallic jingle to it when he ran through the fields. Often, if his collar spun round too far, and the disc rested to the side of or on the back of his neck, Nelson would paw at it to spin it back onto his chest. This was not because he had an annoying itch, but more likely that there was a *fille* in the vicinity and he was trying to make himself as presentable as possible for her. He was refining that very manoeuvre for an approaching female, ready to introduce himself, when he was upturned and bowled over by a very small, very fast, very hairy object.

~ What now, Rascal?

~ Nothin'. Just came to say hello. How's Medallion Dog today? Still tryin' to hide the grey hairs? Hey, Nelson, guess what happened to me? Been kicked out of trainin' school again. That's three times now! Anyway, what happened was we were all herdin' our guardians together in really tight circles, an' it was all goin' really well. But then another dog tried to herd my guardians instead of his, so I grabbed his back leg an' we ended up in a fight. Then me an' my guardians were kicked out. Again!

~ It's nothing to be proud of, Rascal. If you would stop being such a boisterous little beast, you might not keep being expelled.

~ Who cares? Waste of time if you ask me. It's all pointless, borin' lessons. Do this, do that, do the other. An' for what at the end? A few tasteless biscuits. I'm too old for that, Nelson.

~ Evidently not. You could learn a lot, Rascal, if you tried.

~ You reckon? They've taught me nothin' so far.

~ But they have. You just don't know it.

~ Like what then?

~ Okay then ... so ... so how did you discover the old herding technique? It's not as if you've ever spent any time 'in the wild', is it?

~ *They* never taught me that! That's in my genes – it comes natural.

~ All right then, smart dog, how is it that you *apparently* know French dog-speak?

~ Ha! You've been dyin' to know that since the first day we met, *n'est-ce pas*? Ever since I shouted '*Allez, à bientôt*', you've been chompin' on the bit.

~ Okay, Nelson conceded. Yes, I was a little curious.

~ A little! You were desperate. Come on, be a dog about it, an' admit it.

~ Okay, okay. I was des— ... I am very interested. So how is it then?

They talked until dusk.

Nelson was very surprised by what Rascal had to tell him, and even more shocked that they conversed in French dog-speak much of the time. It had been almost three years since Nelson arrived in England, since he had properly used his native tongue. He had trouble understanding Rascal at first – even though his French was actually much easier to understand than his English was. Rascal helped Nelson out when he became stuck between canine tongues, and prompted him in the right direction. By switching from one to the other, they succeeded in telling each other about their lives. Nelson had to ask Rascal to slow down a lot, however – he was the first dog he had ever met with verbal diarrhoea. But he couldn't help but warm to the little fellow.

Rascal told Nelson of his early days, but much of it was a sketchy memoir, he admitted, because as a pup he was always too busy making a nuisance of himself and acting the fool. He tried to listen to his *maman*, but he had a very short attention span and found it more interesting to play fight and to see what he could get away with.

~ Some things never change, do they, Rascal? Even after ... How old are you anyway? Nearly thirty? And you're still going to school. Or getting *kicked out of* school, I should say.

Rascal's *maman* was, like Nelson's, French, and she had given birth to Rascal and his siblings back in France. During her pregnancy, she was in very poor health – it was an incredibly tough two months for her. She tired easily, and when her pups were born, she found the attentions of five hungry mouths too heavy a load.

One morning Rascal woke but his mother did not.

Nelson's mind drifted, and he wondered about his own *maman*. Was she still alive? Rascal interrupted his thoughts and continued the tale, telling Nelson that during her troubled pregnancy, his mother went briefly to some temporary guardians because her previous ones were unable to cope with her worsening condition. It was there that Rascal and his siblings were born. He only vaguely remembered this home but he told Nelson his surrogate guardians were ever so kind and attentive. He and his siblings were soon shipped off to various homes. The couple who took Rascal – Tom and Gill, living in France at the time, running their ill-fated, soon to be sold, *chambres d'hôtes* business – also took one of his brothers. Rascal told Nelson they originally came from a small village in the Pyrenean mountains.

~ Lachpelle or somethin' *comme ça. Oui.* That was it. *Oui*, Lachpelle – a little village in the middle of the Pyrenees. Not that we saw much of the mountains!

They weren't in Lachpelle for very long at all, Rascal said. They were still very young pups when their new guardians returned to England, taking the two brothers with them. It had been chaotic in their early days and, after the death of their mother, they had spent only a further month or so more in France, so they hadn't had the chance to get to know the area where they lived.

~ They seemed in a real big rush to get out of France, Nelson.

~ Why? France is so beautiful.

~ Dunno. When they first dognapped us, they took us straight back to their house. We were kept pretty much indoors all the time after that – weren't allowed to mix with any dog, or anythin'.

~ I know what you mean. When I was a pup, I wasn't allowed out for the first few weeks either.

~ Yeah! We were only allowed out to pee an' stuff. Mind you, I did most of mine in the house – too cold outside. An' the next thing we know, we're here in England.

~ Rascal? Why did your guardians give you two such similar names, do you think? – Rascal and Rasta?

~ Dunno, really. Rasta reckons it's so they only have to shout one name at us, an' we'll both come back.

~ Yes, well, that would make sense.

~ Not really – I've never been very good at goin' back.

Nelson began to realise that the two of them had a great deal in common, even if Rascal shunned most of it. What was undeniable was that they had so much more to tell. Nelson already had a strong feeling something had brought the dogs together.

~ And not only are we both French, Rascal, but we are both mountain dogs too.

~ Yeah, *peut-être*. But from opposite sides of France, Nelson. Hardly next-door neighbours.

Rascal told Nelson that the reason his mother was in such poor health during her pregnancy was that she had been in a very serious collision with a car. Nelson's heart skipped and he immediately thought of his own recent car accident with monsieur Richard and madame Françoise. Then, inevitably, his mind jumped all the way back to the Alps of his puphood, to Belle and the tourist bus.

Rascal's *maman* had a good but hard life, she told her pups; not allowed to mix much with the other dogs and often kept indoors by her guardians. This reminded Nelson of Alphonse.

~ Just like me on the farm, Rascal, except I was confined *out*doors. You know, I'm sure our destinies have brought us together.

Rascal's response was as eloquent as Nelson should have expected. He yawned wide and long, and looked as though he were chewing one of Timothy's Midget Gems. His reply was no less dismissive.

~ Oh, come on, gramps! Shut up with all that fate stuff, an' let me tell my story, *s'il te plaît*?

Nelson persisted.

~ But how can you ignore the similarities, Rascal? Your own mother was run down by a car, Rascal, and I too was hit by a car once. *And* ... a very good friend of mine – a *very*, *very* good friend, she was kill— ... Well, you know that already, don't you.

~ Yes. *Précisément*. An' there's the difference, Nelson. So please let me get on with my story, an' stop tryin' to make sense of it all. There isn't any! We're just two dogs who happened to meet in a field full of steamin' cowpats.

The tide along the shoreline was rippling slowly inland and the sun was beginning to disappear restfully into the welcoming sea. They were both lying down, looking out over the water, shoulders touching, and chatting away like long lost friends reunited. Rascal suddenly leapt to his paws and shouted into Nelson's ear.

~ Come on, daydreamer, let's go an' roll on a dead seagull. Race you!

Nelson sprang into the air and pounded both his paws heavily onto Rascal's withers to push him down onto the grass before he had chance to set off.

~ Come on then, young 'un. *Pourquoi pas*.

When Nelson finally reached the seagull that Rascal had sniffed out, he was already upside down on it with his legs in the air, rolling around and scratching the parts that carpets and grass can't reach. It took Nelson some time to catch his breath. Rascal rolled off it and looked up at him.

~ *Allez*, go on, old-timer, give it a roll, it's great fun.

~ Oh, I don't know, Rascal. I haven't done this for years. I'm too old for all—

~ Rubbish. Who said you can't teach an old dog new tricks? Here, try this, he suggested as he dived back onto it.

Nelson watched his antics and listened to his endless chatter.

~ Hey, Nelson – d'you know why us dogs roll on dead seagulls an' sheep an' stuff?

~ Of course I do – it's to disguise our scent.

~ Nah! That's not the *real* reason. It's because we know it really annoys our guardians.

Once they had satiated their dormant feral needs, they set off back to their respective homes. But first, Rascal pivoted his back leg and sprayed the carcass. Nelson was not impressed.

~ Why do you have to spray on absolutely everything, Rascal?

~ Just claimin' ownership. Don't want just any old dog rollin' on it. It's mine now.

~ You're welcome to it.

They would part company at the canal bridge. Rascal would continue along it back to his house and Nelson would return directly home across the fields. It gave them a little more time to talk, a little more time to get to know each other. Nelson was grateful for those extra minutes with his new *ami*. Especially when Rascal shocked him with some news that had his heart pounding with excitement. Was it truly possible?

~ 27 ~

Side by side, Nelson and Rascal trotted briskly along the canal towpath, dodging walkers, bicycles and pushchairs as they went. Rascal was chatting almost as fast as they trotted, stopping only briefly to yap at a couple of bicycle tyres and a few swans safely on the far side of the water. Up onto the humpback bridge they detoured.

Nelson had probed Rascal all the way from the shore, and was keen to hear more about his life. He was humbly intrigued by how Rascal had managed to maintain such an impressive level of bilingual dog-speak – especially when he had spent so little time in France as a pup. Rascal put it down, mainly, to living with Rasta all his life, and to the long brotherly walks that they took.

Like Nelson, Rascal and Rasta were very proud of their French roots, and of their *maman* too. She had told Rascal and Rasta and their siblings all about life – though usually only in short fits and bursts – and about how wonderful *les montagnes* were and how she loved to stroll in them. But it tired her to tell her stories for too long; she needed rest and sleep.

~ Pity *we* never got to see the mountains, Rascal complained.

Rascal never had the chance to really get to know his three other siblings properly, due to their earlier-than-usual separation from their mother. None of them had ever met their father, nor did Rascal remember their mother ever talking about him. Nelson told Rascal that his father too had fled the camp – another common link that Nelson pointed out but Rascal dismissed. Together they sullied the names of their respective fathers they had never met. It felt good for them both, a release of pent-up feelings from the past, and they both howled abuse at the sky. Nelson had to ask Rascal to curb his tongue a little, and for him to explain a few of the more colourful terms he used.

From what Rascal told him of his brief time in the Pyrenees, Nelson had to agree it did sound very special. But not as special as the Alps. Nelson suggested, jokingly, that they should return to France to take a trip into the Pyrenees and to Rascal's place of birth. Then they could traverse *la Belle France* to the Alps and Nelson would take him on a tour of all his old haunts. They could argue and fight about whether the Alps or the Pyrenees were best.

~ *Les Pyrenées* of course! boasted Rascal.

~ How do you know? You just said you never saw them. *Les Alpes!*

~ *Les Pyrenées!*

~ *Mais, non! Les Alpes!*

~ *Les Pyrenées!*

...

But that was highly unlikely to happen, Nelson admitted.

~ *Impossible!* he said.

~ Why is it impossible, Nelson? You're not serious are you? You mean you've *never* been back to France?

~ Of course not, Rascal! How could I? I'm a dog. How would I get there?

Rascal cocked his head and looked at Nelson as though he were deranged. He then proceeded to tell Nelson how his guardians made regular trips to their holiday home in France – at least once or twice a year. And, '*naturellement*', the brothers accompanied them every time.

The information hit Nelson harder than any of Alphonse's sweaty work boots ever did.

~ How could you? That's not possible! Is it?

~ Course it's poss—

Rascal didn't have chance to finish what he was saying, such was the urgency with which Nelson hightailed it home. As he disappeared from view, Rascal shouted after him.

~ *Seigneur!* Where've you been hidin' all these years?

When he finally arrived home, he was physically and mentally exhausted. And he was starving. But that was the last thing on his mind. When he burst in through the patio doors, he ignored his dog bowl and sprinted straight into the lounge. He was ecstatic and began jumping and weaving around the lounge like a prancing horse, shouting at Richard and Françoise.

Richard frowned at him above his overgrown eyebrows.

'What's got into you, Nelson? You're like a cat on hot bricks.'

Nelson ignored him and threw his paws up onto the sofa where madame sat.

'Nelson! Down!' she shouted. 'You know the rules. No jumping up on the chai—'

With her unfinished sentence hanging in the air, Françoise threw her hand quickly up to her mouth and clasped it tightly. With a screwed-up face, she continued talking from behind her palm.

'*Rich*ard! He *stinks*. Goodness me, where has he been? It smells as if he has been rolling in something dead. Oh, he is disgusting! Quick, get him in the bath before he smells out the house.'

While she was mumbling behind her palm, Nelson carried on with his hysterics, but suddenly monsieur grabbed him from behind, scooped him up and carried him into the bathroom. Richard dumped him unceremoniously in the bath and knelt down beside the dog. Nelson knew exactly what was coming and yapped his disapproval.

~ No, no! I don't need a wash. I had one in spring!

Nelson squirmed within Richard's hands and tried to climb out of the bath, but his claws had no purchase on the slippery surface. Richard reached for the hose.

~ No, wait!

Too late. The sudden blast of water made Nelson jump. He

quickly closed his eyes and tried to cover them with his ears. Nelson knew to expect rough treatment and braced himself accordingly. Monsieur was very heavy-handed, not at all as gentle as Timothy used to be.

Richard agreed with his wife's diagnosis. 'Boy, you do stink, Nelson. Well, I suppose you *are* due a good bath. After all, we can't have you going on your first ever trip abroad smelling like that can we, eh? Mummy— Fran is right.'

Nelson loves water almost as much as he hates having a bath. He, Sherpa and a few other Alpine friends had once agreed unanimously that dogs are simply not supposed to smell clean. That was a cat's vocation not a dog's! Even though Sherpa did admittedly pong beyond all acceptable limits, none of them ever chose to point it out to him. It had taken Nelson ages to achieve his latest unique aroma – the seagull just added to it – and monsieur was, in Nelson's mind, trying to take away his identity. Nelson's friends wouldn't recognise him for weeks, and Rascal would surely make cruel fun of him. His neighbours wouldn't trust him any more and *les filles* would think he was some kind of oddball.

~ No, monsieur, I tell you, it's an infringement of my canine righ—

The water jetted under his chest and stopped him in mid-complaint.

~ Hey! Easy with the undercarriage, will you. It's fragile down there. Give me that! Give it to me.

He turned round and tried to snatch the showerhead from Richard's hand but he raised it above Nelson's head and sprayed him on the back. Nelson spun again and attempted to pull at the shower hose with his teeth but Richard managed to keep it clear of his snapping jaws.

'Keep still, dog. And get *off*! You're not having it. You *need* a bath, I tell you. It's only water, for goodness sake. Come here. There, that's better, now stand still and relax. I bet you've never been to France before, have you? It will be a great little adventure.

And who knows, you might even meet a lovely French filly. I did! But that was ... oh, more than thirty years ago, now. Keep still, will you! And stop that grumbling, you dopey dog.'

~ That's enough. I'm clean now. Give me that!

'Nelson, get off. Let go! So, how do you feel about that, then? Nice little trip to France. We haven't been on holiday for a while – I spent a little too much of my retirement money on the TVR, you see. We thought it was about time we visited again. Nelson, keep still, I tell you! The more you fidget, the longer it takes. And stop chewing the shower hose!'

Richard reached behind Nelson and directed the spray up and under, between his back legs. Nelson didn't like his lower regions being power-blasted so he sat down in the bath to protect them.

'For God's sake, dog, will you stop sitting down. I can't wash you properly like that. Stand up. My dear mother always told me not to forget my bits. The same applies to you, I'm afraid. Now come on, stand up!'

~ Hey! Get *off* my tail!

'Come on, you dopey dog, stand up so I can wash you.'

~ Off – the – *tail*! Oww!

'That's better. Now stay standing, will you. No! I said stay standing up! Nels— oh, blow you, you fool. Anyway, I've been saving the pennies for a while now so that we can go over for the summer. We've rented a lovely little *gîte*. It sounds wonderful. Stand up, for goodness sake, dog! Mumm— Fran's mother and father have stayed there several times and they recommended it – it belongs to friends of them, so we got a very good deal. They're from Marseille, you know. I bet you would like to come with us wouldn't you, lad? Keep *still*, I tell you!'

Nelson had no intention of keeping still.

~ Monsieur, will you stop talking and hurry up and get this over with. I must be done now. I smell disgusting. Weeks without friends again.

'You do look comical all soaped up like that, Nelson. No, don't sit down. Don't sit— I need to rinse you through.'

Françoise entered the bathroom.

'Is everything okay in here, *chéri*? It sounded very much like you were having a little *tête-à-tête* with Nelson. And did I hear you calling me "Mummy" to him? Who is the "loopy" one now?'

~ 28 ~

Nelson took to Rascal's brother immediately. Rasta had a mature head on still-young shoulders, was very sharp for his years, and he had none of the volatility or recklessness that his younger sibling thrived on. Although Rascal had 'graced' the world with his presence only slightly behind Rasta – he was the second of the five to be born – the differences were remarkable, both physically and in character. Rasta was taller in the leg, and stockier with it. His beard was a little longer and shaggier, but his body hair was smoother than Rascal's was. He didn't run as fast or as far as his brother, but that was more Rasta's choice rather than genetic make-up – his legs were meaty strong and built like massive pipe cleaners. Even when Nelson was in his prime, Rasta could probably have outrun him. His hybrid features gave him a slightly uncoordinated look, and again Nelson pondered his two new friends' debatable parentage. But Rasta was all the same a handsome dog and, unlike Rascal, he wasn't burdened with an impossibly bright pink, impossibly long tongue that refused to stay indoors.

Nelson felt so good to be around the young brothers, and their mix of characters took years off him; it enabled him to have the best of both worlds – all in a twin hairy black package.

Rasta told Nelson a little bit more about the brothers' time back in France. The guardians were lagging behind as usual and Rascal was foraging, causing chaos in the woods. The local rabbits hated it when he was in the neighbourhood.

Their walk and talk was interrupted when they drew level with the weir and heard a loud, enthusiastic calling. Rascal's high-pitched call was unmistakable.

~ Hey, you two! Look at me. Watch this!

Rascal ran along the wall of the weir to its very centre, where the water gushed down through the narrow channel. He yapped again, hurled himself off the end and cried out with excitement.

~ World's first flyin' dog. Yee-hah!

He landed in the water with an impressively loud bellyflop and disappeared beneath the surface. He didn't reappear for some time. Nelson was concerned.

~ Is he okay, Rasta? He's been under a long time now.

~ *Oui, oui*, he'll be fine. He's a very strong swimmer, he can stay under for ages.

~ I hope so. I'm a fairly strong swimmer too – I used to love a good swim! – but I couldn't ever stay under that long. Are you sure he's okay? Should we go in and see?

~ *Non*, he'll be fine, Nelson. He'll be— ... Look, there he is, downriver under the railway bridge. He's just showing off. Again!

~ Thank goodness for that. Do you jump off the weir as well? It looks fun. Maybe I'll have a go later.

~ I've done it once or twice with Rascal, but it's not really my thing. He goes swimming every time we come here, once he's finished terrorising the rabbits; but I'm not as strong a swimmer as he is. And it's a bit dangerous. There are lots of canoes on the river, especially at the weekends. There's no chance they can see him in that dark water. And he never looks before he jumps. He's so carefree, not a worry in the world.

Rascal appeared behind them.

~ Scared you there, didn't I? Come on, you two, come an' have a go. *Allez!*

~ Maybe later! Rasta and Nelson replied simultaneously.

~ Suit yourselves, Rascal said, and ran back to the weir.

Nelson and Rasta watched him throw himself off the wall again and into the rushing water. This time he would be disappointed that his audience ignored his acrobatics and breath-holding skills, and instead carried on their relaxed walk.

Some time later, much further along the riverbank, they heard the muffled calls of Rascal well before they saw him. He appeared through the bushes with a pair of jeans in his mouth, tripping up clumsily over the legs as he dragged them along. He dropped them onto the ground in front of Rasta, as proud as can be, his thin tail waving like a hypnotist's finger.

~ Look what I found! Some old rags to play with. Come on, you two frumps, anyone for a game of tug o' war?

~ Rascal! bellowed Rasta. Where did you get those?

~ Somebody left 'em lyin' aroun' on a canoe. Why?

Rasta ordered him to return the jeans, but Rascal was reluctant to relinquish his prize.

~ I'd better spray 'em first, though, eh? – stop some other dog claimin' 'em.

~ No!

A little way further along the path, Rasta spotted a friend of his and so excused himself for a while. Nelson waited for Rascal to catch up after returning the jeans, and he then attempted to strike an agreement with him. He worried about Rascal's endless tricks, but moreover, his reckless jumping off the weir. Nelson tried to persuade him it could be very much in his own interest to calm down and mature a little. And in Nelson's too – he still bore the wounds from their head-on collisions.

~ I hope you don't mind me saying this, Rascal, but I really think you need to slow down a little bit and stop doing so many dangerous things. You worry your brother, you know. You've already more than lived up to your name, so don't you think it's perhaps time to mature a little? What I think you need is a ... a sort of role model. A kind of father figure. And—

~ I presume you mean *you*, do you? Last thing I need is a role model or father figure, *merci beaucoup*. You might well be old enough to be my father – *for sure!* – but I've already got Rasta.

He's just like you – always havin' a go at me. No wonder you two get on so well. An' anyway, *father* was a complete—!

Nelson accepted he was wasting his time. Rasta soon rejoined them, which Rascal took as a good excuse to disappear again. Rasta watched his brother hurtle into the trees.

~ I wonder what he'll come back with next. The canoeist will probably still be in the jeans this time.

As they approached the next bridge over the river, something Rasta had said earlier came back into Nelson's head and puzzled him. Because his mind had been more on Rascal's weir jumping, he had missed it the first time. He was glad to have Rasta back to settle his curiosity.

~ Rasta? he asked with a wrinkled brow and raised eyelids. Did I hear you correctly earlier? When you were telling me about your time as a pup in France, did you say it was in *les Pyrenées* or *les Alpes*?

~ *Les Alpes*. Or at least that's where I think it was. Why, what's puzzling you, Nelson?

~ Well ... a while back, when Rascal and I were discussing puphoods, guardians, and where we all came from, he told me that you two were from the Pyrenees, not the Alps. So—

~ Pyrenees. Alps. Who knows, Nelson? It could have been anywhere for all we know. *Maman* didn't make much sense in her final days, as you know.

~ But that's amazing, Rasta! That's marvellous. If you are from the Alps, we could have been neighbours! Are you sure you can't remember where you were born? Rascal said it was in a place called Lachpelle. It has to be fate! It has to be. I told Rascal—

~ Yes, I know. He told me you were a bit of a believer. Well, he wasn't as polite about it, but I think that's what he meant. If you don't mind me telling you so, Nelson, I think you're a bit of a dreamer too. No disrespect. No offence meant.

~ None taken, Rasta, but—

~ *But* nothing, *mon vieux*. Anyway, we don't know if we are from the Pyrenees or the Alps. Or anywhere else for that matter.

All I remember about those early days is a clean den and then *maman* leaving us all alone. And then being collected by our guardians. *Maman* mentioned something about her previous guardians but we never knew them. And who knows what she was really telling us, the mess she was in. Is it *that* important to you? I think Rascal is right about you, *mon ami*. Not only are you a faithful hound, but you're a bit of a fateful one too. He has a point, don't you think?

~ No, not really, Rasta. I—

~ Okay, look ... even if we do accept everything that you want us to believe, would it change anything? Our paths never crossed in France, did they?

~ No, but—

~ And even if we were from the Alps, we certainly never met your Belle. I'm sure we would have remembered her if we had. She sounds really special. But she was kill— ... Sorry, Nelson. She died well before we were even born, didn't she?

~ Yes, true. Her name wasn't really Belle, you know. That's just what I called her. I never knew her real name. I never thought to ask; she was always Belle to me.

~ So, none of it really fits, does it? And, *mon ami*, does it really matter *that* much to you?

~ Yes. No. Yes ... I suppose you're right, Rasta. What *does* it matter? The main thing is we are friends now.

~ *Exactement*. Now, what were you telling me about that big old dog in the Alps? What was he called again? Sher—? Rascal! Rascal! Take those underpants back now!

~ 29 ~

It was a typically hot July in the hamlet of Tourèze, deep in the South of France. Nelson was on his summer holidays with Richard and Françoise. *La Belle France!* It wasn't home any more; England was home, but *Zut!* It was good to be back.

Their holiday home could not have been better situated, nor could it have been more suitable for an inquisitive dog. It boasted plenty of rooms in which Nelson could hide his bones and Richard's slippers, and there was even a large utility room that he claimed as his own and installed his basket and blankets. No sign of any *bagàdos*, though, which was fantastic news.

The terrace at the back of the house was a daylong suntrap, but with just enough patchy shade for Nelson to follow around during the long, hot days of summer. It was on two levels: the lower one was a gravelly courtyard where the family ate lunch and prepared the evening barbecues; the upper level was a grassy haven, nestled up against a small cliff face that sheltered the garden from the wind. There was even a small swimming pool that Nelson wasn't allowed in, but he never was a stickler for rules.

He spent a lot of time inside the house during those sweltering afternoons of summer. His guardians thoughtfully closed the shutters for him. It was a stifling dry heat, especially for Nelson as a black dog, and he found it very hard to keep cool. He left a sweaty trail of paw prints when he padded around the house restlessly. He felt for all those poor tourist dogs, whose owners left them in cars for hours on end.

The *pièce de résistance* was the view from the front of the house. Nelson was treated to an ever-present but ever-changing panorama of the Cirque de Tourèze. The window ledges were a little too high for him to see over, so Richard had placed a large footstool in the window bay for him to sit on to survey his kingdom. The magnificent *cirque* that his vantage point oversaw was what the French call a '*chaos*' – a large jumbled area of jagged rocks and cliffs in, appropriately, total and utter chaos. All dotted in a heavy covering of forest. A local dog told Nelson that it was created in one single night by a team of fairies. Nelson almost believed him, but his tail told the truth.

It was impossible not to become lost in the *chaos* – 'the jungle' as the local dogs called it – but that was at least half the fun. After all, as long as Nelson was back in time for his barbecued *merguez* and chipolatas, the rest of the time was his to fill. Even after three months in Tourèze, there were still undiscovered nooks and corners, and areas of the jungle into which he had not ventured. And there was one particular area he did not intend to visit ever again – he recognised the tracks and droppings of wild boar anywhere. The rest of the *chaos* was much safer, a labyrinth of little paths and ravines he could take in search of the next encounter, aroma or memorable experience – like the cactus that he accidentally sat on.

His favourite times of day were early mornings when monsieur and madame were still having their lazy breakfasts. The air in the *cirque* was so cool and fresh. He also liked the evenings when all the day tourists had left.

In the mornings, it was very peaceful, but still Nelson had to tread carefully and watch his back as, in the heart of the jungle, he met other early risers. Rabbits, deer, squirrels and birds of prey with *very* sharp claws. There were always a few village cats too, on the prowl for unsuspecting birds and mice.

During the daytimes, it was human visitors who tramped the rock paths and forest routes, which was good for supplementing his early breakfasts. It was a very busy place during the summer months; in the village, there was a convivial bar and restaurant that was popular with day-trippers and, when the weather was good, it was crowded with walkers, cyclists and motorcyclists.

Early evenings, when the crowds had gone away, the real *spectacle* began. The sun began to dip behind the cliff at the rear of the *gîte* and it coloured the rocks of the *chaos* magically. Richard and Françoise positioned themselves in the windows for the light show. Nelson sat on his stool, with one of his guardians caressing him absent-mindedly, and together they watched the rocks change from shade to shade as the fiery sunset pigmented the sky.

Nelson met plenty of French dogs during his stay and, even at seven and a half, he showed he still had plenty of energy to take his new-found canine chums exploring in the jungle. They often accompanied him on his long treks up to the top of the *cirque* and beyond, to where they could see the beautiful lake. And if any of them ever wanted to come back to his place to meet the guardians, then they were always made welcome.

~ ~ ~ ~ ~

July and August reluctantly gave way to September. Nelson's trip back to his homeland was almost over – they had only two weeks left.

It was late morning and he was returning from a long exploration through the *chaos*. Although it was mid-September now and the temperature was noticeably cooler, Nelson was exceptionally thirsty. But that was perhaps more his nerves than fatigue. Not only had he completed the full tour, including the stiff climb up to the stunning viewpoint over the lake, but he had barely escaped yet another physical disagreement with one of the resident boar. She was most displeased when Nelson had disturbed her snuffling in the undergrowth.

~ *Zut alors!* he said to himself, out of breath, once he had reached a safe distance from her. They can run awfully fast, those *sangliers* – but not as fast as I can.

He reached the road at the lower end of the village and set off up it for the kilometre walk back to civilisation. He knew that opposite the village bar was a roadside fountain where he could both quench his eager thirst and cool down. It was a small, sculpted wall fountain, where the water cascades from a lion's mouth into a trough.

When he reached it, he jumped up onto the bench alongside and climbed straight into the trough. The water was delightfully refreshing but just too deep for him to lie down in, so he had to make do with sitting. He panted happily and, with great relief, he dropped his bottom to rest on the cool stone base of the trough. It was with regularity that he called in for a little bathe and a big drink.

The owners of the bar opposite usually put a little bowl of water outside the bar for thirsty dogs, but Nelson preferred the cool flowing water – the *eau de fontaine* tasted so much better. Sitting in the water, he was able to drink from the trough, but other times he took it directly from the lion's cascading mouth. All he had to do was lift and turn his snout a little, open his mouth and gobble greedily. Passers-by stopped and watched and laughed. Had they never seen a dog having a drink before? They usually gave him a friendly *Bonjour* and a pat on the head. Nelson always tried to return their vocal greetings, but he often had a mouthful of water. And it was very difficult to wag his tail underwater.

After a few moments of lapping, he paused. Something had disturbed him.

He thrust his snout up in the air. His ears twitched and swivelled on high alert. His tail tried to twitch but couldn't.

What's that smell? he thought.

He had picked something up on the warm air that he recognised. It was a very familiar smell, but he couldn't quite place it. He stretched his nose even higher up into the air, flared open his nostrils and sniffed rapidly. Yes, definitely something he knew. Lunch? *Une fille?* In fact, it wasn't one lone smell that he recognised. It was several. All mixed together, but separate. So many of them and all so familiar. So familiar. He couldn't quite see over the lip of the trough, so he temporarily dismissed the smell in favour of his thirst. No, can't place it. Oh, well, never mind – back to more important matters. He stretched up again and drank from the lion's mouth.

He heard a voice from the bar across the road.

'Father, why is that dog kissing that lion?'

~ ~ ~ ~ ~

Nelson took them all back up to the house for lunch, and for the rest of the day his tail never stopped talking. The adults chatted incessantly too, swapping stories old and new. Timothy and Nelson sat together on the terrace, watching, listening, being close. Nelson had more than a few questions for monsieur David, but because he could see and smell that he was as overjoyed to see Nelson again as Nelson was to see him, he didn't pressure him.

Earlier, when they first hugged at the bar – after David had recovered from the shock of bumping into 'Ozzy' again; in France of all places! – he had been surprised to see his old dog was actually wearing a collar, and intrigued that he was called Nelson. When Ljana had first cuddled and stroked Nelson, something metallic on one of her fingers caught on his collar.

'"Nelson"?' mused David. 'That's an original name for a dog. And you've even got a collar on as well. Wow!'

'It is a much better name than Ozzy, father. Do you know, father, that it is exactly one year ago that Oswald ran away from you up at the Tower? I was twelve years and six months and fifteen days old when he ran away. He must have run a very very long way to get here all on his own.'

In the afternoon, they took Nelson for a ride on the motorbike. He sat in the sidecar with Timothy, who held him tightly between his knees. While David and Timothy were preparing the motorbike for their trip out, Nelson sat with the two women on the terrace. Richard had gone upstairs for a lie down – Nelson had sensed he was a little off colour again.

'I am very worried about *Rich*ard,' said Françoise to Ljana. 'He has been having some terribly bad headaches these previous weeks. I keep telling him we must visit the *docteur*, but he insists we wait until we return to England. He is convinced it is simply too much sun, but I am not so sure I believe him. I hope he is right. So, my dear, how do you like this part of *la belle France*?'

'Oh, it's simply beautiful. We were hoping to come last year, but with David's work, we couldn't fit it in. He's a bit of a bike nut, as you may have gathered, and one of his friends talked about how this region was perfect and that there was a famous motorbike circuit here. So here we are. David gets to do his coveted circuit and see Lake Salagou, Timothy can practise his French and I can spend some quality time with the two of them. And some beach time of course. And—'

'Sorry, my dear, what was it you were saying? *Excuse-moi*, I was far away.'

The boys rode out of the village and into the heart of the countryside, all the way up to the lake. They parked at the far shore and found a grassy knoll overlooking the water. They sprawled out on the grass and relaxed. Nelson found a perfect little spot in between father and son and enjoyed their joint attention and caresses. It made him feel very special to think that monsieur David and Timothy had spent a whole year looking for him. Had they come all this way to take him home with them? Should he go with them? He still missed them both so much, but his home was with monsieur Richard and madame Françoise. They needed him. He needed them.

Timothy stopped stroking Nelson and folded his arms.

'Father, are we going to take Oswald home with us now that we have found him again?'

'No. No, Tim. We won't be taking him home with us, I'm afraid. If we did, it would ... it would cause far too many problems. I'll explain it all to you one day, Tim. And we can't take him because he has a new home now. He has a good home with Richard and Françoise. He's *their* dog now. They're his family.'

'I am glad you see it my way, father. I think I have missed him but it would not be a good idea now that he has a new family.'

'No, son. You're right. It would not be a good idea.'

'But it is very good to see him I think.'

'It is, Tim, it is.'

'And it explains one thing very clearly, father.'

'What's that, Tim?'

'Why even when I concentrated very very hard I still could not see Oswald next to mother in the stars and planets on my ceiling.'

David's eyes watered and, instinctively, he reached over to put his arm round Timothy's shoulder. But when Timothy flinched and pulled back, he stopped short. Simultaneously, father and son reached over Nelson to tickle an ear each. Oh, how he had missed that! Then David pulled Nelson close and spoke to him.

'So, it's Nelson now is it?' David ruffled Nelson's scruff affectionately. 'Come on then, *Nelson*, let's see if you're still the old Ozzy we used to know. Still as mischievous as ever, are we? On your feet then, dog – let's see just how playful you really are.'

David leapt to his feet, picked up a large stick and threw it into the lake.

'Go on, boy. Fetch it!'

Nelson looked up at him, rolled his eyes and let out a little groan.

~ Do you really think I'll fall for that old trick again?

~ ~ ~ ~ ~

Nelson's chance meeting with his old guardians was over, and fate had left with them on a big motorbike.

October soon arrived. With it, Nelson felt ready to go home – home to England. Not insomuch as he had had enough of France, *au contraire*, but because he desperately wanted to see Rascal and Rasta – especially now he had something truly marvellous to tell them.

They both always made fun of him when he mentioned fate and

destiny, but he vowed not to let their prejudices stand in his way this time. He knew he couldn't hope for a sensible response from Rascal, but he was reasonably optimistic he could appeal at least to Rasta's sense of logic.

They arrived home late. They were all very tired after the long journey, so they went to bed as soon as Richard and Françoise had unloaded the car of personal belongings, wine, cheese and olives. Monsieur was visibly shattered, Nelson noted with concern, so he helped his guardians as much as he could and carried all his own bedding into the house.

The following morning, Richard was up almost as early as Nelson was, and he immediately commenced tending the garden that had been neglected while they were away. Françoise busied herself with unpacking and putting away, and sifting through the mail that had piled up behind the front door. After less than an hour, Nelson and Richard came back into the house; Richard had a pained expression on his face and was massaging the back of his neck and his right temple.

'I've got another one of those blasted headaches, darling. It feels as if I have a golf ball lodged in the back of my neck. I think I'll leave the gardening for now and go for a little lie down.'

'And I will call the *docteur* first thing on Monday morning, *chéri*. I will have no buts this time.'

'Oh, don't fret, Fran – it's probably just the travelling and change of climate. I'll be fine after a little rest, you'll see. And anyway, by the time I get a damned appointment, it will have passed over.'

'That may well be true, *Rich*ard, but we are going anyway.'

'Whatever you say, dear. But I'm sure it's nothing.'

Richard went upstairs, Françoise carried on her sorting. Nelson took the opportunity to head out and run over to tell Rascal and Rasta his wonderful news. He hadn't slept all night. He was too excited.

It was around that time of day the brothers took their usual weekend ramble along the river to the crook, so he would probably be able to join up with them for the latter part of the morning. He caught them upriver of the weir, strolling along the old railway line. He spotted Rascal first. Somewhat uncharacteristically, he was walking calmly alongside Gill's heel. Oh, dear, thought Nelson; Rascal has been a naughty dog *again*, and is on his best behaviour.

~ Not for long! *Not for long!* shouted Nelson as he sprinted along the path.

He bounded up to Rascal and took the opportunity to reap a little revenge. From behind, Nelson launched himself onto Rascal's back, landing squarely with both paws, knocking his legs from under him, down into a muddy ditch.

~ Hey, kiddo, how are you today? I'm back! And I have *so* much to tell you. How was *your* summer? Mine was absolutely brilliant. And you'll never, ever guess who I met in Fran—

~ Rasta's dead, Nelson. My brother's dead.

~ 30 ~

Nelson's walk home was a long solitary one. His paws were as heavy as his head. He went straight to bed. He saw madame only briefly; monsieur, he presumed, was still in bed resting. He didn't even call in to see how he was.

Rasta and Rascal were out walking one weekend in September and were playing alongside the river, hiding from Tom and Gill, and swimming in the water. The brothers were having a super time in each other's company. Rasta was in a lively mood as they both raced along the weir, fighting to be first in. He jumped enthusiastically through the air just ahead of Rascal, both of them bellyflopping gracelessly into the water, both yapping as they landed. Yap, splat! Yap, splat! Rasta stayed underwater even longer than Rascal did. When Rasta resurfaced, the canoe hit him square on the side of the head.

Rascal saw it happen, heard the dull thud of fibreglass on bone and watched his brother disappear under the canoe and back into the dark water. He swam as fast as he could with the current to reach Rasta and finally caught up with him downriver, floating under the old bridge. With great effort, he managed to push Rasta to the riverbank. Tom and Gill ran back down to the bridge and Tom waded into the river. He lifted Rasta from the water and held him close. Blood was seeping from one of his ears.

Nelson cried into the evening and through the night. Françoise tried to console him, stroking him, and asking what was wrong with her *petit*, but he rejected her efforts. He couldn't block the scene from his mind no matter how hard he tried. He could see it all so clearly. All he kept imagining was the noise of the canoe thudding against Rasta's skull. And he could hear Rasta's voice telling him how he worried about Rascal and the weir and the canoes and ...

Over and over, again and again, like the ticking of the clock in the kitchen.

~ ~ ~ ~ ~

Rascal and Nelson didn't see each other for quite a while. Rascal preferred to deal with things in his own way. This was his grief, and who was Nelson to offer empty wisdom and reason. Yet, Nelson could not deny his own selfish disappointment and despair at not having the chance to tell the brothers his truly revelatory news from France.

After a few more weeks, Rascal and he began to resume their walks and chats, and Rascal slowly regained some of his old ways. He slowed down in many ways. He didn't have the same levels of boundless energy any more and he played fewer tricks on Nelson. Events had matured him. He never went swimming off the weir again. In his head, he was a wiser dog, tainted by the death of a close one. Nelson knew precisely how he felt. Rascal became a little more like his dear brother. Even though it was in a diluted version, Nelson was grateful to have his best friend back. Inside he was still Rascal. Rascal by name, Rascal by nature. Nelson was proud of him, and he tried to tell him so. But he hadn't thought out his praise carefully enough.

~ I really am very proud of you, Rascal – the way you have dealt with this. And, if your father could see you—

He stopped himself quickly. Definitely not a wise analogy. Fortunately, Rascal didn't pick up on it, but Nelson would have to be much more careful in future if he didn't want to jeopardise anything. He had to handle Rascal carefully. He continued hastily.

~ If your mother were watching over you now, Rascal, she

would be very proud of you too. She is probably up there right now, I'm sure, high above a snow-fringed Alpine mountain, watching over you, and over Rasta too.

~ Hope so. But it would be a Pyrenean mountain, not an Alpine one.

~ Yes, well, perhaps. But Rasta told me you were from the Alp—

~ Pyrenees.

~ Alps.

~ Pyrenees!

~ Alps!

~ Pyren— Oh, forget it, Nelson. What does it matter?

~ Rascal, it does matter. It matters a lot. One day I'll— ... you'll understand.

Nelson was upset by Rascal's reluctance. His head dropped and he blinked rapidly. It troubled him, but he didn't have time to dwell on it because Rascal was suddenly full of energy again.

~ Hey, Nelson! Guess what? You know that little Jack Russell pup in the village? Rizla, the one with the stumpy tail? Guess what I saw him doin' yesterday. He was tearin' through a field of sheep like a nutter, screamin' at 'em. *Mint sauce! Mint sauce!*

~ Rascal, that joke is nearly as old as I am. It's not funny any more.

~ Oh come on, will you. Lighten up!

~ It's just not funny, Rascal. It's not ... it's ...

~ So why you grinnin' like that then, with your tongue hangin' out? I can see it in your eyes. You do find it funny, but you just won't admit it. Typical French. Come on, you old frump, it won't hurt you. Let it out, dog!

Such was his joy at seeing Rascal full of life again that Nelson simply couldn't resist. They were soon both on their backs rolling around, laughing and kicking each other with their legs in the air. It was like being pups again.

~ Look at you, gramps. Havin' fun for a change. An' not a dead seagull in sight. I'm proud of you too!

~ It's good to have you back, Rascal! Nelson managed to say.

Nelson jumped up, pinned Rascal down on the grass and sank his teeth into his back leg. Rascal's response was to break wind in Nelson's face, which made them both roll around even more.

~ Rascal! Have you been on the liver again?

~ Nah! It's that new Pedigree Chum stuff my guardians have got me on. With rabbit. It repeats on me.

~ So, finally you get to eat rabbit – even if you didn't catch it yourself. Congratulations! You deserve a pat on the back for that, but I'm not coming anywhere near you, not with those evil pongs. They're worse than monsieur's when he thinks I'm out of range.

~ ~ ~ ~ ~

Christmas came and passed and they entered another year. Nelson enjoyed his Christmases because he was able to eat turkey for several days afterwards.

On New Year's Day, they all went out for a good long walk along the river. Nelson took Richard and Françoise with him; Rascal brought Tom and Gill. It had been too long since the adults had seen one another, so the dogs were very pleased to get them all together again for a stroll.

In the pale blue sky, the sun was shining and there was a light covering of frosty snow in the fields. It wasn't snow like in the Alps, certainly not enough to have snowball fights or to go sledging, but it was fun for Rascal and Nelson to roll in and cool down after their exertions. The humans didn't join in much but the dogs had a great time.

Only part-way into the walk, however, Nelson and his guardians had to excuse themselves to go home. Richard could feel one of his headaches coming on: what he had come to term his 'mithering migraines'. It had been several trouble-free weeks since the previous episode, so it came as quite an unwelcome return. Nelson could see madame was very concerned. So was he.

'We have already been to the *docteur*,' Françoise told Gill and Tom. 'Several times in fact. He gave *Rich*ard some very strong painkillers and told him to take it easy. And they did some tests at the hospital as well, didn't they, *chéri*? Fortunately, the results were – how do you say in English; it always confuses me – positive or negative?'

Tom spoke.

'It is a bit confusing, isn't it? Negative is good, positive is bad. Well, if the results were negative, then that's good news. Isn't it?'

'I don't really know. We would like to know for sure what it could be. The *docteur* says *Rich*ard is in very good health for his age … except for his headaches. They have even done tests on his heart, you know. And they were pos— … negative. They were all okay. But I cannot help but worry. The *docteur* has said he would like a second opinion and has also recommended some further tests to check for anything more. But he says there is probably nothing to worry about. We are waiting for another appointment now, aren't we, *chéri*?'

'Yes, and knowing the NHS, it will be *next* Christmas before I get to see anyone. If I were a dog, I'd be in tomorrow!'

~ ~ ~ ~ ~

Richard's headaches, although infrequent, became worse. The doctors were still at a complete loss. A few weeks later, he was called into the hospital for more tests, including an MRI brain scan. The results were 'all clear'. Richard was sent home with nothing more than a pocket full of painkillers.

On one occasion in March, while Nelson and he were out walking in the fields, Richard fainted and collapsed. Nelson called out for help and ran round Richard in circles. The field was deserted and no one heard. Nelson set off at speed back to the house to find madame. But before he reached the gate onto the farm track, he heard monsieur weakly calling him back. He had woken up and was sitting on the grass, dazed and confused. He spoke to Nelson and assured him he was perfectly fine, but Nelson sensed he wasn't revealing the whole truth. He didn't smell at all well.

'Don't worry, lad. I'm okay now. I just felt a bit dizzy all of a sudden. The field started spinning, and then ...'

They sat for a while longer until Richard recovered. Nelson sat close by his side, pushing his warm body against Richard's. He was trembling. Richard eventually stood up on unsteady feet and they carried on their walk.

'Come on then, let's be off. We don't want anyone seeing this daft old chump sitting down in the middle of a field, do we, eh? And we'll not mention this to Fran, shall we not? Mum's the word. Don't want to worry her too much, do we, lad?'

Another month passed with no more fainting episodes, but then one day in April, while doing some gardening, Richard passed out again. The garden began to spin, and Richard fell, hitting the back of his head on the flagstones of the patio. Françoise and Nelson both heard the crack from the kitchen and rushed outside. When finally he came to, and Françoise had managed to help him sit up, Richard's eyes were glazed and he was very confused, like a little lost child in need of a parent's embrace. Françoise held him steady and inspected him. So did Nelson. There was a nasty gash on the back of his head, and it was bleeding badly. Françoise positioned Richard comfortably against the wall, got up and set off inside the house to call an ambulance. Nelson stayed by his side.

'Wait, Fran, wait,' whispered Richard in a shaky voice. 'There's no need for an ambulance. I can drive to the hospital. It's only a bump on the head.'

'A bump? A bump! *Mon Dieu, Rich*ard! I heard your head hit the ground from inside the house. You will do no such thing!'

'Well, you drive then. I don't need an ambulance. They have enough to do without some dithering old fool with an egg on his head bothering them.'

'*Rich*ard, you are a stubborn old Englishman. Where are the keys?'

Nelson accompanied them to the hospital and waited in the car. When they eventually came back out, monsieur appeared much better and assured Nelson he felt fine and dandy. Pulling a broad grin that just about concealed his nervousness, he patted the large dressing on the back of his head. Françoise shook her head in disapproval, worry etched across her face.

'Let us hope we get the rendezvous to see the specialist soon. Then at least we will know what it really is, *n'est-ce pas*?'

Patting himself on the head again, Richard said: 'You know what they say, Fran – "Where there's no sense, there's no feeling". Eh, Nelson? What do you say?'

Nelson wagged his tail excitedly.

~ ~ ~ ~ ~

It was a lovely summer's afternoon, mid-June. Nelson and Richard were in the garden again. Richard was in high spirits: he hadn't suffered any fainting episodes for two months. But Nelson knew it all still troubled him. He could sense monsieur was keeping something secret from him. He heard it in the tone of his voice, and saw it in his eyes. Nelson was unaware, however, that monsieur was waiting for yet another appointment for yet another test. Would they ever discover what was wrong?

The next planned test was the one that had involved strapping Richard to the infamous, rotating bed unit – what he told Tom sounded like a 'mediaeval torture rack'. It was something he had dreaded: he alone knew just how terrible his migraines and spinning worlds were and he had not been looking forward to having such an episode forced upon him. Secretly, he had hoped it wouldn't work.

Richard was filling the bird table, scraping the leftover breadcrumbs from lunchtime onto it. He filled up the birdbath with water. Nelson liked to jump up against it, planting his paws on it to drink from the bath, but he wasn't allowed to, so he had to do it when they weren't watching. The birds didn't like him drinking out of it either and often dive-bombed him and rapped his snout with pointy beaks, chirping obscenities at him in their incomprehensible language.

Richard collected a spade and a few gardening implements from the shed and began digging round a small bush. It looked as though he was planning to remove it, which worried Nelson; not because it was strenuous work for monsieur, but because it was one of Nelson's favourite ports of call.

Françoise was busy in the kitchen cooking. Through the open windowpanes, Nelson could smell that she was preparing for one of her Chinese banquets, something they did from time to time, and she usually did most of the preparations in the afternoon. This meant she could spend more time chatting and drinking too much in the evening.

Nelson wandered inside to investigate. Chinese was never his favourite cuisine, he found the sauces a little too rich. He liked the rice and the drier dishes, and those deliciously crunchy spring rolls, but for the rest, *non merci*. He could smell the first of the spring rolls frying. Françoise used only the finest quality pork and chicken, and the herbs and spices she used made Nelson drool puddles on the kitchen floor. He usually sat in the same spot when she was preparing any food, waiting eagerly for any spillage, so she often put one of his old after-walk towels under him so he could dribble at will.

Richard entered the kitchen, whistling. He stepped over Nelson, went to the cooker and leant over the spring rolls.

~ Hey! No queue jumping! shouted Nelson, as he prodded monsieur's calf with his paw.

'Don't worry, Nelson. I'm not here to steal your treat.'

Richard turned to look at his wife.

'You know, darling, we really should get around to buying one of those deep fat frying machines. They're so much safer than that old pan you use.'

'Yes, I know, *chéri*. But the old habits die slowly. And it hardly seems worth the expense. It is not as if we ever deep fry anything else, *n'est-ce pas*?'

'True. But all the same, next time I'm in town, I'll see how much they ar—'

They all jumped when they heard the telephone ring. Françoise picked it up.

'It is the hospital, *chéri*! There has been a cancellation. They have an appointment for the experiment if we can make it there in half an hour. *Allez!* We will have to be quick.'

'The torture chamber, you mean! Oh, well, I suppose I can't put it off any longer.' Richard looked down at Nelson. 'They say it's a dog's life, but I wish I had yours, Nelson. Right then – the Dark Ages here we come.'

Nelson realised something very important must have happened because monsieur and madame hurried manically around the house, closed the door through to the hallway and grabbed the car keys from the hook. They dashed out of the back door in a flurry. All he received in explanation was a quick pat on the head from them both, and then monsieur pulled the door closed on him and left.

~ I'll wait here then, shall I? Nelson grumbled. Oh, well, no bonus spring roll for me this afternoon. What shall I do with myself for a few hours shut up in here?

He sighed heavily and plodded into the sun lounge to sunbathe against the patio doors. The sun warmed him through and he dozed off.

When he woke up, he felt too hot in the sun, so he moved to a shadier part of the sun lounge. But it was very warm there too ... even in the shade.

What was that smell? Oh, yes – the spring rolls! He could hear them bubbling, dancing merrily in the boiling fat. Should be ready soon. He dribbled and smacked his lips in anticipation.

Nelson's afternoon siesta was one of his well-practised rituals, so it was no surprise when his snout and eyelids soon became too heavy to hold up. He nodded off again, and drifted into a pleasant dream ...

Part 3

The End of a Journey

~ 31 ~

The present day, a fine December morning

An unexpectedly warm and beautiful December morning probes its way through the patio windows into the sun lounge, where Nelson lies dozing in his basket. He has been awake a good while already, pondering and daydreaming, but he's in no rush to get up.

When Françoise entered the kitchen, Nelson didn't bound up to her to welcome her with his usual morning spark; she had to go into the sun lounge to solicit any form of greeting at all. Richard followed her into the kitchen a few minutes later and let Nelson outside; then they assembled for breakfast as they did every morning.

'You're quiet this morning, Nelson,' he said. 'Don't worry, lad, breakfast is on its way.'

Habitually, Nelson was given one Weetabix for breakfast, but he pestered Françoise for a second one by standing stubbornly at his bowl, looking up expectantly. He had never bothered her in this way before and it puzzled her, but she didn't dwell on it too much, and simply crushed up another biscuit, pouring on an extra helping of milk.

'You *are* hungry, *mon petit*,' she commented absent-mindedly. 'This is good, though, because you will need your strength today. We are going for a good long walk on Bowcragg Fell. You like this one, don't you? We have to make the most of the English weather, and today is *beautiful*. I like this global warming. *Rich*ard will no doubt make us have the roof off the car, won't you, *chéri*? I had better take my hat and scarf. *Bon*, I will prepare some sandwiches then.'

She busied herself preparing food, filling the flask and organising Nelson's usual travel bowls of water, light mixer-lunch and some carrot and cucumber. Richard gathered the raincoats – 'One never knows, darling' – the camera, binoculars and maps, and stuffed them all into the rucksacks.

Nelson relaxed on his full stomach and lay on the sun lounge floor watching the activity. He seemed lost in his own thoughts. Françoise noticed his eyes held a blank stare. Normally, they twinkled with curiosity and enthusiasm, but today they were dull and vacant. It concerned her a little, but she knew the fresh winter air would revitalise him. Probably hadn't had much sleep, she thought.

Finally, they were ready to go. Richard clapped his hands twice as a signal.

'Okay then, people. Are we ready to go?'

'I think so,' replied Françoise. 'I think we have everything. Did you pack the camera?'

'Of course. Right then, let's be on our way. Come on, Nelson, look lively then, lad.'

Nelson stood up and walked to the back door. But when he got there, he didn't rush past them or push his way out into the garden. He sat down firmly on the floor and stared up at the two of them. When he met Françoise's eye, he stared hard and cocked an ear. It was a penetrating stare and Françoise felt a strange little shiver ripple through her. Richard noticed an uncharacteristic look in the dog's eyes too.

'What's got into you this morning, Nelson? A bit under the weather, are we?'

Nelson's response was to stand up, turn round and walk slowly back to his basket. He climbed into it and lay down. The couple were at a loss and followed him.

'Come on, lad, what the heavens is the matter? It's a beautiful day out there.'

'*Chéri*,' said Françoise. 'I have the impression he doesn't want to come. I don't think he is feeling very well.'

'Whatever *do* you mean, darling? Of course he wants to come. He's a dog! He's just—'

'No, *Rich*ard – he is not like he was. He is not as young as he used to be, you know. Like all of us, *n'est-ce pas*? I think he is perhaps a bit, how do you say? – off the colour. Look, his eyes are so empty, and his nose is very dry. Perhaps he is getting a bit of a chill. He obviously doesn't want to come with us. You can take him out for a little leg stretch when we come home, *non*?'

'But, Fran ...'

'Come on, *Rich*ard. Look at him. He cannot be bothered with it. Look, he is falling asleep as we speak. I will put his basket out on the grass then he can enjoy the sun here for the day. You prepare the car and I'll be with you in a moment.'

'Are you sure, dear?'

'He will be fine. It is not the first time we have left him in the garden is it? We can leave the door open for him. Can you get his lunch out of the rucksack – we can leave it with him in case he is hungry later.'

Since the fire, Richard and Françoise had never again left Nelson confined in the house. If ever they went out without him, they always left the patio door slightly ajar for him to exit and enter as he pleased. Yes, it was risky to leave the door open, but their back garden was hidden from prying eyes – and they wouldn't dare leave the doors locked and the dog inside. They had thought briefly of putting a Nelson-sized dog flap in the back door, but they worried about next door's cat sneaking in and the two of them fighting while confined inside.

Françoise gestured to Nelson to get out of his bed, which he did. He watched her as she took it outside and placed it on the grass at the edge of the patio. He followed and climbed back in, sat down and looked up at her, snout angled high, ears directed forwards. He lifted a paw. Françoise took this as a gesture of curiosity on Nelson's part, but he knew it to be more a thank you.

'You will be fine there, Nelson, *mon petit*. Don't worry, we are not dragging you up the hills today. You can have an easy day here in the garden, and we will—'

'Here we are then, lad. How about that for waiter service,' said Richard, who placed the food and water by the side of Nelson's basket.

Nelson sniffed uninterestedly at it and turned away.

Richard stroked Nelson's head and said, 'You'll be all right then, will you? Fran, let's not bother with the Fells today, let's go somewhere a bit nearer then he's not on his own too long.'

'Okay, *chéri*,' she mumbled, her thoughts far away from what her husband was saying.

They both gave Nelson an affectionate stroke and made to leave. Richard turned on his heels, walked through the gate and headed round the corner to the car. At the gate, Françoise turned round and returned quickly to Nelson as though she had forgotten something. She crouched low to him and cupped his head between her hands, holding his chin up to her face. They held each other's stare for a long moment. Then Françoise lowered her head and placed a long kiss on Nelson's furrowed brow.

She had no idea why she had done it, or why a tear fell from her cheek and landed on Nelson's head. She had even less of an explanation when she said to him in a small whisper, '*Je t'aime, mon petit*. We both do.'

Slowly she rose and left the garden, refusing to look back, even when she thought she heard a tiny whimper.

~ ~ ~ ~ ~

Earlier

The gentle December dawn taps on the window and on Nelson's heavy eyelids, beckoning him to wake up and profit from another day. He stands up in his basket, stretches his neck and legs and gazes vacantly out through the patio window.

Three and a half years it's been since the house fire, he reminds himself. Three and a half wonderful years. And all thanks to Rascal. How can Nelson ever thank him?

But Nelson has not been entirely truthful with Rascal over recent years. He has some secrets that he kept well hidden from him, safely buried during their long years of friendship. But along with all his old bones, it is time for those hidden truths to be uncovered, dug up and revealed. Although there is nobody with him to share and understand his thoughts – Richard and Françoise are still sleeping – he is convinced he can pacify his guilt and eternal doubt by airing them. His conscience will be as clear as the December sky.

He finds he is graced with an enthusiasm that he has not felt in quite a while and he is very grateful that Rascal is not with him, for he might act rashly and reveal everything to him.

He lies down and sighs long and happily to let out his final *pensées*. He knows that once his mind is purged, he will bid the world and all its memories a very fond *Adieu*, for his time is now. His deep sigh and long exhalation confirm he has accepted that every dog must eventually pass away. But he is in control. It is Nelson who makes the final decision – not fate. There is no call for sorrow, he tells himself. He has been a very fortunate dog, and he knows that a star called *maman* has been following him along his long and winding journey.

He woke up earlier feeling a restful calm spread throughout his body. His muscles were so relaxed he thought his skeleton had dissolved during the night. When Françoise finally rose from bed and entered the kitchen, Nelson wasn't in the mood for a boisterous display of energy. When she called him in, he ignored her jovial invitation, turned away lethargically and buried his snout under his blanket. She came in to see him and called his name again, ruffling his head gently. Without even lifting his snout, Nelson sighed heavily and looked up at her with a preoccupied eye. He had a lot on his mind and a long-standing burden to unload.

When Richard arrived later, he was not as considerate as his wife was, and he would not take no for an answer, even when Nelson looked up at him dolefully from his basket, putting on his best saucer-eye look and flattening his ears. Richard spoke insistently and encouraged Nelson out into the garden for his morning rituals. Then Nelson went for breakfast. With a raised paw and an insistent whine, he stood stubbornly at his bowl for the extra Weetabix and even managed to secure an extra helping of milk. Perhaps the weight of his decision ran as far as his stomach. A strange final meal, but his Weetabix would see him along. Madame gazed down at Nelson with a strange look that he had never seen before, but he was too busy wolfing down his breakfast to pay her mood much attention.

He was aware that monsieur and madame were preparing for a family hike somewhere but Nelson knew he didn't want to go with them. Not today. He lay on the sun lounge floor watching their activity lazily, but lost in his own faraway thoughts. After he had turned down their repeated invitations to accompany them, he was relieved to watch madame carry his basket outside and place it on the patio in its usual spot. Ever since the fire, this was something Nelson noticed they always did when they were going somewhere he was not invited, and if the weather was good. When the weather was bad, Nelson's basket would remain inside, but still they would leave the patio door slightly ajar so that he could go outdoors whenever he wanted to. Or needed to.

When they finally left, Nelson sat and watched them. He knew he could go inside if it turned cold or rainy, but the day was already bright and sunny. He knew he would not be going into the house ever again. He was moving to a new home. He watched as his guardians walked down the path to the car. He would not see them walk back up it. He was very sad to see them go, but he was equally ready to make his own trip. As they rounded the corner and walked out of sight, madame turned her shoulder as though to look back to him, but she stopped herself. Nelson let out a little whimper – one that said all he wanted to tell them.

He hoped they would come to understand his decision. He hoped, too, that Rascal would accept he had to leave without saying goodbye. Without telling him. He tried to concentrate on his thoughts of Rascal, but his mind was distracted by something madame had done before leaving the garden. She crouched down to Nelson and cupped his face in her hands. Then she whispered something soothing into his ear.

Nelson appreciated the words and especially that little kiss on his forehead, but it had taken him completely by surprise; she didn't normally do such a thing when they went out for the day.

After a while, Nelson turned his thoughts away from the gate. He wiped a little sleep from his eyes, sighed deeply and climbed out of his basket. He studied it for a long while, frowning as he did so. Then he stepped slowly back in. He pawed deliberately at his blankets, shuffling them around a little until they were plumped up and perfect. He turned three full circles to be as close as possible to *maman* and then he flopped down with a noisy smack of his jaws and another heavy sigh. Nelson would not be leaving his basket again – as far as he was concerned, he was in his final resting place. He wasn't feeling sad or lonely, he had his memories to keep him warm and his special secrets to keep him company. And the reassurance that, in a dog's world, dreams really do come true.

Rascal and Rasta always refused to believe Nelson's claims of fate and destiny. Their unwillingness to accept that they could all have been from the Alps was very hard on him, but that was the brothers' choice and Nelson tried to accept it. All they would ever admit was that they were unsure whether it was the Pyrenees or the Alps from where they came. That was all it had taken for Nelson's doubts to take root, for their story to start gnawing at him. He clearly remembered Rascal's uncertainty. And Rasta had *never* known the name of their village – he had no recollection of it. Initially, Nelson had accepted Rascal's own version that he and Rasta were born in a village called Lachpelle in the Pyrenees, but when Nelson began fishing for more evidence about their lives, he asked Rascal once again. Rascal still couldn't remember exactly.

~ Nelson, it was years ago.

~ Was it Lachpelle, Rascal?

~ Yes, that's it.

~ But are you sure? Could it have been something that sounds very much like Lachpelle, but wasn't? Like La Chapelle?

~ I said yes, didn't I? It's the same thing.

~ Rascal, was it Lachpelle, or could it *possibly* have been something like La Chapelle? La Chapelle?

~ It's the *same thing*, Nelson!

Nelson knew he was wasting his time pressing Rascal further.

~ Never mind. It's nothing.

But it wasn't.

La Chapelle – or La Chapelle d'Abondance, to give it its official title – is a village in the Alps and not in the Pyrenees. And what's more, it is situated only a short run along the valley from the village of Abondance, Nelson's own village. The locals simply call it La Chapelle.

His suspicions were further aroused a few weeks later.

Rascal and he were sitting on the shoreline, side by side as they often did, watching the sun set over the ebbing tide. They were both in high spirits and were reminiscing about their puphoods, their *mamans*, and any particular friends or relationships their mothers had.

~ *Non*. Like I said before, Nelson, she never really told us much. Reckon it was because she couldn't remember half of it after her accident. I do remember once, though, she mentioned a dog she knew ... but that was just a silly story really. Just some dopey dog from down the valley. Sounded a bit of a weirdo. Used to wander aroun' dressed up in a bizarre contraption stuffed full of baguettes or somethin'. Bit of a nutter. An' he even got beaten up by a sheep once, apparently. A *sheep!* Wish I'd met him, he sounds a real laugh.

~ Yes ... yes indeed, Rascal. They can be a rather odd breed, those Alp— ... those *Pyrenean* hounds.

Nelson had his proof. They had been neighbours after all. Rascal and Rasta's mother had even heard of him, from as far afield as the next village! He was famous – albeit it for something he would rather have forgotten.

Nelson knew he wouldn't be able to persuade the brothers to accept this part of his story – they would just make fun of him again as they always did. So, he was prepared to leave it at that. And that's what he did. At first. But something was still nagging at him, like a big fat flea on his back, and it would not leave him alone.

Just before Nelson went to France on holiday, Rasta had recounted their mother's accident to him. When Nelson had discussed it with Rascal a couple of months previously and Rascal said their *maman* was hit by a car, they were chatting in a mix of both French and English dog-speak. When Rasta told him about the same incident, he told Nelson in French. Nelson didn't register anything significant at the time. But when he pondered it again while on holiday in France, he was struck by a subtle difference between their versions. He believed Rascal had said it in English, but it must have been a jumbled mélange of English and French. It had to be!

~ *Maman* was hit by a *car*.

Not a car, but *un car*. In French, a *car* is a coach or a bus.

Nelson's mind recoiled and shot back to the Alps of his youth. He watched Belle disappear under the tourist coach.

In a split second, he understood why Belle had been so excited when she ran across the road that day to meet him. His head started to spin and his paws began to sweat. He tried hard to make sense of the numbers but he struggled with the reality. Slowly, events came into focus. Belle's accident, his third manniversary. Rascal and Rasta, born the same year. In April. *Mon Dieu!* Was he still in the Alps when Belle gave birth? Nelson shivered.

His heart was pumping and he was panting with excitement. He forced himself to sit down and he attempted to gather his thoughts. The rest fell into place.

There was a veterinary practice in La Chapelle d'Abondance. It was where Nelson was dragged to as a young pup, where the man in the blue coat poked and fiddled. Surviving her accident, Belle was taken to the same practice for treatment. That's why the brothers remembered everything was so clean and it explained why there where so many guardians. It was there that Belle gave birth to their pups. And then she died.

It confirmed why the brothers had little beards. Belle was a Patterdale Terrier, a breed that, as a young ignorant pup, Ombré had never heard of. How could he have? – a Patterdale in the French Alps! Rascal and Rasta, Patterdale-crosses. Now Nelson knew exactly what they were crossed with.

~ ~ ~ ~ ~

Perversely, Nelson had spent the first months of his friendship with the brothers trying his utmost to convince them they were all brought together by the kindly paw of fate. Then, after he finally worked it all out and discovered the wonderful truth, he spent the rest of his life hiding it.

He planned to tell them both everything as soon as he returned from France. He was so excited and eager to return. But he was very nervous as well, because how would they take the news? What if they didn't want him to be their father? What if—? What if ...? But his excitement never waned, and when he jumped onto Rascal's back that day along the river, he was bursting to blurt it out.

Rasta's death sobered Nelson with a jolt and forced him to take stock of the situation. How would Rascal take his news now? Nelson came very close to telling him so many times, but he always stopped himself. During the fire, when Rascal and Nelson stared at each other through the window, Nelson felt the depth of Rascal's own suffering. He saw the pain and despair in Rascal's eyes when he thought he was losing a friend to the flames. What would it have done to him to think he was losing his father? After Nelson pulled through, he promised himself he should never tell Rascal.

He almost slipped up once or twice after that, in conversations when he was preaching to Rascal about role models and father figures. But as Rascal was always so unapproachable on that subject, Nelson knew he shrugged it off as nothing more than an over-concerned gesture from an older friend. He would never in a million dog years have registered its real significance.

Nelson has to believe that what he did was right. It will help him to rest easy, knowing that his bloodline continues. Although his own time is over, his life will continue through Rascal. He knows Rascal won't disappoint him – he is as popular with *les filles* as Nelson was.

Nelson wants to rest now. All this has tired him out. It's time. Time for him to go. When he lowers his head and closes his eyes for the very last time, he feels humbly proud of what he has achieved. Even if his family tree is yet a budding sapling, Belle truly blossomed on it and gave dear Rasta a beginning to his short but memorable existence. And, *bien sûr*, Nelson assures himself, he can always count on a certain cheeky little Rascal to water it.

Part 4

Le Fin ...
A New Beginning

~ 32 ~

Tom and Gill visited Richard and Françoise to pay their respects. Naturally, they took Rascal along. After laying a tiny wreath on the soil, the adults went into the house. Rascal stayed in the garden – alone with his thoughts and a small patch of freshly turned soil with which to share them.

In the house, Tom and Gill had something very important to discuss with Richard and Françoise, something that could not wait. They had a huge favour to ask and a monumental decision to make.

Rascal stood in front of Nelson's grave, pawing ever so gently at the earth. He knew his friend was under the soil, he could feel his presence. He stepped back a little, lowered his front paws, then his back legs, and he lay down on the damp grass. He rested his chin on the soil and let out a long whimper to air his thoughts:

~ *Salut, mon ami.* Hope you don't mind me disturbing you, Nelson, but I just wanted to tell you something. You always used to take the time to listen to me, so I hope you can find a little bit more now.

I know I always made a lot of fun of you, an' I know I was hard work some of— ... *most* of the time. But anyway, I just wanted to say I'll ... I'll miss you, Nelson. I will, really.

I know it's all part of growing up an' all that, losing someone, but when you lose someone close, it's like a big chunk of you is missing – you know? Like when you told me about how that Bazou dog bit someone's backside off. Well, it's just like that, except it's not your backside. It's more like a big piece of your insides that's missing. Which is really weird, because even though some of your insides are missing an' they feel hollow, they actually weigh more. D'you know what I mean?

It's not right you've gone. It's so much easier to leave than it is to be left behind. That's the only selfish thing you've ever done in your whole life.

Life's cruel sometimes, I reckon. First I lost *maman*, an' all my other brothers an' sisters. An' then I lost Rasta. You know we never knew our father – we never knew anything at all about him. Probably a loser, like we said. An' now I've lost you, my best friend ever.

Why couldn't I have gone first? Or we could've all gone at the same time. Or something. I wish we'd had chance to say goodbye. Why didn't you tell me you were going, Nelson? But at least you went quickly – unlike *maman*.

Hey, hang on, though, gramps. I'm not gonna go all soppy on you, because I know you'd start analysing it all. But I just wanted to say I'm really sorry for all the times I laughed at all your ideas an' ignored your suggestions; I was only having a bit of fun. You know me: Rascal by name, pain in the butt by nature. One day, I'll grow up. Promise! Don't expect me to rush it, though, but one day, I'll make you proud of me, Nelson. An' I think Rasta will be too. Well, I hope he will.

We were great buddies, weren't we? Remember the first time I got you to roll on that dead seagull on the shore? An' that time when you an' Rasta said I couldn't wee on that canoeist's jeans. Well, I knew you'd say that so I sprayed them first, just in case. An' all the time Rasta telling me what to do, an' you going on an' on about role models. I bet you didn't even realise – knowing you, so wrapped up in your crazy ideas an' fate an' all – but after you came back from France an' you were droning on about all that father-figure stuff, I'm sure you actually thought you *were* my father, the way you talked sometimes. The sun must have gone to your head.

Crazy, eh? You never really did tell me about your holiday, did you?

I know I never ever told you this, Nelson, but when you did do that, it actually made me feel really good inside, you know. Really close. But I was too scared and too proud to admit it to you. Can you imagine what you would've said if I did? Yeah, well, that's *pre*cisely why I didn't.

An' remember when we used to sit on the shoreline watching the sunset? We'd sit side by side an' stare out across the bay, chatting, telling stories, enjoying the peace. Well, when I'd let you have any! I felt really close to you those times, you know. When we sat so that our shoulders touched, sometimes a shiver ran down my back an' it made my hair stand on end. I never told you *that*, either. But I can tell you now.

An' you know something else, gramps? If I ever did have a real father, I'd want him to be just like you.

~ ~ ~ ~ ~

Inside, Tom and Gill were explaining their predicament. Tom had been offered an overseas posting as part of his employment. Since their return to the UK, Tom had gone back to consultancy work. He was doing very well for himself, which was how they had been able to buy their holiday retreat in the Aveyron. If he took the overseas position, it would mean they would need to go to live in the Philippines for at least a year, perhaps more. They knew they could not possibly take Rascal with them – 'They *eat* dogs over there!' exclaimed Gill. Tom was prepared to turn down the offer unless they could find a temporary home for Rascal. It was an incredibly tough decision for them to make, to have to leave their dog behind, but it would be foolish to reject such an offer. Wouldn't it?

Richard and Françoise were touched by the suggestion. They were surprised too that Rascal's owners had put so much faith and trust in them.

'We don't exactly have a good track record, do we?' said Richard.

He wasn't so sure it would be a good idea. The couple said they would think it over, but they could not guarantee anything. Richard's main concern, which he didn't voice, was that he simply didn't want another dog. He knew it would be impossible to replace Nelson, and he didn't want to even try. He knew he would grow too attached to a new dog, and simply could not bear the loss of another. He was already sure his answer would be no. But 'of course' they would think about it, they said.

Still outside, gazing thoughtfully at Nelson's resting place, Rascal was unaware his future was being discussed; though he had sensed his guardians had something preying heavily on their minds – he thought he could even smell it.

His thoughts were interrupted by a very deep but lacklustre voice from over his shoulder. A tall boy was walking along the side of the house. Behind him were a man and a woman. Clutching her mother's hand tightly, a little girl of two shuffled slowly along.

Rascal jumped up on high alert and instinctively shouted at the four humans daring to invade the grounds of his departed friend. It wasn't a vicious shout, just a warning to them. He needn't have wasted his breath; no sooner had the warning left his vocal cords than he knew they meant no harm. He smelt the goodness in them.

The boy crouched down on the grass alongside the house and called to Rascal in a voice that the dog thought rather odd and uninviting. But he was very intrigued, so he approached the boy warily for an introductory sniff. He let the boy stroke him behind an ear. There was a tenderness and warmth in the touch that Rascal liked immediately and he cocked his head to one side to better enjoy the caress. He let out a little grunt to voice his approval and enjoyment.

'Do not worry, Mister Dog, we are not going to hurt you. I have brought my family with me to give Nelson some presents. My sister and I are going to put them on his grave so he knows we still think of him all the time. Nathalia never met Nelson but I have told her all about him and it took me a very long time. But he was called Oswald when he was with us. Father told me that he was not going to keep in touch with Oswald or Nelson but when Nelson died he told me he had done. He told me a very very big fib but I have forgiven him this time. You actually look a little bit like Nelson did, Mister Dog. Father, do you think he looks like Nelson did?'

'Yes, Tim, he does a bit.' Then to Rascal: 'Come here, boy, let's have a look at you then. So, are you Richard and Françoise's new dog then? They soon got *you*! You've some pretty big shoes to fill, little fella, I'll tell you that. What's your name then? Let's have a look at your collar. Ah, Ra— Ras— Keep still, will you. Rasc— Goodness me, you're a frisky little devil. Tim, look, he even has a little white patch on his chest like Ozz— Nelson did. So, it's Rascal, eh? I'll bet you are!'

Rascal was enjoying the attention from this kindly man. He carried a distinct smell of engine oil, but it wasn't off-putting in any way. But he was distracted by another smell: that of the woman standing next to him. She smelt much, much better than engine oil. Rascal made a full tour of her, stretching up on his hind legs to smell the parts he couldn't reach, and the ones he wasn't supposed to. The woman laughed and gently pushed him down. Rascal nibbled her fingers; they tasted delicious. He yapped his appreciation.

He wondered if Nelson had ever known these people, because they were obviously friends of Richard and Françoise. Could they be the previous guardians he spoke of so much? Whoever they were, Rascal decided he liked them.

He watched the boy take the little girl's hand in his. She held her brother's hand tightly, giggling as Rascal sniffed around her. He walked her directly over to Nelson's grave. He crouched down, still holding the girl with one hand. In the other hand, he held a plastic box. From the box, the boy pulled out some items. Rascal couldn't see what the boy was doing because his body was in the way, so he approached stealthily and burrowed his nose under the boy's arm, between him and the girl.

The boy had placed several small carrots and some pieces of cucumber on the grave. Rascal's curiosity had the better of him and he pushed through to the grave and sniffed eagerly at the offerings.

Timothy tapped Rascal's rump. 'These are not for you, Rascal, they are for Nelson. But you can have a small piece of one because you seem like a good dog to me. Would you like some carrot or some cucumber?'

Timothy made to offer Rascal a five-centimetre strip of cucumber.

'Tim, I don't think he'll like that,' said David. 'Nelson was a bit of a one-off, I think. Cucumber is not something dogs normally ea—'

Rascal plucked the cucumber from Timothy's hand and chomped it eagerly.

'Well, now there's a thing. Go on, son, you might as well give him the carro—'

The small carrot disappeared into Rascal's mouth.

Rascal was just as surprised: Nelson had never once mentioned that he liked carrots and cucumber. Timothy fed Rascal another few pieces and then held both hands up with his palms open like stars.

'All gone, Rascal. The rest are for Nelson.'

David walked to the front door and rang the bell.

Rascal placed his paw on the boy's knee and let out a little yap. Then he jumped clear and began darting around agitatedly. His curiosity was running wild. This was a mystery he needed to solve. He shouted at the visitors and then ran to the back door and into the house. A moment later, the front door of the house opened and Françoise appeared. Rascal was at her heels, yapping impatiently.

Everybody went inside, gathered in the lounge and drinks were served. Rascal continued to run round in circles, from one person to the next, determined to work out how the puzzle fitted together. He ran to Timothy and nudged him insistently with his snout, prodding him with a paw.

Suddenly, a huge grin appeared on Françoise's face as she looked first at Timothy and then to David. She appeared almost as excited as Rascal.

'David ...?' she said. 'You wouldn't be interested in dog-sitting this adorable little monster would you?'

About the Author

‘*I think, therefore I write. If only I could keep things in that order.*’

Born and raised in the North of England, Tony Lewis now lives in the South of France, dividing his time between there and ‘home’. He loves (*almost*) all things French, professes to be at least *semi*-bilingual, and enjoys the simple pleasures of cycling and exploring the local countryside in his faithful walking boots.

He lives with his Belgian partner, Ludmilla; they currently have no cuddly dogs, no children (cuddly or otherwise), but share their hamlet hideaway with an outspoken cockerel and his four hens, and a family of uninvited wild boar intent on destroying the garden.

Author's Note

I wish to express my immense gratitude to the following people. Ludmilla, for her tireless reading, re-reading and invaluable critique. All the individuals who have taken the time to read and comment on my book, and for allowing me to reproduce their kindly words for review purposes. Matador, for their invaluable support, advice and knowledge. And to you the reader, for sticking with Ombré all the way.

A final word to offer my heartfelt thanks to my canine chums past and present. Naturally, to Jinny and to Carter who, aged just nine years young, had to be put to sleep with kidney problems whilst I was finalising this book. To Sam, Denzel and Brandy, and to the countless other inimitable dogs I have met over the years, without whom there would have been no inspiration or reason for this book.

~ ~ ~ ~ ~

For more information, please visit:
www.ifonlyicouldtalk.co.uk
www.troubador.co.uk